DAHLIA BLACK

ALSO BY KEITH THOMAS

The Clarity

DAHLIA BLACK

A Novel

KEITH THOMAS

LEOPOLDO
& CO

ATRIA

New York   London   Toronto   Sydney   New Delhi

LEOPOLDO & CO

ATRIA

An Imprint of Simon & Schuster, Inc.
1230 Avenue of the Americas
New York, NY 10020

First Leopoldo & Co/Atria Books hardcover edition August 2019

LEOPOLDO & CO/**ATRIA** BOOKS and colophon are trademarks of Simon & Schuster, Inc.

For information about special discounts for bulk purchases, please contact Simon & Schuster Special Sales at 1-866-506-1949 or business@simonandschuster.com.

The Simon & Schuster Speakers Bureau can bring authors to your live event. For more information or to book an event, contact the Simon & Schuster Speakers Bureau at 1-866-248-3049 or visit our website at www.simonspeakers.com.

Interior design by Dana Sloan

Manufactured in the United States of America

10   9   8   7   6   5   4   3   2   1

ISBN 978-1-5011-5671-7
ISBN 978-1-5011-5673-1 (ebook)

For Fremder Gorn

DISCLOSURE

How One Woman's Discovery

Led to the Greatest Event in

Human History

KEITH THOMAS

⭐ KLEINZEIT HOUSE PRESS

Kleinzeit House Press
New York, NY

First hardcover edition August 2028

Interior design by Miranda Caliban

Manufactured in the United States of America

1 3 5 7 9 10 8 6 4 2

FOREWORD

W hen I was nine years old, my father took me to Cape Canaveral to watch the launch of the Voyager 1 probe.

Dad was an engineer at NASA and that got me, a wide-eyed, space obsessed girl, a front-row seat to the send-off. I never forgot the experience of witnessing one of mankind's greatest achievements. And that memory was the spark that pushed me to be better. It was what led me to speak to you now, as the President of what used to be called the United States of America.

That was all long before the world was transformed, before the panic.

Before we witnessed the very first Elevation of a human being . . .

In 1977, the whole world turned towards the stars. We wanted to believe there was intelligent life somewhere out there. And we hoped that if we could reach them, maybe they'd reach back. Voyager 1, this satellite dish with bristling antenna, was a message in a bottle. Our way of letting the galaxy know we existed. That we were out here if anyone wanted to find us.

Over the next forty years, the probe flew past Jupiter and Saturn before it drifted into the void, swallowed up by a silent universe. Or so we thought . . .

Truth is, our message didn't go unheard.

The universe reached back and changed everything. Not with war or an invasion but with a whisper. Almost overnight, all that we knew transformed.

And I saw it happen.

In 2023, we witnessed the first Elevation of a human being.

It began, as most dramatic things do, with a single person.

I'm looking at a photo of Dr. Dahlia Mitchell right now. It is sitting here, framed on my desk. She is younger, mid-twenties, in the photo than when I met her. Her eyes are green, her hair long and crimped, and she's smiling. Happy. I have no idea when it was taken, but my guess is shortly after she got her professorship at the University of California, Santa Cruz.

Dahlia's history is a tragic one.

She was an army brat. Her family moved fourteen times over the next eighteen years. Her father, Arthur, an African American chemical engineer with the Army Corps of Engineers, fell for a German girl, Giselle, while he was stationed in Europe.

Dahlia only enjoyed Fort Polk for two years, barely long enough to learn to run, before the family—Dahlia, mom, dad, and her older brother, Nico—uprooted to Augsburg, Germany. A whirlwind followed: Oklahoma, Kansas, Hawaii, Virginia, Bavaria, Seoul, and back to Augsburg.

During the brief time we spent together, she told me she was introspective growing up, obsessed with books and history. A curious kid, she uncovered new and exciting things in every place the family encamped. And, like her mother, Dahlia learned languages easily. She spoke three by the time she was ten. She remained a bright, easily awed child well into her early teens, when her mother committed suicide.

Dahlia took her death hard.

After her mother's suicide, Arthur withdrew and Nico and Dahlia had to fend for themselves. While Nico rebelled, Dahlia focused on her studies—primarily astrophysics and chemistry.

An ambitious and clever student, Dahlia impressed her professors and received a full ride to earn a PhD in astrophysics from Cornell. After graduation, she took a professorship at the University of California, Santa Cruz, where she was, by all accounts, very productive but not very happy.

But I'll let you hear that from her.

This book is a testament. Not to my presidency or my administration but to the people behind the scenes, the people who averted us from even bigger disasters or steered us out of harm's way. When Keith Thomas first approached me about participating in this book, I told him I was hesitant to get involved. The times he wanted to document were trying for me politically and personally. Revisiting these events, even after five years, was emotionally draining and, in some cases, quite upsetting. Still, I agreed and I'm convinced he's been able to capture some, if not all, of what made the Finality the sea change of all sea changes.

While I know a lot of people who've been left broken by the Elevation, I have also met just as many who are excited by the prospects of starting over. Future generations depend on us not making the same mistakes our ancestors did. Regardless of which political philosophies you ascribe to or what religion you practice, I think we all can agree we'd like to see less bloodshed and more kindness. We have an opportunity to rejuvenate our planet. A lot of folks around here, they've already begun: all the food I eat, all the water I drink, it comes from down the road. From local farms, local reservoirs, and the air . . . well, it's amazing how clean the air is.

Of course, we're not without lingering, serious problems. Nearly 70 percent of the western United States is still without power and more than 50 percent of the South suffers from rolling brownouts. Medical care is still an ongoing emergency, and fuel issues limit our growth.

But we are a strong people. We're clever; we're resourceful. And, like those who have left us, the 122 million souls who joined the Ascendants five years ago, we are brave.

I hope that, going forward, we can learn from the events before, during, and after the Elevation. I know the world is a much smaller place. But it was a small place before, and I am confident it will become a much bigger place again. It won't happen in the next five or ten years but five hundred and a thousand. I sincerely hope that when we rebuild—and we will—we do it a little more carefully.

I spent several years working on an autobiography but refused to use a ghostwriter for assistance. At the end of the day, I realized that I just didn't have the patience or the temperament to see it through. I've agreed to let Mr. Thomas use excerpts from this unfinished work in this book. The portions he's chosen are fairly wide-ranging but I think get at the heart of what I was attempting to record.

When Voyager 1 was launched, we were optimistic that the future held only great things for humanity. While it is true that the Voyager is still drifting out into the vaster reaches of space, with no signal back, no sign of ever having existed at all, I want us to get back to that original optimistic place.

While we know we are not alone in this universe, we also know that we are unique. That should be celebrated. And in the pages to follow, I think you will find quite a bit to celebrate.

Sincerely,
President Vanessa Ballard
June 25, 2028

INTRODUCTION

This is an oral history of how the world ended.

It took me twenty-three months to write this book.

The world we knew ended in just two.

On October 17, 2023, an astronomer, not particularly well-known or widely published, named Dahlia Mitchell discovered a signal emanating from a distant point in the galaxy. That signal was a pulse, sent by an unknown intelligence, and came to be known as the Pulse Code, as it contained data in incredibly advanced cryptographic cipher.

The Pulse Code was not a message. It was not an attempt at communication from some distant civilization. It was a Trojan virus—a biological tool that altered the brains of roughly 30 percent of the human population. Those changed by the Pulse Code could see and hear things the rest of us couldn't: gravitational waves, ultraviolet light, the very movement of the Earth itself. And that was only the beginning of their capabilities . . .

This event was dubbed the Elevation.

Many of the Elevated died—their bodies unable to keep up with the incredible transformation going on inside their heads. Some of those that survived went insane. Others isolated themselves from the rest of humanity, sequestering themselves in anticipation of an event that would see them transition from our world to another.

That event was called the Finality.

There have, of course, been many books written about the Elevation and the Finality—some focused on the science, others on the sociology; all of them approached the subject in suitably reverential ways. This was, after all, the biggest event in human history, changing humanity forever. Three billion people—gone.

So why add to the pile of books about this ultimate event?

Especially as someone known primarily as a novelist and filmmaker?

The other books, documentaries—even the disastrous feature film that came out last year—attempt to tell the story of the Elevation as a whole; they take the 20,000-foot view. But I think this is a story that needs to be told from a personal place. At the end of the day, it's the story of us—all of us. This oral history provides a platform for the voices of those who were there from the very beginning.

But there is one additional thing that makes this project unique:

This book contains portions of Dahlia Mitchell's diaries.

For a long time, they were presumed lost. While many people made it clear in interviews that Dahlia was a consummate diarist, no one had ever seen the books. Because they weren't books. Dahlia, true to the digital age, recorded her diaries via posts on a private website only accessible via a password. To my knowledge, Dahlia never shared that password with anyone.

About three years ago I got an email from a professional hacker who goes by the sobriquet S4yL4Frit3. Like a lot of hackers put out of work by the tech collapse that followed in the wake of the Elevation, S4yL4Frit3 was looking to make some side money by trawling through abandoned servers. (As an aside, it is estimated that over 3 quindecillion bytes of data—that's a 3 followed by forty-eight zeros—remain un-accessed in world servers.) S4yL4Frit3 stumbled onto Dahlia's diaries quite by accident; it was just one of several million private blogs archived on a "dead" social media platform (similar to the largely forgotten Twitter and Facebook) swept up in one of S4yL4Frit3's data hauls.

Being a fan of a certain horror thriller I'd written a couple years ago, S4yL4Frit3 sent me the diaries. Being something of a news and science junkie, S4yL4Frit3 knew this was something special. Not the sort of thing to just dump on the Net or toss to a few of the remaining news networks. The message I got from S4yL4Frit3 was simple: "Do this thing justice."

After I read the diaries, I knew that was exactly what I had to do. I spent the next eleven months traveling the country and compiling interviews with people who had witnessed the incredible changes that roiled our country firsthand. I was fortunate to talk to powerful voices like President Ballard, the country's first Independent president, and unsung characters like Thomas Franklin Bess, a witness to one of the first Elevations.

I also gained access to recorded interviews and transcripts from numerous sources. Some were transcripts from recordings made surreptitiously by both government and nongovernment actors. All of these pieces, intermixed with the one-on-one interviews I personally conducted, paint a true picture of transformation.

On both a global and also a personal level.

As Dahlia changed, so changed the world.

Telling the story of the Elevation was never going to be easy.

I knew that I wasn't going to be able to touch on each and every angle—the wars that erupted in the Middle East, the disasters in Singapore and Austria—but I covered the history as best I could. And have provided footnotes as well.

There will be surprises here.

Some of what I discovered hasn't yet been exposed.

And some of it will be disturbing.

While many of us were aware that there were people inside President Ballard's administration fully against her plans, we couldn't have known how many of these agents were entrenched in our government, like hidden cancerous cells, for many, many decades. I know I'm not the first to discuss the existence of the Twelve, but I am the first to speak to several of its former members.

There will be controversy in these pages as well.

Some of my contacts are people that history will not remember fondly. A lot of you might be angered to see their names again in print. I assure you that I am not airing their opinions to generate buzz but to give rationale, a way of seeing the Elevation, which very nearly ended our existence.

As the folk anecdote goes: The worst divisions are from within.

However, this is in many ways Dahlia Mitchell's story. I didn't want that to be lost in all the political or scientific turmoil. Just like all of us, Dahlia was someone caught up in the chaos of the Elevation, someone looking for safety, looking for comfort. Despite her scientific breakthroughs and the startling abilities she discovered within herself, Dahlia was a dreamer and remained one until the end.

I dedicate this book to all the other dreamers out there.

Keith Thomas
February 2028

THE PULSE

1

EDITED TRANSCRIPT FROM AN FBI INTERVIEW WITH DAHLIA MITCHELL

PALO ALTO FIELD OFFICE: RECORDING #001—FIELD AGENT J. E. MUDDOCK

OCTOBER 23, 2023

AGENT MUDDOCK: Please state your name, brief biographical history, education, marital status, and profession.

DAHLIA MITCHELL: My name's Dahlia Mitchell. I was born at Fort Polk, Louisiana, but was raised all over the globe, pretty much. Army brat. I have one brother, Nico. My parents were divorced. My father died about ten years ago from an illness. My mother . . . uh, my mother committed suicide. I went to UPenn and then did my graduate studies in astronomy at Cornell. I am single and I'm . . . well, I was, an astronomer at the University of California, Santa Cruz.

AGENT MUDDOCK: And what was your area of expertise there? What were you researching and teaching students?

DAHLIA MITCHELL: I did my dissertation on how we can use gravitational lensing to map the distribution of dark matter in relation to galaxies. We use gravitational lensing to find galaxy clustering, and if we look at that clustering in relation to dark matter fields, we can get a sense of the position of the galaxies. If that makes sense . . .

AGENT MUDDOCK: I'm not an expert. Please tell us what your most recent research subject was. The work you were doing before the event.

DAHLIA MITCHELL: Same topic. Just . . . just studying it differently. You know the expression about not seeing the forest for the trees? Well, it was sort of the opposite of that. I was too focused on the forest, on the larger whole. While I was looking at galaxies, what I really needed to do was focus on the spaces in between to find out how dark matter ties together the universe. Even though dark matter's still essentially theoretical, there are ways to study the effect that dark matter has on gravitational waves and other ... well, transmissions that are beaming their way across space. I was scanning as much of the sky as I could, collecting radio bursts and hoping those would give me a better understanding of how dark matter was operating. That's it in a nutshell.

AGENT MUDDOCK: And how was this work received at the university?

DAHLIA MITCHELL: You know, it's tough doing research on something that, for the most part, is only rumored to exist. I mean, that's been changing pretty rapidly, but there's still this bias out there against research that's seen as fundamentally impractical on a basic science level. Harder to get the funding and the grants when you're looking into something people can't see, computers can't even measure, and that might not actually exist the way you imagine it does.

AGENT MUDDOCK: So it's safe to say that your work hasn't been championed within your department? We've interviewed Dr. Kjelgaard and he doesn't speak as highly of your work as he does of your colleagues'. Is it true that you were asked to suspend your dark matter work in the days leading up to discovering the Pulse signal?

DAHLIA MITCHELL: Yes, that's true.

AGENT MUDDOCK: And so the night that you made this discovery—technically you were not supposed to be at the radio telescope observatory. You were not approved to run an experiment—

DAHLIA MITCHELL: That isn't exactly correct. I had been approved, just a few weeks earlier, to run the tests that I was running that night. At the last minute, my ... my superior decided that I should just shut the program down—

AGENT MUDDOCK: It was in fact the board that made the decision.

DAHLIA MITCHELL: On my superior's recommendation, yes. But I had prior approval and I saw it only as a chance—like a last-ditch effort, really— to complete a project that I had spent the majority of my professional life working on. You have to understand, there are very specific criteria that go into these sorts of observations. If the weather is off or the dishes aren't properly calibrated, then you're looking at significant, potentially disastrous delays. I couldn't afford to miss the moment. No matter—

AGENT MUDDOCK: No matter the fact that your boss had told you to stop. He had specifically told you not to continue the experiment that night.

DAHLIA MITCHELL: Yes. That's true.

AGENT MUDDOCK: Seems a little convenient, doesn't it? You're told not to pursue this avenue of exploration, and you dismiss your superior's judgment as flawed, you go ahead with the project as you had originally intended, and then you make the single most important discovery in recorded history . . .

DAHLIA MITCHELL: No. No, it didn't happen . . . What exactly are you suggesting?

AGENT MUDDOCK: That it is possible that there is a very good reason you made this discovery. You went up there that night, in direct violation of an order not to proceed with the experiment, the readings, the manipulation of equipment, for the express purpose of, quote, unquote, "making this discovery." Is it possible, Dr. Mitchell, that you created the data that you claim to have stumbled across?

DAHLIA MITCHELL: Of course not. That's outrageous. I would never do anything like that. I take my work as seriously as anything. I can't believe—who would even suggest something like that? You've seen the data, right?

AGENT MUDDOCK: The data you were studying—

DAHLIA MITCHELL: The data from the Pulse. You've had it for weeks; you've been studying it the whole time. If not you, then the people on your team. I couldn't fake the math found in that signal. I couldn't fake that level of sophistication—

AGENT MUDDOCK: You're intelligent. Transcripts from undergrad and graduate school show exceptional levels of dedication. And, let's see, one of your advisors here wrote, and I'm quoting, "More than any of my students, Dahlia has the ability to think far beyond the edges of the box. She sees things most of us, even myself, miss. Dahlia is the sort of student who will in time discover great things." Perhaps this signal is something you, quote, unquote, "discovered" as well?

DAHLIA MITCHELL: That is absurd. You're taking a random quote that has nothing to do with this and trying to reapply it. The information contained in that pulse, the code at the heart of it, is . . . even the most out-of-the-box thinker could never come up with something like that.

AGENT MUDDOCK: Or maybe it just seems that way. Maybe it's just gobbledygook, like glossolalia. Are you familiar with the Voynich manuscript, Dr. Mitchell?

DAHLIA MITCHELL: No.

AGENT MUDDOCK: It's a manuscript, singular and strange, that has been dated back to the 1400s. Supposedly, it is some sort of alchemical textbook filled with medieval science experiments, anthropological observations, a treatise on botany and zoology, and explorations of human reproduction. I use the word "supposedly" because no one, no expert, knows for sure. The Voynich manuscript is written in an unknown, likely made-up language. It has never been translated and likely never will be.

DAHLIA MITCHELL: Okay . . . I don't understand what you're getting at . . .

AGENT MUDDOCK: It won't even be successfully translated because it isn't a language at all. It has all the corresponding structure and look of a language, but it isn't. It's gobbledygook. Glossolalia. Speaking in tongues.

And yet brilliant mathematicians, linguists, cryptographers, still try to decipher the Voynich. People have given up decades of their lives attempting to crack the uncrackable. This code you discovered, maybe it is the same thing.

DAHLIA MITCHELL: No. You're wrong. I didn't make it; I couldn't have made it. I suggest you take a good look at the Pulse Code. A good, hard look. You'll say—and your experts are going to tell you the same in a matter of days, maybe hours—that this wasn't a hoax or from a deranged astronomer.

AGENT MUDDOCK: Then what is it, Dr. Mitchell?

DAHLIA MITCHELL: It is the one thing you're not willing to open your mind to; the one thing that you want desperately not to believe . . .

2

I think I found something tonight.

Writing that sounds ridiculous.

Like I'm back in undergrad, convinced I'd just made some huge breakthrough when I "discovered" an unusual fast radio burst out of Centaurus A.* How silly, right? Thankfully, Dr. Zivkovic† let me down easy. He didn't want to quash my enthusiasm. Of course, the burst I'd found was first seen in 1934. It was rediscovered every day, a thousand times a day. Still, that thrill when I first heard it—there was nothing to match that. I wanted to feel it again. To think that maybe, just maybe, I'd discovered something no one else alive had ever come across. Unmapped territory. The great beyond . . .

I got the same feeling tonight.

And so far, I haven't found a single reference to this location, this signal, before. I've checked the University databases, SIMBAD, SDSS, NASA's ADS, NASA/IPAC's NED, and come up with nothing. This location isn't a new stretch of space. It's old territory, pored over for centuries. Dead space, as they say. Literally the last place you'd expect to pick up something new. That's why, despite what happened, I still have my doubts. I always have my doubts . . .

---

* First noted in 2007, fast radio bursts (FRBs) are transient but intense radio pulses from deep space. Usually lasting only a few milliseconds, the vast majority of recorded FRBs are of unknown origin. Many originate from distances as far away as 1 gigaparsec, or 3 billion light-years.

† Dr. Emil Zivkovic, an astrophysicist at Cornell University. He was Elevated.

—

My day didn't start well.

"Sucked" is a better word for it.

During my morning lecture on dark matter—the same intro lecture I've given for nearly three years and could recite verbatim in my sleep—Frank walked in. By the look on his face, he wasn't thrilled at the thought of catching my attention. The board meeting had been two nights earlier, and I'd been waiting on pins and needles for him to tell me what was going on. Ominous silence, no matter the situation, is never a good sign. Especially with Frank.*

So I stopped by his messy office—does this guy ever straighten up?—after the lecture let out and sat in front of his desk. He fiddled with his pen for a moment, pretending to look over some papers as he got up the courage to break the news to me: "Dahlia, the board's scaling back your dark matter project."

I reacted like he'd just swung a bowling ball into my stomach. It really was that dramatic. Hurt. Frank shook his head and waved his hands, trying to make it seem like none of it was his idea, but that didn't last long. He eventually just set his teeth and gave me the bad news. "The interim analysis isn't supporting your thesis."

No shit.

That was why I'd fought the board about doing an interim analysis in the very first place. It was unnecessary and likely to result in some significantly skewed numbers. Turns out I was right, of course. I told Frank that I was dealing with 300 terabytes of data. In only three months I'd more than doubled our mapping progress. Looking for dark matter wasn't exactly easy; it's called dark for a reason, because, in the vastness of space, it's pretty much invisible. But sometimes it's the invisible that matters most. Goofy thought, but it's true.

Think of all the things we can't see that touch our lives every day: air, gravity, emotions, faith . . . Dark matter is the equivalent of these

---

* Dahlia is referring to Dr. Frank Kjelgaard, an astrophysicist and dean of astronomy and astrophysics at the University of California, Santa Cruz.

things but in outer space. More than that, we think it makes up most of the known universe; it is the very fabric that holds the celestial bodies in their places, the source of gravitational waves.

Not that Frank was listening. He never is.

No, he just went on with his speech, expecting me to roll right over. Not only did he bring up the fact that I've got "a heavy course load for the year"—I bet he'd never point that same fact out to Colin or Fredrick—and that shifting my focus might actually be advantageous. He didn't suggest, as he had before, that dark matter wasn't the worthwhile endeavor the rest of the astrophysics community had built it up to be. That always grated on me most. Still, I bet if I'd pressed him he would have told me I'd been wasting my life. Don't even go there, Dahlia . . .*

So I suggested that I run one more test: the Bullet Cluster.[†]

Frank scoffed and said Milgrom had ruled it out years ago.[‡]

I argued Milgrom wasn't using the right tools.

But Frank was beyond listening. Whether the board had truly made a decision or it was just that Frank was tired of defending my work, he was passive-aggressively telling me that I was done. It took pushing but finally he just said it: "I need you to start shutting down your project tonight."

And that, as far as he was concerned, was that. I left the room in a huff and Frank could call the board and tell them it was done—that their little problem child astronomer was being relegated to the back of the class. Not only was tenure likely going to be delayed if not taken off the table outright, but I was looking at a long slog to get approval for any additional project. Could the day get any worse?

As I walked back to my office from Frank's, I realized what I needed

---

* Dahlia is talking about two other, younger astronomers at the University of California, Santa Cruz. Both male and both, at the time, less accomplished.

† The Bullet Cluster consists of two groups of galaxies slowly smashing into each other a few billion light-years from Earth. A lot of astrophysicists think the Bullet Cluster provides very compelling evidence for the existence of dark matter; it's complicated how, exactly, but it has to do with the mass of the Bullet Cluster.

‡ Mordehai Milgrom, a physicist, argued there are other explanations for the mass "issues" related to the Bullet Cluster. Some people agreed with him, others didn't.

to do. I wouldn't be shutting down the dark matter observation of the Bullet Cluster. I decided I would run it and damn the consequences. I was given time at the observatory, allocated the staff and the computer time, and I was going to use it.

Dad would've been horrified. Sorry, Dad.

After wrapping up some additional paperwork and grading some papers, I jogged the three-mile loop around West Cliff. My time was mediocre but I got my miles in. It felt good to move, just sweat out that stress. At home I showered, poured a glass of red, and then considered which microwave meal to eat (pasta or masala) when Nico[*] called. Right on time, big brother.

I told him what had gone down and like usual he tried to talk me out of doing anything rash—a little too late for that, though. "I'm going to fight this thing, Nico." He suggested, always playing Devil's advocate, that maybe, just maybe, I had made a mistake and Frank was onto something.

"Nico," I said, "I need you on my side."

He laughed and asked if I wanted him to kick Frank's ass for me. I said that wouldn't be necessary and that if Frank's ass had to be kicked, I could certainly be the one to do it, thank you very much.

Nico, being Nico, followed up with something about him and Valerie[†] and the kids coming down for a visit. I couldn't think of anything worse. But, really, it was just another excuse for him to be worried about me. Ever since Mom . . . well, we know how that whole situation played out. Nico worked through all those emotions no problem; he got a therapist, he confided in his wife, and worked it all out. Not even a year after and he was like he was before—maybe wiser, maybe more humbled, but himself. Me, not as much.

It was like we were riding out a storm together. He navigated it perfectly, got to the other side, in the warmth and the sun. But I'm still back there, right in the heart of the storm—beat down, frozen. Nico expects me to turn it around overnight. He expects me to pick myself

* Nico Mitchell, Dahlia's older brother.

† Valerie Mitchell, Dahlia's sister-in-law.

up and say, "That was rough but I learned a lot about myself." Right, like that's how I've ever approached things. I pick myself up but I keep moving straight ahead. Introspection isn't one of my charms.

Two hours later, I left for the desert.

I got to Big Ears* early, just to get started on some of the experiments my grad students were running. Clark Watts† was there, working on Dr. Jacob's‡ field triangulations but likely saw the night as a way to catch up on his reading. Clark's smart but has never been the most motivated student. I doubt he'd argue the point. I wonder if that's how my profs saw me. Trying but not really.

When I arrived at the control building I found Clark using fitsplode§ to pull spectral line data for one of the other grad students. He was busy enough that he barely noticed me. I cleared my throat, said good evening. Clark looked up at me, a bit bleary-eyed. Clearly he'd been catching some z's.

"Didn't think you were coming up," he said.

"Need to finish something."

Clark just nodded and went back to his work but watched me out of the corner of his eye as I pulled together some printouts of my spectrum analysis of the anomaly we'd picked up in October.¶ I showed Clark the area I'd isolated and asked him what he made of it. Like Frank, he thought the Bullet Cluster was old news and the anomaly was just that—an incongruity.

"It doesn't mean there's something there," he said.

---

* "Big Ears" is a nickname for the Owens Valley Radio Observatory in Big Pine, California. It consists of several massive radio telescopes—white "dishes" arrayed in a valley. These are used to "listen" to the universe.

† Clark Ashton Watts was a graduate student at Santa Cruz. His research with Dr. Kjelgaard involved X-ray binaries. After the Finality, he chose to pursue a career in landscape architecture.

‡ Dr. Andrew Jacob, a senior lecturer at Santa Cruz, was an expert on the Wild Duck Cluster, a group of over two thousand stars. Dr. Jacob was well liked by his students and peers. He died in the early stages of the Elevation.

§ A program that pulls spectral line (used to identify molecules present in stars, galaxies, and gas clouds) data from binary FITS (Flexible Image Transport System) tables, the most commonly used digital file format in astronomy.

¶ Dr. Mitchell is referring to a "signal" or "spike" that she'd identified previously. Classified as an anomaly, it was determined to be a fast radio burst unrelated to the Pulse and likely emanating from a supermassive black hole in the Milky Way.

"I'm not suggesting there's something there," I replied. "I just need to understand why we've gotten this data. I don't think it's an error and I'm not jumping to conclusions either. Aren't you in Dr. Rafael Tirso's* class? I took his class, too, just eight years ago. I'm sure he hasn't changed much."

He nodded.

I reminded Clark that Rafael had one point he hammered into the brains of his students: a section of space, no matter how small, can never be fully ruled out. Dead space is never really dead. With that, I pulled rank and asked Clark to recalibrate the K4 telescope. We were going to scan the Bullet Cluster again. That's when the truth came out. Or at least part of it . . .

Clark confirmed that Frank had told him not to let me redirect the telescopes. He figured I might try to run this last look and wanted Clark, a grad student, to stop me, a professor, from doing it. As soon as those words left Clark's mouth, he knew how silly and demeaning they sounded. I wasn't to be trusted with this equipment? Why not just change all the locks in the lab? Why not blacklist me on some astronomy website for heretics? It was unbelievable.

Clark keyed in the codes and turned the K4.

I didn't even want to talk to him again after that. I was too angry, too worried I'd just explode at him. That wouldn't look good. It's never professional to let out your rage on students. Just had to suck it up and refocus. So I did.

And three hours later, it happened.

Three sixteen to be exact. The machines were ticking away, I was going over some of the axion clump research that Hertzberg at Tufts[†] had been doing while Clark was making his way through a never-ending pile of Frank's undergrad essays. Ready for my second coffee of the evening, I went out into the hallway to grab a cup. Clark didn't want one; he was happy with his Red Bull.

---

* Dr. Rafael Tirso was an astrophysicist at the University of California, Santa Cruz. He studied neutron stars and passed away during the early stages of the Elevation.

† Dr. Wallace Hertzberg was an astronomer whose research at Tufts revolved around dark matter axions. Dr. Hertzberg lost both his eyesight and hearing during the Elevation.

The espresso machine, however, was finicky.

It was one of those ancient vending machines with the horrible Styrofoam cups that held scalding-hot, watery coffee. My only dollar was at least ten years old and had clearly been through someone's wash. It was soft and folded and there was no way the machine was going to accept it. Every time I put the dollar in, it slid back out silently. I'm not sure why I've been so fixated on that moment. It's so meaningless, so banal, and yet, when I think back on that moment—the one minute that changed everything—I see the coffee machine and the failed dollar. I was frustrated and growing angry. I'd never kicked a vending machine before, but just as my sneaker was about to crash into the side of the machine, an alarm went off.

It's not unusual to hear alarms at the radio telescopes.

Sometimes it's a calibration issue; sometimes there's something picked up by one of the other pieces of equipment. This, however, wasn't an alarm I'd heard before. Not loud like a smoke detector, not wailing; it was more an insistent and irritating chirp. Sounded like a toy bird. The kind a cat plays with.

I ran back into the control room, where Clark was freaking out.

"We got an anomaly here!" Clark shouted.

He pointed over to a monitor displaying a spiky, EKG-like line, and there, right at the peak of one of the waves, was a break in the line, a spot where the background data was missing because something new, different, had punched its way through. Here is little squiggly drawing of it I did. Terrible, I know.

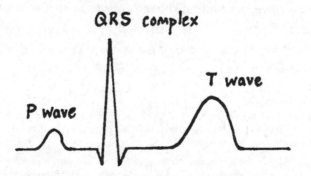

Clark said, "I think it's a fast radio burst."

"Could be," I said. "Or some other random signal. Get me some specs."

Clark started analyzing it.

"Looks weird to me," he said.

"Don't jump to conclusions."

"I'm not but . . . Seriously."

He was right. This wasn't a fast radio burst. It was pulsating.

I made sure Clark was recording it, then ported the signal over to visualization. It didn't look like much; it was coming in blurry. Clark and I did some on-the-fly engineering to rig a monitor that would show us what was coming in. Dad would have been proud. It took a few minutes, but when the Pulse finally showed up on the screen it . . . it was beautiful. That sounds funny, talking about data on a monitor. But it was. Even someone who couldn't tell a fast radio burst from a pair of old socks would think so. It was elegant . . . so organic . . .

And buried inside the Pulse, contained within its oscillations, was a code. A series of numbers, letters, and symbols like dots and triangles. Clark and I watched with our mouths open as these digits streamed across the monitors. I wrote as many of them down as I could, but . . . the series was incredibly complex and long.

"This is coming from deep space," I said.

Clark was too stunned to speak.

"Where's the ETI confirmation binders?"[*] I asked.

He had no idea what I was talking about, so I had to pull myself away from watching the monitors and dig in a closet. Luckily, I found them. These were instructional binders given to the University by the SETI Institute[†] a few years previously. They were covered in dust and I doubt anyone had looked at them since they'd arrived. I flipped through one and found the page I needed.

---

[*] "ETI confirmation" refers to extraterrestrial intelligence. Dahlia is talking about a binder of information from SETI (see below) used to determine if an "intelligently generated" signal has been sent by an extraterrestrial culture or mind.

[†] "SETI" stands for the "search for extraterrestrial intelligence." The first modern SETI experiment was set up in 1960, while the nonprofit SETI Institute itself was established in 1995.

"'Hypothetically, in interstellar communication, a radiation pulse would appear in more than one iteration with consistently massive maximum dispersion measures,'" I read aloud, then looked up at Clark. "It's data. A message . . ."

Clark was befuddled, "You're not actually suggesting—"

"I'm not suggesting," I said. "I'm saying. This pulse was broadcast by something or someone outside of our galaxy."

His response was perfect: "Holy shit."

3

AGENT RANGER: Take us through the night, as far as you remember it.

CLARK ASHTON WATTS: Okay, well, I was up at Big Ears for my shift. This was just a normal night. One of three nights a month that I'd go up there, make that long drive, and then crunch numbers, analyze some of what we'd picked up during the week, and try and get some of my other work done. Just routine work.

AGENT RANGER: And you weren't expecting Dr. Mitchell to be there?

CLARK ASHTON WATTS: No. I, uh, I wasn't sure who else might be up there. The professors rotate on their own schedule and sometimes swap shifts, depending on the project they're working on. I wasn't surprised to see Dr. Mitchell come in but I expected her to be there to look over some of the other projects that we'd been running, maybe catch up on the dark matter data scan.

AGENT RANGER: But she wasn't there to look over other projects or catch up on older data, correct? She wanted to run an experiment.

CLARK ASHTON WATTS: She asked me to recalibrate and move one of the radio telescopes.

AGENT RANGER: And what did she say the purpose was?

CLARK ASHTON WATTS: To look at the Bullet Cluster. It was related to her dark matter research. She knew that Frank had asked me—well, told me—not to let her move the telescopes. But I did. I moved number three and, uh, a few hours later we picked up the signal. That's when it happened.

AGENT RANGER: Where was Dr. Mitchell when the signal was intercepted?

CLARK ASHTON WATTS: She was in the building getting coffee. We heard the alarm at the exact same time. I'll be honest with you, I didn't know what it meant at first. I figured something was wrong with the equipment. But it was functioning normally. The alarm was us picking up the signal, getting a reading. I'd never actually been in the building for one of those. It was a rush.

AGENT RANGER: Were you at all concerned? Frightened? Nervous?

CLARK ASHTON WATTS: Me? No. No way. Cool as a cucumber. Nothing really spooks me.

AGENT RANGER: And the two of you analyzed what you'd received?

CLARK ASHTON WATTS: Yeah. Right away.

AGENT RANGER: Though it didn't go as planned, right?

CLARK ASHTON WATTS: I wouldn't word it that way. No one plans to get a thing like this. I mean, maybe the folks over at SETI would have been prepared—they have protocol for these sorts of things—but I assumed at first that it was something terrestrial bouncing back. We've seen that before; it's common. But it was clear within minutes of analyzing the signal that it wasn't beamed from Earth.

AGENT RANGER: How, then, did you determine this signal wasn't from, say, a celestial event like the explosion of a supernova or two colliding stars?

CLARK ASHTON WATTS: We ran the metrics, but it wasn't until we'd gotten the signal through some of the more advanced software, particularly using time delays on some of the correlated particles emitted from the astronomical sources near our site in the Bullet Cluster. What I'm saying is we ran all those tests and the results came back negative for celestial events. This FRB, this *pulse*, was clearly not a natural event. Dr. Mitchell said it seemed it was *intentional*. That's the word she used.

AGENT RANGER: Can we shift gears for a moment? You mentioned in an earlier interview with several of our colleagues that you had concerns about Dr. Mitchell.

CLARK ASHTON WATTS: That was related to what Dr. Kjelgaard had mentioned. Like I said, he didn't want her touching the telescopes. He'd already asked her to stop her research, and he thought . . .

AGENT RANGER: Thought what?

CLARK ASHTON WATTS: That she might push it, you know? Like she wasn't going to give up too easy on finishing her dark matter research. She'd spent months preparing for it. Dr. Mitchell's hardheaded. I mean that in a good way. Frank knew it too. He told me to not let her go ahead with it. But having me protect the place is like using a Chihuahua as a guard dog.

AGENT RANGER: I see. However, you raised other concerns, correct? We're more interested in what you communicated to Dr. Kjelgaard several weeks before this event. I think we have a copy of the notes he took of your meeting here. Let me bring them up . . . Yes, here. You expressed some apprehension about Dr. Mitchell's mental state. Is that correct?

CLARK ASHTON WATTS: That was just a . . . I think maybe it was me being a little overconcerned, you know? Mental state is also . . . That suggests crazy, right? I never thought Dr. Mitchell was crazy or suffering from some . . . It was—

AGENT RANGER: You suspected she was abusing pharmaceuticals.

CLARK ASHTON WATTS: I was worried, okay? I have some friends, people I went to school with, who got addicted to pain pills; an ex-girlfriend back in Ohio. Me, I never hit anything harder than some ibuprofen. Honestly. In my mind, we've become kind of soft . . . People don't put up with pain the way they used to. Life's hard, right? That's—

AGENT RANGER: Mr. Watts. Focus. Why did you think Dr. Mitchell was abusing?

CLARK ASHTON WATTS: Okay. I'm sorry. It's just . . . Never done this before. She kind of had some tells. Mood swings, nothing major, but when she was happy, she was *real* happy. Dr. Mitchell was never the fanciest dresser. She's an astronomer. But over the last year or so she kind of let herself go. Not in a bad way, just wearing a lot of sweats and not much makeup. She also put way too much sugar in her coffee. I know that sounds like no big deal, but I've seen that before. Opioid addicts, they're big on the sweets.

AGENT RANGER: You never saw her taking any prescription medications?

CLARK ASHTON WATTS: No. This was just a hunch.

AGENT RANGER: But it was enough of a hunch that you reported it to Dr. Mitchell's supervisor. That's not a minor step to take.

CLARK ASHTON WATTS: Listen . . . I want to be as forthright with you as possible, okay? I am telling you everything I know. I just need some . . . I want some guarantee that—

AGENT RANGER: As we explained at the outset, Clark, this conversation is entirely confidential. Everything you say to us will be off the record, so to speak. Neither Dr. Kjelgaard, Dr. Mitchell, nor any of the staff at the University of California, Santa Cruz, will be made aware that we are even meeting. And I should remind you that you are under oath. This is a criminal investigation. Now, please go ahead.

CLARK ASHTON WATTS: I wanted to impress Dr. Kjelgaard. I wanted to be his inside man, okay? I noticed stuff going on with Dr. Mitchell and I could have kept it to myself but . . . information is currency, right? It's not strange to want to impress your boss. All of us are looking for a way to get ahead. I'm just a grad student, but I'm looking at a crowded field out there. And to tell you all the truth, I haven't always been the most stellar student. So, yeah, that's why I told Dr. Kjelgaard. Honestly, it was just as much out of concern for her health, you know, as well as me getting a leg up—

AGENT RANGER: Is it possible that Dr. Mitchell was abusing prescription medications when she located the Pulse signal?

CLARK ASHTON WATTS: I don't know. Maybe. I mean . . . if you're addicted, you don't stop, right? I don't really see how it would matter though. We found that signal. I analyzed it right there in the room with her. I ran the programs, watched them do their thing. No matter whether she was high or not, the Pulse was real. It *is* real.

4

EDITED TRANSCRIPT FROM AN FBI INTERVIEW WITH DAHLIA MITCHELL

PALO ALTO FIELD OFFICE: RECORDING #001—FIELD AGENT J. E. MUDDOCK

OCTOBER 23, 2023

AGENT MUDDOCK: You said you didn't know the signal was extraterrestrial at first. You assumed it was just another space signal.

DAHLIA MITCHELL: Right, at first. We see these things, random noise generated by the universe all the time. Astronomers have picked them up for . . . centuries, really. Fast radio bursts, most of the time. In every instance, it's a noise generated by some natural phenomenon. Usually something exploding.

AGENT MUDDOCK: But not in this instance.

DAHLIA MITCHELL: That's what we figured out. Like I said, though, at first I assumed it was just some of the same background noise we'd always seen.

AGENT MUDDOCK: Okay, and then what?

DAHLIA MITCHELL: So you're not going to accuse me of falsifying it?

AGENT MUDDOCK: No.

DAHLIA MITCHELL: First time I was dragged in to talk, they made it pretty clear that they thought I had something to do with the Pulse. Like I'd either faked it or somehow knew about its location and only released the data when it was professionally advantageous to me. Which is the most absurd thing imaginable.

AGENT MUDDOCK: We're not interested in exploring that angle further at this moment. Please tell us what happened after you'd verified the signal data.

DAHLIA MITCHELL: To be honest, I sat on it for a while. I wasn't convinced I was really seeing what I was seeing. Analyzing these things takes a while. There are sounds radio telescopes picked up three decades ago that still haven't been deciphered. I figured this would be another one of those, something grad students would crunch numbers on for the next few years. Turns out, I was wrong.

AGENT MUDDOCK: Yes. And how exactly did that realization come about?

DAHLIA MITCHELL: I did some initial analysis. When we find something, we take all the proper measurements and record them. We're pretty tempered people—

AGENT MUDDOCK: Explain.

DAHLIA MITCHELL: It's not like the movies—not like we look through a telescope and suddenly see something and all shout "Eureka!" But after my initial analysis, even as cursory as it was, I was certain: this was unlike anything I'd ever seen. But even knowing that, even seeing it right there in front of me, I needed someone else to analyze it and tell me that it was what I thought it was.

AGENT MUDDOCK: Can you be more specific about what you thought it was?

DAHLIA MITCHELL: It sounds silly saying it out loud. I ran through every conceivable option—from an FRB, like we discussed, to an unknown type of cosmic radiation or a celestial collision—but it just didn't fit any of those things directly, And, frankly, it was so . . . purposeful. That's why I thought it must be a transmission from an unknown intelligence outside of our galaxy.

AGENT MUDDOCK: From an extraterrestrial source.

DAHLIA MITCHELL: Yes. That was my first thought. But that idea itself opens an entirely different can of worms. I let my mind go there for a few minutes; certainly Clark and I talked about it, but it was just . . . it was too much. So I did what I was trained to do when confronted with anomalous and shocking data, data that simply doesn't fit: I stepped back, got serious, and analyzed it. Tried to find what I was doing wrong. But everything checked out.

5

FRANK KJELGAARD, PROFESSOR OF ASTRONOMY

LOS ANGELES, CA

MAY 9, 2025

Dr. Frank Kjelgaard is a burly, unmarried sixty-five-year-old who moved to Los Angeles from Santa Cruz about three years ago.

An astronomer, Frank taught at the University of California, Santa Cruz, for fifteen years. He always considered himself a scientist first and a teacher second, an approach that guaranteed grant monies but also resulted in poor student reviews of his teaching. He told me that he once went online to see how he was ranked compared to other professors at his school. He was not happy with what he saw.

The Elevation brought Frank a lot of unwanted attention. People, mostly on-line and anonymous, blamed him for not trusting or listening to Dahlia Mitchell when she told him she'd discovered the Pulse Code. There were death threats. He was even "SWATed." An angry denizen of the dark web called the police, claimed to be holding hostages, and gave the cops Frank's address. When the SWAT team kicked in the front door, Frank was in bed and terrified.

When the country fell apart in the immediate aftermath of the Finality, Frank tried to maintain a semblance of his life. He awoke at 6:00 a.m., dressed in a suit and tie, and went to work at the University. Though there were no students, Frank continued his research until the power went down. After that, he went to the library on campus and caught up on reading during the daylight hours. Eventually, he was asked to leave by police who'd been ordered to lock up the campus to prevent looting.

Bored at home in Santa Cruz and infuriated with the pace of recovery, Frank chose to move to Los Angeles, where a number of academics—including several astronomers and astrophysicists—had set up camp around the famed Griffith Observatory. Here, they reminisce, plan new projects, and plot how they'll eventually gain access to working modern telescopes should the opportunity arise.

I meet with Frank on the steps of the Observatory on August 7. It is a hot day and the city of Los Angeles sparkles below us. The Pacific beyond is so still, it resembles a pane of glass. Frank smokes an old-fashioned pipe as he speaks and looks out over the city below us. Ten years earlier, it would have been a sea of congestion: cars baking in the late summer heat as they inched from jammed intersection to intersection; the sidewalks crammed with people; the skies buzzing with passing planes, helicopters, and drones; the air hazy. Two months before Dahlia discovered the Pulse, there was a traffic jam on I-405 that lasted a record-breaking three days.

Now the city is silent.

There are only a handful of cars darting by on the streets below us. Most of the people traveling across the city are on bikes. With the population of the city only a fourth of what it once was, the place has largely been given back to nature—and nature's taken as much as she can get. The Los Angeles River, a few years ago just a concrete trench with a few inches of water in it, is now a raging torrent. Palm trees have taken root on rooftops. There are large flocks of birds, thousands strong, nesting in the abandoned office buildings along South Grand Avenue.

Dahlia came to me the morning after she'd found the Pulse.

She looked as though she hadn't slept, which of course she hadn't. I was used to seeing Dahlia fired up. She was a passionate teacher. Many of her students came to me in the months that followed the discovery and told me personally of how she'd touched their lives. This was before everything happened, before all the changes. Like most of us, I was personally affected by the Elevation: I lost a wife, a daughter, and my brother-in-law.

I realize there are others, people who lost just as much as I did or even more. For a long time, and I'm okay admitting this now, I blamed Dahlia for what happened. I know how that sounds. She's a national hero of sorts, a global one, but until all the information came out about the other signals, I held Dahlia liable for bringing it on us. Sort of an extraterrestrial Pandora, but instead of opening a jar,* she opened the entirety of the universe.

Despite spending a good portion of my life staring up at the sky, I never was one to hope we'd see anything, find anything, other than new stars and new astronomic events. I never believed there was another intelligence out there. In my mind, there was always only us. We were a miracle in the vastness.

The funny thing—the thing that no one else wants to say—is that still might be the case. After the Elevation, after the Finality, we, the survivors, remain alone here . . .

Frank pauses here, exhales a plume of smoke, and looks off at the ocean. A few seconds later he clears his throat and picks up where he left off.

When Dahlia showed me printouts of the signal, I was confused.

She said, "We've been looking at gravitational lensing† this whole time, but when I recalibrated the telescopes for radio emissions, we found it."

Only I wasn't seeing what she was seeing.

"It's a pulse," she said, pointing at several lines of the code. She continued, "This isn't like Gran Sasso‡ or Minnesota,§ Frank. This pulse didn't come from background processes. It's not bouncing in from a terrestrial source."

Then she leaned forward and told me: "This is the one."

The *one*.

I asked her if she was familiar with Martin Keane.

She shook her head.

I said, "Of course you're not. No one is. He was a third-year grad student

---

* This phrase is usually rendered as "Pandora's box" but the mythological source for the idiom states that it was, in fact, a jar and not a box. Apparently in ancient Greece, things of value (or in this case powerful evil) were stored in large clay jars, not boxes of any sort.

† "Gravitational lensing" refers to the fact that mass bends light. The gravitational field of a massive object, like a planet, bends the space far around it. Even the light rays passing by will be bent. Astronomers can look for this bending light, dubbed lensing, to identify distant objects. Dark matter, Dahlia's field of study, bends light in similar ways, though it is itself invisible.

‡ Gran Sasso is a reference to Italy's Laboratori Nazionali del Gran Sasso, an underground research center for physics studies.

§ Minnesota Institute for Astrophysics.

at MIT when he stumbled across an alien broadcast. Made the papers. It took four years to figure out he'd mucked up his measurements. Today, he gives lectures on how most of the presidents since Nixon are secretly reptilian aliens."*

Dahlia said, "This isn't a nutcase conspiracy theory. This is verifiable data."

I reminded her that she'd just told me she altered the calibration of the telescopes. That, in her words, she'd "fixed them."

I told her it wasn't a challenge.

I told her I'd given her an opportunity to move to another project and instead she came back with this garbled code that convinced her it was sent by an alien intelligence. She was exasperated, as expected, and stormed off.

Which is what I was hoping she'd do.

Frank pauses again. I can tell he's going to reveal something big, so I wait, don't pressure him, let it form inside his mind. Several reporters before me had approached Frank with questions about his dealings with Dahlia Mitchell, the finding of the Pulse, and what transpired after. Frank is clearly uneasy.

After Dahlia left, I took the data she'd given me and made a few calls.

I'm telling you this now because . . . well, it's been long enough. I've kept this information secret for too many years.

I took the Pulse Code that Dahlia gave me and sent it to a contact I had at the National Geospatial-Intelligence Agency. You've probably never heard of them and, honestly, I'm not sure anyone is in that department any longer. But at the time, they were tasked with providing all geospatial data—analyzing Earth's features, both man-made and natural. What they do is tangential to what we do. They focus down, we focus up, but we have a lot of tools and technologies in common. My contact, however, wasn't involved in the geospatial work. That was his cover.

---

* The whole "reptilian" conspiracy theory movement was born in the late 1980s. Like most conspiracy theories, it is a hodgepodge of esoteric thought (nineteenth-century spiritualism), fear of government overreach, New Age cosmology, and pulp fiction. The general thesis is this: sometime in the distant past, bipedal lizard people came to Earth and now reside in underground bases across the globe. From these bases, they control (and/or have replaced) various politicians, well-known actors and musicians, and even royalty.

I never knew his real name, though I'd met him in 2021.

Never knew what agency he truly worked for. This was a guy who came out of the shadows, literally, and then vanished back into them. He said his name was Simon Grieg. He approached me at a conference at the Capodimonte observatory in Napoli.[*] He'd read some of my work, notably the papers I'd published on the effects of pulsars on gravitational waves. We chatted for a while about astronomy and bitched about funding and then he suggested I call him when I was next in Washington. He gave me his card and it all looked quite official.

When I found the card in my desk drawer twelve, thirteen months later, I grew curious. I ran a few searches on Simon and everything seemed to check out. He was a government employee, an expert in geostationary satellite imaging, and had worked for NOAA, among other agencies. According to what I found online, he was married, had two daughters, and lived in Reston, Virginia. Turned out, of course, that none of that was true.

I was in Washington three months later for a meeting and gave Simon a call. He and I met for dinner at a vegetarian restaurant (my preference) and he told me he'd gotten involved in something that I would find *intriguing*. Apparently, there were deep branches of the government, offices I'd never heard of, that had been tasked with dissecting signals received from outside our galaxy.

We're talking fast radio bursts, largely.

What followed was the strangest conversation I'd ever had in my life. Simon said that his colleagues had picked up signals that they believed were from outside our galaxy and intentionally designed to get our attention. Communication. I was skeptical, of course. This is exactly the kind of UFO nut stuff that I'd been dealing with since before graduate school. Roswell, Levelland, Tehran, Rendlesham Forest, the "triangle flaps"[†]—I knew enough to dismiss them all. Mass hysteria, confusion, poor reporting, eyewitness error, the list of explanations was endless. And yet, Simon was clearly not

---

[*] The Astronomical Observatory of Capodimonte in Naples is part of Italy's National Institute for Astrophysics.

[†] UFO believers regard all five of these events as foundational—cases of UFO sightings that scientists, historians, and other experts haven't "proven" to be hoaxes or misinterpretations of common experiences (e.g., planes or planetary bodies mistaken for extraterrestrial aircraft). Of course, scientists and historians would argue that these cases are easily explainable.

one of these people. I told him I needed proof, and, well, that's when he showed me something.

It was a few weeks after our meeting in DC. I was in New York for yet another meeting and he called me up. I agreed to meet him in Maryland. I rented a car and drove to an office building in Silver Spring. He met me in the lobby.

First thing I noticed when I walked in was that he had armed body-guards. Simon handed me a bottle of water and then led me to the elevators. We rode to the tenth floor. There, we went down a hallway to a closed door. He produced a key and opened it. I stepped inside an office largely devoid of furniture. There was but a single standing desk in the center of the room. On it was a laptop computer. Simon, without saying anything, pressed the return key on the laptop and . . .

Frank needs reassurance from me that the information he's about to give won't result in an investigation or potential criminal charges. I show him the letter I received from my attorneys about this project and those I interview. As he reads it over I remind him of what he already knows: the world has changed.

At this point, there is no one interested in punishing people who may have withheld information in the lead-up to the Finality. And the court system is a tenth of what it was, 82 percent of prisons have closed, and the few remaining district attorneys certainly have better things to do. If Frank wants to talk—if he wants the truth about the Pulse, the Elevation, and the Finality to finally be told—it's now.

He continues:

There was video.

It was filmed in a research lab. There were no exterior shots. I saw workbenches with technical equipment on them, computer monitors, the usual stuff. There was a chair in front of the wall. It was simple, plastic. Two people came into frame, both wearing hazmat suits and masks. They stood on either side of the chair, arms folded in front. I couldn't see their eyes because of their visors. Then a third person, also in a hazmat suit, walked into frame, and propped up a young woman in a chair. She appeared very ill.

The girl was maybe fifteen, sixteen, but not much older than that.

She had deep bags under her eyes, and long, dirty-blond hair tied back in a loose ponytail. Her skin was tanned but pockmarked and scarred. The scars resembled those you might see on someone who'd been cutting him- or herself. I had a niece who did that. She struggled with addictions for most of her life and . . . well, it's not important.

Then the person in the hazmat suit, I'm guessing he was a male, the one standing to the left of the chair, produced a small tablet computer. He held it up so the camera could make it out and the camera zoomed in.

The man pressed a button on the tablet screen.

First, there was a number. I believe it was 0304. Then a card that read: "Trial Sonora." Then the tablet displayed a code that ran across the screen, left to right. The code was complicated. Not as complicated as what Dahlia found but similar. I can't describe it more than to tell you that it was a series of letters, numbers, and simple shapes. It ran in three loops, each maybe twenty-two seconds long.

The man signaled to the second person standing to the right of the chair. This person, female would be my guess, leaned over and signaled for the girl to turn around. She did, though it was clear that the movements were painful.

The man then reached down and opened up the back of this girl's hospital gown, revealing her skin. There were visible scars, just as there were on her arms and legs. The camera zoomed in on this girl's spine.

At first I couldn't make out what the purpose of this was. The girl's back seemed fine, outside of the scars and some discolorations of the skin.

And then she moved.

I can't . . . I can't guarantee that it wasn't faked.

In this video, the girl had *two spinal columns*. They . . . they moved with each other, twisting with her body as she bent from side to side. When she leaned forward, her spines were even more pronounced.

The video ended.

I was in shock. I'm still left speechless thinking about it, honestly. This was many years ago. Years before the Pulse, before Dahlia even joined the University. Simon Grieg, of course, knew the video would upset me and leave me confused. I think he also knew that it would frighten me. Frighten me enough to listen very carefully. I'd asked Simon for more information on the video. What was wrong with the girl? A mutation? A genetic aberration?

He said, "Both."

I asked about the tablet computer, the code it showed.

Simon told me it was directly related to the girl's condition.*

Then he closed the laptop and led me over to a window. It was sunny out and I could see downtown Silver Spring from the vantage point. Simon patted me on the shoulder and told me that if I ever found a coded transmission from outside our solar system, a fast radio burst that appeared directed or designed, I was to send it to him directly. For this, I would be paid quite a bit of money. There was an added benefit. Simon was very clear: I was in the inner sanctum. I knew more than I should. If I wanted my family to be safe, happy, healthy, I would agree.

And I did.

I learned later, after the Elevation, that eight of my colleagues, at various universities around the globe, made the same agreement with Simon.

Obviously, when Dahlia showed up with that pulse, I needed to be sure of what it was. I needed to be confident in my judgment. I also needed for her to try and let it go. She couldn't, of course. That's why the whole world changed.

I sent the Pulse information she'd given me to Simon.

He already had it, I'm certain.

But I did what I'd agreed to do in 2022. There was a direct deposit into my bank account five days afterwards for the sum of $250,000. I was also sent a final message, my last communication with Simon, whoever he was, that my family and myself were out of harm's way.

I didn't believe it, of course.

Three weeks after the Elevation began, after my niece started suffering from worsening symptoms, I quit my job at the University and moved here. We bought a house and the land around it and got as far from the rest of the

---

* The video that Frank describes has never turned up publicly. I searched long and hard for it, utilizing every lead I could find. Frank was never able to provide any more information about the video other than what I've recorded here, so it remains something of an enigma. It is possible that he invented the story—maybe to confuse folks snooping around his personal history—or that what he saw was a complex fabrication, a video designed to scare him. Otherwise, the video was real. If so, it hints at a very dark prehistory to the Pulse and the Elevation.

world as possible. I wasn't escaping the Elevation; I was running as far as possible from Simon, from the bureaucracy behind him.

I suppose that makes me weak. I never reached out to Dahlia, not directly, though I should have. I was impressed with how nonjudgmental she was. Dahlia never denigrated me in the press. She never lambasted me as the cliché boss that just doesn't get it, the one who forces the strong-willed employee's hands.

You see, there's always a story behind the story.

I had a small part to play in the history of the Pulse Code and what happened to our world after it was discovered—a small but important part. It's okay that people remember me as Dahlia's boss, a forgotten astronomer, but I think it's important that they know the larger picture too.

This might have started with Dahlia's discovery.

But she was not the first: there were many before her.

6

And so it begins.

I haven't slept in nearly thirty-three hours. I haven't been tired either. Is that bad? Outside of running to the bathroom (when my bladder was quaking 'cause it was so close to rupturing) and refilling my coffee and microwaving a few pieces of day-old pepperoni pizza, I've been in my seat at my desk in my office poring over the data from the Pulse. This is crazy!

The Pulse is unlike anything I've ever encountered.

I sound melodramatic saying it but . . . it's true. So true.

As a kid, I never got into science fiction. Growing up, my father would take us to movies off base. He had a thing for the spectacle flicks—the ones with special effects and all the ooh-and-aah moments. Nico got really into Star Wars. Had the pj's and all the toys. I preferred the moodier movies, the ones that felt more plausible, more real. Nerdy, right? Maybe it was because of what was going on with my mother—with all of us—but I wanted to see people dealing with real world—this world—problems. That sort of escapism didn't do much for me.

If I wanted aliens, I wanted something truly alien.

The things in the sci-fi movies, they were always just another version of us—maybe with a few more bumps, different-color eyes, or three heads. But they met in bars like us. They drank alcoholic drinks the way we do. They fought, they fucked, but they were human in every way except shape and language.

Even as a kid I knew it wasn't realistic. If there was other life out in the cosmos, it wasn't going to look or act like us. If we ever even saw them, that is. No, aliens—if they existed—might be so unlike us, so vastly different, that we might not even recognize them as living. Forget space amoebas or creatures of light; we're talking beings that don't even live inside our spatial planes—beyond invisible.

The kind of beings that would send the Pulse.

And the Pulse Code hinted at an intelligence I could barely fathom.

Not necessarily superior, though it was, but utterly unlike our minds. We think linearly. Our consciousness is immersed in time. We are creatures of schedules and calendars. Of lifetimes and cycles. Our math, our physics—they're the result of our time-bound brains. It is the lens through which our world and our lives make sense: things are born, they live, they die, repeat, repeat, ad infinitum.

And yet, the intelligence behind the Pulse Code was beyond time.

I can't even explain how I knew it but I did.

I felt it. Right in my chest. Just this release . . .

And even though I couldn't translate the code—I couldn't even figure out how it began or the mathematics it was composed of—I realized right away that it was both impossibly ancient and crafted only seconds before I found it. That sounds crazy, I know. Frank would see it and shake his head, say it was a mistake. Best I can describe the Pulse Code was like looking out at the ocean: the waves hitting the beach at your feet are finishing what the deepest ocean currents started generations earlier. All right there, in one immense, overwhelming vista.

Too poetic but . . . you get the image, right?

Frank was useless as usual.

Not only did he doubt that I'd discovered anything worth looking at, he wasn't even willing to give it any more than a second glance. So I stormed out of his office and went back home. I showered. I had a glass of wine. Thank God for wine. And I tried to see his point of view. I honestly attempted to clear my mind and approach the data with a new perspective, antagonizing it as though someone told me at the outset that it was a hoax. And you know what? I came to the same conclusion as before.

If it was a hoax, it was the most beautiful hoax I'd ever seen.

And I believed it fully.

It's funny, because I used to make fun of Mom for being gullible. She'd forward every chain letter email she'd get—usually they promised all sorts of luck and happiness—and was convinced that good things would come from it. When good things didn't, she was crushed. Now here I am, convinced that I've just uncovered contact with an extraterrestrial race based on a single scrap of impossible to decipher code. But . . . but . . . this is different.

It always is with me, isn't it?

But, God, I was such a wide-eyed child, so naïve about the world. So protected from human failing and misery. I remember judging each of the cities we lived in by their libraries. Augsburg, Honolulu, Seoul . . . I can't picture the downtowns now, but I can still see the interiors of those libraries as though I was sitting in them at this very second. So many wonderful moments of discovery in those stacks. The thrill of finding a book that I'd never even heard of, covering a topic that I didn't even know existed . . .

Well, that was heaven to a nerdy little girl like me.

Of course, those bubbles I inhabited—moving from town to town, house to house, school to school, library to library, and book to book— would never have existed if my mother hadn't created them. After Mom died, Nico and I went through her journals, working together to translate them using our combined German knowledge. We didn't need much to see all that sadness, all that bitterness.

If she were around, she'd be pissed at me about the pills.

I know they're a problem but . . . I'm getting better.

It's true. It really is. I feel . . . I'm just more focused than before. I don't need all the emotional bullshit . . . They give me that little boost I need to get through the day. Nothing more. I could live without them, I . . . I just don't have the strength right now.

Besides, if I quit, I worry that I'll end up disillusioned. Not as a housewife with drug issues but as an astronomer who jumps reck-

lessly at every opportunity to find awe in the world again. That's why I research dark matter, isn't it? I'm always looking for that moment of discovery, that rush of new knowledge. Doesn't get more enticing than matter that might not even exist.

Nico likes to say I search the stars to find myself.

He loves platitudes and aphorisms and summing up complicated ideas in bumper sticker–sized bites. Though Nico would never admit it, he'd probably feel a very deep satisfaction in forwarding chain letters. So, yeah, he'd boil me down to a sound bite of psychology: Dahlia spends all her time staring up into the night sky because she's lost here on Earth. That's exactly how he'd say it.

And maybe he's right.

Maybe I have been lost.

But now . . . I've been found.

We all have.

7

JON HURTADO, FORMER NSA ANALYST
SALT LAKE CITY, UT
JUNE 13, 2025

*Though he lives in Los Angeles, Jon Hurtado and I meet in Salt Lake City, where
he's attending a conference.*

*That might sound strange, considering this is a city that still suffers from
rolling brownouts and rarely has Internet speeds exceeding 2 megabytes per
second, which is, even before the Elevation, considerably slow. The organizers
of this conference, however, want to highlight these technological disparities.
This is a meeting of entrepreneurs and former government officials eager to get
in on the ground floor of what they see as the future, reunited United States of
America. Whether or not they can convince Texas and Alabama to come back
to the table, however, is a matter of ongoing debate.*

*But while Jon has fascinating things to say about rebuilding our country,
we're not here to discuss them. Jon was one of the few people who were close
to Dahlia Mitchell, and his insight into her character and decision-making is
crucial to our understanding of the Elevation and the Finality. It must also be
said that Jon was there, in the thick of it, when the long-rumored organization
the Twelve was exposed.*

*Jon was Dahlia's lover. Well, former. They dated for several years—going
so far as to move in together for a brief, tumultuous time—before breaking up
but staying friends. That's unusual. Most couples, after the split, they just can't
move forward in any way emotionally; in my experience, there's always one
party that just can't let go. But Jon and Dahlia were different. What split them*

apart was physical distance and intellectual pride. They simply met at the wrong time. Both chasing careers, neither side willing to let their passions for work go. For her, it was the research and the academic ladder. For him, the deep dive into the clandestine work of saving the world. Star-crossed lovers indeed. They kept in touch over the years they were apart, texting, emailing, even calling every now and again. Even though neither of them had room for the other in their life, they weren't willing to fully let go.

When Dahlia discovered the signal and Dr. Kjelgaard wasn't willing to listen, Jon was the next best person to turn to. That history—that emotional connection—was, for all intents and purposes, the thing that changed the course of Dahlia's life the most: if she hadn't come to him with the signal, it might have been forgotten.

For a while at least.

Jon Hurtado, the son of two Mexican immigrants, was in ROTC in high school. He followed in his father's footsteps and joined the military. (His dad, Luis, was a second lieutenant in the Mexican army.) Jon served in the second Iraq war as a radio operator, intercepting enemy text messages and radio broadcasts, and coordinating air strikes through cell tower pings.

After the war, the Office of Tailored Access Operations (TAO), the NSA's warfare intelligence-gathering unit, recruited him. As an analyst in the ROC (remote operations center) at Fort Meade, he monitored and infiltrated computer systems before being promoted to overseeing their virus containment unit—a "digital jail" where malware is safely broken apart and analyzed. Successful at TAO, Jon was recruited by the CIA to work on cyberwarfare programs and relocated to California.

We have coffee in the lobby of his hotel. He is now a thin and youthful forty years old with a trim, graying beard and a full head of hair. Jon is dressed down in jeans and a hoodie. He has a cast on one hand, the result, he tells me, of a biking accident. ("I was biking with a friend around Silver Lake and ran straight into a deer—the place is overrun with them now.")

Dahlia is something else.

It's funny saying that.

Makes it sound like she's going to walk in the door any minute. I'll be sitting on my porch and hear the door close behind me and turn expecting to see her but . . . it's nothing. No one. Even though it's been two years, when I talk about her, I refer to her in the present tense. I can't help it.

It's not like she actually died, right?

You asked me about how it all started. The signal. The code. The discovery.

The way most people remember it, the whole thing began with *her*, with that one moment inside a radio telescope observatory.

It's never really the truth, though.

That's just how we remember it. Her face was all over the news. It felt like she woke up that morning as a nobody, a well-liked but not-well-published professor at one of the West Coast colleges, but by that evening she was the most talked about human being on the planet. And this was before it all happened, before anyone had any idea of the truth.

Dahlia wasn't one for fame.

She was after the information.

Frankly, she'd spent most of her career focused on the deepest recesses of space. Not the exciting parts, you understand? Not the black holes and the supernovae and the comets and the stars. But the spaces in between. You know how you see these photos of the Milky Way and it's dense with planets and suns, like someone spilled sugar across a black stretch of cloth? Well, that wasn't where she was looking. Her research, it was in the places where the stars were so far apart, no craft would ever reach them.

This was just dead space. Forgotten, forgettable, empty.

The kind of emptiness that gives you nightmares.

As a kid, I used to have these falling dreams. Usually happened in the seconds right after I fell asleep, right after I closed my eyes. I'd feel the floor whip out from underneath me and I'd be tumbling into nothingness. Not down a cliff face or a staircase but just straight down into the void. Heart pounding, I'd jolt upright in bed with a gasp. Suddenly awake and terrified, filled with adrenaline.

The first time Dahlia told me about the empty spaces she studied, I thought about those dreams.

I imagined falling into those gaps.

You'd fall forever there.

Funny, I think I even told her that.

I had this image of myself falling, growing old, getting some long beard in my spacesuit, and dying and becoming this skeleton tumbling through space for the rest of eternity; a speck amongst specks.

Dahlia called me a romantic after I mentioned it.

She said it wasn't anything like the way I described it.

The way I worried about it.

Apparently, you can't fall in space. Not technically, anyway.

In space, direction doesn't exist. Just like time doesn't. All these things we make assumptions about down on Earth, they're illusions in space. You don't fall because there is no up and there is no down.

Anyway, this was two years before the discovery.

Dahlia was up for tenure review and was pretty stressed-out.

I met her at a party.

No idea really how our paths crossed that night.

It was a thing at someone's houseboat docked at Pier 32. My friend Charles, a contractor with the agency, invited me on a whim and I had nothing better doing, so I figured some wine and cheese with a bunch of hipsters on a houseboat would be a change of pace. I'd spent the last year crunching numbers at NASA's Langley Research Center, isolated in a windowless back room, glued to a computer monitor fifteen hours a day. Having a drink on a houseboat, watching the sunset, seemed a pretty nice escape.

Turned out, Charles barely knew the boat's owners himself. He was dating a woman who'd been invited. They broke up two weeks after the party.

Anyway, I felt as though I was crashing the scene—a lot of pretty boring people crammed into a boat talking politics, art, movies, and small batch beers—and so I stepped out and walked the dock for a few minutes.

The lull of the waves slapping against the boats, the stars sparkling up above—it wasn't a romantic moment but it felt like it could easily have been the setting for one . . . And then she walked in.

"The Seven Sisters."

Dahlia moved down the dock towards me, pointing up at the stars I'd been glancing at a few moments earlier.

"The Pleiades," she continued, "the seven daughters of one of the Titans. It's an impressive cluster of stars. The brightest of them are easily hundreds of times more luminous than our sun."

I looked up at the stars. They certainly seemed luminous.

"I did not know that," I said.

Then I turned back to Dahlia. She had her hair pulled up and was wearing a black dress. That was one of the few times I'd ever seen her in makeup and contact lenses; she was striking regardless. I hadn't been in a relationship, at least anything meaningful, for a few years. I wasn't actively looking either.

You know that old chestnut about not finding what you're looking for until you stop looking for it? Well, that's always been true for me.

That night was the start. We talked until dawn, forgot all about the party. Turns out that she wasn't supposed to be there either. Just like me, a friend had invited her out. She found the conversation boring and needed air.

Dahlia and I were together for two years and two months.

We had our ups and downs. I traveled a ton, effectively living on the East Coast for a stretch of it, and she worked ridiculous hours. That led to a fair amount of tension—times I wanted to see her and she wasn't available, other times she was hoping I was free but I had to travel. I wouldn't say our fights were anything unusual. We're both tough people to love.

I still am.

We broke up on President's Day.* I was in a foul mood—I'd been called in to work an extra shift—and she had had a tough conversation with her brother. She was really hurt and wanted to talk through it all, get it off her chest. Only, I wasn't emotionally available. I couldn't have been bothered to tell her that, though. She came to me crying, I was barely listening to what she said.

She blew up. Stormed out.

That was it.

I was in such a bad mood that I didn't chase after her. Didn't call either.

I regret that asshole decision to this day. Took me some therapy sessions, talking with friends and my folks, to realize how badly I'd blown a pretty great thing. I was full of myself, figured she'd come back to me. But Dahlia is strong—strongest person I've ever met. She knew she could do better than me.

---

* Jon went so far as to show me his dog-eared calendar from that year. On the entry for President's Day he'd written, in blue, "Over with Dahlia."

So you'll imagine my surprise when she called October 19, 2023. I can't ever forget that date.

She told me she needed to talk.

Needed someone she could trust.

I'll tell you, I cried after I hung up the phone. That call, I don't know why it got me so emotional, but it did. Maybe I was in a bad place, maybe work had really beaten me down, but I needed the uplift of that message—that I meant something to somebody. That I was someone she could trust.

I met her at the Black Bear Diner in Monterey.

She looked great. Comfortable.

I slid into a chair across from her and complimented her shorter hair.

She jumped right into it and handed me a flash drive.

"This is going to sound nuts," she said, "but last night I found a pulse that enveloped the entire planet. We've had brushes with unusual deep-space signals before, but they've always turned out to be evaporating black holes or solar flares."

"Or microwaves," I said. "I read about some astronomers who got all excited about a crazy powerful signal. Turned out it was just someone re-heating a bowl of pho in the break room...."*

I smiled, expecting a giggle.

She didn't crack.

"What's on this drive isn't a microwave. It's not a black hole or a solar flare[†] either. I've run the numbers over and over. It keeps coming up the same."

"What exactly do you think it is?" I asked.

"Contact," she replied.

Dahlia let that sink in for a second.

Then she continued: "This pulse is from outside our galaxy, Jon, and it is the most complex piece of mathematics I've seen. It's beautiful. Mathematics means language, Jon. It's a message. To us. But . . . we'll need a supercom-

---

* True story. Australian astronomers were puzzled for over a decade by a strange signal they'd been picking up. They thought the interference was due to lightning strikes or something else coming from the upper atmosphere. Turns out it was a microwave oven in the break room.

† Solar flares are most often associated with "coronal mass ejections"—a release of plasma (and magnetic field) from the sun. These frequently interfere with electronic systems on Earth—a real bugaboo for astronomers.

puter to get anything out of it. Took me all night to just review a fraction of the data."

I told her she should take it to NASA or SETI.

"I gave it to Frank. He shot it down. I don't trust my people, Jon, and my people don't trust me. You're the only one I do trust."

I swallowed hard hearing that. "I work for the NSA. We're not exactly known for our honesty."

Dahlia reached across the table, took my hands in hers.

"Please, just review it. If the data's garbage, you can forget I ever brought it to you. You can call me crazy too."

"Fine," I said, "but I have one condition. Dinner at Banzai Sushi on Friday. I'll pick you up. Dinner. That's it."

Finally, she smiled. Dahlia said, "I just handed you a flash drive with what could be the most important discovery in human history . . ."

"And I'm offering you some kick-ass sashimi and a few good jokes."

She agreed and then left.

I'm not ashamed to admit I did a little victory dance, right there in my seat.

When I got home, I made a copy of the flash drive. Felt a little paranoid doing it, so when I went to hide it, I didn't put it in any one of the usual places—not the lockbox or the sock drawer. A friend in the FBI once told me to hide stuff inside boxes of cereal.

That's what I did with the copy.

Tucked it into a bag of Cap'n Crunch.

I brought the code in to work the next morning. Dahlia warned me to be careful with it. She didn't want it vanishing into the government black hole, winding up in some file or drawer somewhere in Reno. She wanted me to give it to someone that I trusted—someone who would recognize the importance of it.

So first thing I did when I got into the office was show it to one of my coworkers, Zach Jaffe. He's something of a clown, a bit paranoid, but he's the best coder that I know. If anyone was going to get a read on this thing, it was him.

You know what happened after that.

8

AGENT PENDARVES: Please state your name and occupation for the record.

ZACH JAFFE: Well, I'm Zach Jaffe and I'm thirty. I work for the government.

AGENT PENDARVES: Please be more precise, Mr. Jaffe. What do you do for the government and how long have you done it?

ZACH JAFFE: This is being recorded?

AGENT PENDARVES: Yes. Let me remind you that not only are you under oath but that you're facing obstruction charges that carry a maximum sentence of twenty to twenty-five years in a federal prison.

ZACH JAFFE: Hey, I'm just asking, okay? I'm the one that came to you guys, right? I'm the one who wanted to share what I know.

AGENT PENDARVES: Again, tell us what you do for the government.

ZACH JAFFE: NSA. Coding. I mean, that's the long and short of it. You can dress up what I do in all the fancy technical jargon that you want, but I code. I used to get my digital rocks off cracking company and government databases. I used to say that I was looking for evidence of conspiracies—you know, CIA agents smuggling drugs into the inner city or assassinations that the public didn't know about[*]—but really that was just my way to dress it up. I wasn't actually looking for anything; I just liked being inside, you know? Anyway, I'm making this story too long. I got caught. Cops raided my apartment when I was at my desk, in my underwear, eating a Hot Pocket. They told me I was looking at something like ten years in prison. I made a deal and, well, after working for them for free for a couple years, I got to liking the gig. Worked my way up the NSA and the ROC.

AGENT PENDARVES: The ROC?

ZACH JAFFE: Remote operations center. I was in the Office of Tailored Access Operations. We were the specialists behind the specialists. Need someone to design a specific virus for a piece of equipment at a hydroelectric dam in Iran? We could design that and, even better, we could figure out a way to get it across the air gap. We were the *other* badasses with beards. SEALs kind of claimed that look first, but . . . we wore it better.

AGENT PENDARVES: And you worked there with Jon Hurtado . . .

ZACH JAFFE: Yes and no. I mean, he wasn't in my department. Jon was more on the analysis side of things. His job was locating targets and mine was the infiltration. He and I did a few jobs together though and we got along. Shared an interest in music and trying to keep a punk attitude at the NSA. Wasn't easy.

AGENT PENDARVES: Jon brought you the Pulse code for analysis, correct?

ZACH JAFFE: I got a thumb drive from him. Way he set up the story was simple: he said that the information on the drive was picked up by a radio telescope in Cali. He wanted to see if it matched anything we

---

[*] Zach's referencing a conspiracy theory associated with the crack epidemic of the 1980s and 1990s. According to those who believe the theory, cocaine was smuggled into the United States by the CIA and taken to America's inner-city neighborhoods hit hardest by the drug war. Why? The CIA was using the money to fund the Contras, a revolutionary group seeking to overthrow the socialist junta controlling Nicaragua. Some historians think there could be truth to the conspiracy; others see the whole crack "epidemic" as a moral panic, a sort of media-fueled delusion like "Satanic ritual abuse" cases and UFO abductions.

had in our database. I reminded him—gently, of course—that we're at the NSA, not NASA. That's when he said he needed it to be under the table, so to speak. I want that clear, okay?

AGENT PENDARVES: I think we understand. He brought it to you with the idea that you'd be reviewing it secretly. This was not considered a government project. It was to be outside of your daily work routine. Yes?

ZACH JAFFE: You put it perfectly. So he hands me this thumb drive and asks me to check it out. And that would be fine if we were at my apartment, when I've got shit—I mean, my stuff—contained. But we're at work. And at work, my supervisors are tracking every single one of my keystrokes.

AGENT PENDARVES: But you had a work-around.

ZACH JAFFE: Of course I did. He had to flatter me a bit. I like to know that I still have that special touch. Anyway, I circumvented the tracking software on my machine and opened the data he gave me and had a look-see. I'll be honest with you, my first thought was that someone was pranking him. I mean, the stuff on that drive, it wasn't any coding language I was familiar with. It wasn't our stuff; wasn't anyone else's stuff either. Just random looking, bizarre, and that meant dangerous. I was actually fascinated by it but didn't want to dive too deep into that rabbit hole, you know? You guys must be familiar with the Max Headroom signal intrusion, right?

AGENT PENDARVES: No. Does it relate to our conversation about the Pulse Code?

ZACH JAFFE: I wouldn't be bringing it up otherwise. No, seriously, it gets at what I'm telling you. See, in the late 1980s there was this weird thing that happened in Chicago. People were just hanging out, watching the 9:00 news or whatever, when the screen suddenly flicks out and this dude appears in a Max Headroom mask. He was kind of a cult TV figure at the time. So this guy shows up in a homemade studio set, bobs around to strange electronic buzzing sounds, and then is gone. We're talking about someone hijacking a TV signal, and there was a code embedded in the intrusion signal—

AGENT PENDARVES: Mr. Jaffe, please, we're talking about—

ZACH JAFFE: I know, I know, this is going to be important later. Hear me out, okay? There was a code hidden under the Headroom thing. It was super-sophisticated and almost no one knows about it. Me and a bunch of like-minded folks on deep-Net sites, we analyzed that code and found it was like a numbers station—a code for spies to broadcast from inside the CIA. The stuff was too cryptic to understand; I was able to make out a few words. Something about "mutation" and "throughout all time" and then a group name, something I'd never actually heard of, called the Twelve. The people I was picking apart this code with? They started dying. Yeah, accidents, overdoses . . . Crazy shit. Long story short, the code that Jon brought in, it looked like that Headroom intrusion code, and, frankly, I was a little bit worried about seeing it. So I didn't look too hard.

AGENT PENDARVES: The information you gleaned from the Headroom code—what did you do with it? Did you forward it along, or . . .

ZACH JAFFE: No. Like I said, that stuff had some bad mojo around it. People were getting killed—

AGENT PENDARVES: You said they had accidents, overdoses . . .

ZACH JAFFE: (laughing) Right, right. Don't tell me that you don't know what I'm getting at. I mean, we're talking people who weren't suicidal suddenly up and offing themselves. No notes left behind. People who never fail to take excellent care of their cars who somehow overlook failing brakes. I won't make you read between the lines: I'm saying these folks were murdered and someone, the dreaded *they*, made it looks like accidents, suicides . . .

AGENT PENDARVES: Of course. So what did you and Jon do with the information that Dahlia Mitchell provided?

ZACH JAFFE: So, yeah, I looked briefly at the code on that drive and then Jon asked me to run it against the code we'd picked up in our sweep the night before.

AGENT PENDARVES: Explain that in more detail please.

ZACH JAFFE: That's what we do in Tailored Access: we basically bug the world and record it. Every country, every government, every president—we eavesdrop on them. We're the ears of the world, so to speak. What Jon wanted to do was see if anyone else on Earth picked up the same signal that these radio telescopes did. I wasn't a hundred percent on this, but whatever that code was, it was partial. He wanted to track down the whole thing.

AGENT PENDARVES: And did you find anything?

ZACH JAFFE: Yup. We did. There was another stretch of the same code pulled in by a radio telescope array in Russia. The FSB, the Russian security apparatus, they were freaked out about the code too. Chatter was all sorts of panicked. The Russians, they had no idea where the code was from, but it spooked them because their people suggested it was a cyberweapon.

AGENT PENDARVES: And what did you and Jon think it was?

ZACH JAFFE: We didn't know. The fact that it was picked up from radio telescopes pointed up, like away from our planet, certainly had me guessing. But I couldn't tell just glancing at the code what it could be. Weapon? Naturally occurring high weirdness? Someone's lost pizza order? No idea. But I did know that I wanted nothing more to do with it. So we did what all good government employees do . . .

INTERVIEWER: That is . . . ?

AGENT PENDARVES: We sent it up the proverbial ladder and let our bosses deal with it.

9

KANISHA PRESTON, FORMER NATIONAL SECURITY ADVISOR

SARASOTA, FL

JUNE 25, 2025

Sarasota was never a large city, but now it is essentially abandoned.

The beaches remain popular with tourists, but the few people who do live here are retired or work in the newly galvanized fishing industry.

Five years after the global population dropped from 7.7 billion to 2.5 billion, the fish stocks in these waters have rebounded and are amazingly robust. Hogfish, black drum, king mackerel, red porgy, swordfish, and wahoo are all easily caught off the coast. Walking the white sand beaches of Siesta Key, one sees dozens of small watercraft plying waters that teem with dolphins and manatees.

One of those small ships belongs to Kanisha Preston.

Kanisha, now forty-six, hails from Baltimore and a middle-class black family. A single mom by choice, Kanisha originally attended medical school before switching to law. She graduated from Harvard Law School and went to the State Department. Kanisha then served as senior foreign policy advisor on President Ballard's unconventional Independent presidential run. When President Ballard won the White House, Kanisha was a shoo-in for national security advisor.

Kanisha's daughter, Rose, had special needs, and the expense of caring for her pushed Kanisha nearly to financial ruin. When Rose became Elevated, Kanisha watched with wonder as her daughter's disabilities seemed to simply slough off. Sadly, she did not survive the transition from phase 2 to phase 3.

Though Kanisha had a successful political career and was respected on

Capitol Hill, she is best remembered today as the first political casualty of the Disclosure Task Force. Many questions remain about Kanisha's role in the Task Force's failure to inform the Americans about the first contact with an outside intelligence. While she defended her actions, there were many within—and outside—the Ballard administration that suspected she was a "double-agent," working for both the President and the Twelve—an agency committed to stopping any public disclosure of and/or contact with any alien race. *

One condition of my interview with Kanisha was that I would not broach the topic of the Twelve and Kanisha's suspected contact with its director, Simon Household. I respected Kanisha's wishes at the time. But later in this book I was able to answer some of the questions about her involvement with the Twelve when more research about the Twelve and Simon Household were made available after the Finality. Some are still restricted today.

Kanisha and I met on Crescent Beach.

She allowed me roughly fifty-eight minutes to speak with her, the time it took to walk from one end of the beach to the other.

Deputy Director Broxon told me about the signal.

He'd seen it because someone at the NSA was asked to review it. Didn't take us long to track it back to Jon and then Dahlia, but in those first few hours, when we only knew it was data from a radio telescope, we were stunned.

A signal from space, a message in a radioactive bottle.

The way Broxon told me about it, how breathlessly he described what it meant, I could only think one thing: this is going to change the course of the administration whether we liked it or not.

You need to remember, President Ballard was still in her first term, things were shit all over, and the country was in something of a lull and looking for a boost. In a lot of administrations, depending on the politics of the moment, this was the sort of thing that could have been easily swept under the rug and forgotten.

---

* It is worth noting that the Twelve's opposition to disclosure went beyond just contact with an alien intelligence: they were vociferously opposed to any public revealing of the interception of extraterrestrial signals or interaction with extraterrestrial "culture"—artifacts, communications, etc. If something was found, it must remain secret because, in their estimation, humanity would almost certainly be negatively impacted. This line of thought would, of course, color everything the Twelve did in reaction to the Pulse Code and the Elevation.

I wanted to make sure that wasn't going to happen.

So I brought in Broxon, Chief of Staff Glenn Owen, White House Counsel Terry Quinn, Press Secretary Per Akerson, and Director of National Intelligence Lieutenant General Nadja Chen. We met in the cabinet room at the White House. Per and Nadja weren't exactly thrilled to be there, especially to hear something about "a radio program from the little green men."

They changed their minds pretty quickly when they saw the code.

I explained, as I'd been informed, that this pulse was a thousand times larger than any radio signal that had been picked up before. Even more, it was engineered. Technologically superior to anything mankind could create.

That wasn't bullshit.

Before politics, I'd trained as a physician.

I knew how science worked. There was a logic to this.

Lieutenant General Chen wanted to alert the Joint Chiefs, but Terry put the kibosh on that early. He wanted verification, as though Broxon handing it to us wasn't already enough. In the meantime, he suggested we chase down the best minds in the fields of exobiology, computer science, and astronomy, get their takes on the Pulse Code, and hold off on telling the President anything about it.

I can tell you that once the wheels were in motion, everything happened pretty quickly. There's this tendency to assume that change is slow in Washington, but that's mostly on the policy side. When something big happens, something that potentially threatens the safety and security of the populace, then things happen fast. Orders are given and followed and . . . well, that's what happened here.

We got those experts in fast.

It's funny talking about those early stages. Most of the people who've come to talk to me want to know about what happened later—how we handled the Elevation, the Disclosure Task Force document, President Ballard's struggles. Those first few days after the Pulse appeared are largely a blur. I made a lot of calls, took a lot of meetings, sent an entire continent's worth of emails.

And, to tell you the truth, the weight of it didn't sink in until after I'd left the office. I was a single mother at the time. My own mother took care of my daughter, Rose, while I was working. Sometimes I wouldn't see her for a week or more at a time. That killed me, broke my heart.

I actually had dinner with Rose the night after the Pulse came in. She'd finished her meal and was snacking on some fries when she looked up at me and asked me, "Mom, why is it that every day you go to work, it's to fix things that bad people started? Don't they ever just want to rest?"

Watching her, I realized that for the first time in a really long time I was optimistic. You have to understand, Rose was right. Partially. There were so many bad things happening, and I had to stare them square in the face every day as part of my job in the administration. I don't think I was jaded, but I'd gotten used to seeing the world as fundamentally shitty.

President Ballard arrived on the political scene at a crucial time.

I won't say the world was in chaos, but it felt like it was on the verge of just crumbling apart. The gulf between rich and poor was bigger than it had been in eighty years, the reigning political parties stoked hate on both sides, neighbors didn't talk to each other, social media had us ranting and raving about every little thing that made us angry. It sucked and we needed a change.

When Ballard got into the race, it felt like she'd come out of nowhere.

A true dark horse candidate.

Her newness, her everyman persona—that got people excited. In a good way, a refreshing way. Ballard knew what we were all going through, what we all remembered and wanted to bring back—a hopefulness that the world would get better and that all it would take was a new perspective.

Her winning the election wasn't a shock to me.

Might have rattled the markets and given the career politicians a gut punch they never really recovered from, but people like me—people looking for reinvention—we'd entered a new page in history, and I wanted to be a part of it. There was a lot of talk in the elections before that one about tearing the system down; it didn't work out. Instead of electing people who had vision, the American populace, fed up and sick to death of politics as usual, brought in people with no ambition but their own. Deceived, they retreated even more into rancor and division.

So Ballard seemed real. And she was real.

When I joined the administration, I found a White House that was dedicated to rebuilding, to picking up the pieces, and truly hopeful. When the Pulse Code came in and we all thought it was a message from a culture far more advanced than ours, I felt this warmth in my chest. I felt like maybe the world was going to be an even better place now that we'd been discovered.

I actually thought that: they had discovered us. And, whoever they were, they had plans to make our world better. Surely they did. I couldn't imagine it any other way.

Wow, how wrong I was . . .

Of course, even though Dahlia made the discovery and she's credited with it—rightly, I think—there were other people who found it too. You need to remember that, before the Elevation, we were at this wild moment in history where technology was everywhere and *everything*. It felt like you couldn't go on a date or buy a new pair of shoes without the world recording it somehow.

God, that sounds paranoid, but that's how it was.

 10

ABRAM PETROV, RUSSIAN ASTROPHYSICIST

GRASS VALLEY, CA

JULY 12, 2025

After immigrating to California two years ago, Abram Petrov now finds himself in a double-wide trailer in the heart of the Sierra Nevada Mountains raising horses.

It is certainly not the place this eminent scientist expected to find himself after a rich career in his home country. As other recent histories have detailed, Russia was particularly unbalanced after the Elevation, and, over the years that followed the Finality, it crumbled. We've all seen the images of Volgograd burning and the videos of the riots that savaged St. Petersburg. That was, of course, particularly ugly. Another social media mass hysteria with deadly results—a deepfaked video of Elevated children attacking and killing a couple; it was shared thousands of times, and within hours of its first appearance, the anti-Elevated violence began. * *The well-to-do escaped first, of course. Those with connections to the States jumped on the first flights out of the country. While Petrov didn't have money, he did have strong associations with a number of American universities and notable academics.*

---

* Deepfakes were images or videos that had been computer enhanced using artificial intelligence–based enhancement techniques. First appearing in 2017, these tools were used to superimpose images atop each other. The initial deepfakes were pornography (no surprise) but they quickly manifested as hoax videos: famous people and politicians saying vile or controversial things they never truly said. While programmers quickly developed ways of tagging these fake videos, many escaped into the wild (not by accident) and set off all manner of mayhem. Like St. Petersburg.

The way he describes it, Petrov's last few days in his home country were filled with terror. When rioters appeared on their block in the middle of the night, he and his wife, Sasha, gathered everything they could fit in a couple pieces of luggage, jumped into their battered Lada Kalina, and took back roads to the airport. A journey that usually took them only forty-five minutes stretched out into an almost interminable three hours. Petrov visibly cringes when he relates the story. He tells me that driving through the city that night was like driving through hell itself.

"The things I saw people do ...," he says, shaking his head.

A day and a half later they were in Schenectady, New York, at Union College, where a good friend, South African astronomer Lethabo Pillay, put them up in his apartment. They stayed two weeks, eyes glued to the television, as they, along with the rest of us, watched as Russia tore itself to pieces. From the unnerving riots to the overwhelming military response and the concussive white-hot blasts of the dirty bombs that decimated Moscow. When it was over, Petrov and his wife were citizens of no nation, refugees adrift in a country he'd only ever visited twice.

Their marriage fell apart over the next few months.

Sasha moved back east, to Romania, to be with her sister. Petrov, depressed and feeling unmoored, decided on a radical change: rather than stare up into space, he'd keep his eyes firmly on the ground; hence the move to California and the horses.

It took me several days and multiple phone calls to Petrov's neighbors to track him down. Despite having been in the country only a few years, his English is surprisingly good and he enjoys talking to people, telling stories of his time with the Roscosmos State Corporation for Space Activities and his work on the Pulse in Russia.

There was an English writer, perhaps a poet, who said the following:

The world will end not with a bang but with a whisper.[*]

---

[*] Abram is mistaken. He is quoting T. S. Eliot, whose 1925 poem "The Hollow Men" contains this concluding stanza: "This is the way the world ends/Not with a bang but a whimper." Abram's corruption of the original phrase—which had become quite commonplace and frequently misquoted—makes sense in terms of his intentions. I leave it uncorrected.

That is paraphrasing but the meaning is clear. All the bombs, all the wars, they are tragic but they are human. Tornadoes, hurricanes, tsunamis: these things are a part of the planet—every now and then it needs to shrug its shoulders and let us humans know who is the boss—but they too are predictable. They are the bangs we expect, the ones we know will cause great distress, but we also know we can recover from. Every war ends. Every storm dissipates.

But a whisper . . .

We heard the same whisper from space the night that American scientist discovered it. But, unlike her, we were looking. You see, at the time we had many radio telescopes turned to the same location—the Bullet Cluster—to track down a mysterious signal we had recorded a very small percentage of a few months earlier. When I say it was a small percentage, I mean to say that it was only a few digits—like two or three notes in a song. Not enough to use or analyze but enough to make even the most jaded astronomer curious.

And the jaded astronomer of which I speak? It was me.

I was born in Leningrad. My father was a military man, very diligent, and climbed the ranks quite quickly. He was not what you might expect. He was a warm and loving man who doted on me, his only child. My father died when I was ten years old. It was cancer. I was devastated, as you might imagine. I kept my father's uniform in my closet and I dreamt quite often of wearing it to my own graduation.

Which is exactly what I did when I was twenty-three.

I had a mind for mathematics. Still do. I do not know the reason for it, but I am able to recall numbers better than I can recall even faces. Some have suggested I have a photographic recall, but I do not see it this way. I have a practical brain; whether by training or by biological luck, I have been able to subdivide it into various portions. It is a bit cliché to say, but I relate it to a filing system, the kind you keep in a big metal cabinet. I have a file for languages (I speak three), a file for astronomy, and a file for math.

I used each and every one of these files when we intercepted the Pulse.

It was midafternoon, rather a boring time of day, and I got an alert that something unusual had been received at our site in Pushchino.* It is a massive array of radio telescopes, RT-22s,† near some farms and very much out of the way from prying eyes and ears. Well, it was a massive array. It was destroyed in the months following word of the signal, but that is another story.

Though the information I am about to tell you has certainly been widespread by now, I will give you more of the backstory on it. I do not think that the true history of the Pulse has been—or ever will be—told, despite your best attempts here at documenting what occurred. I am sorry, it is simply too complicated a tale.

Regardless, this was not the first pulse that we in Russia had seen.

The Pulse that Dahlia picked up was the second. The first has, until now, been forgotten in . . . how do you say? The dustpans of history? Yes. Well, this is because we did not understand what we were seeing. Dahlia's brilliance was that she sought to comprehend the Pulse. Our mistake was simply trying to record it and leave the understanding to others. This was how things were in my country at the time.

The very first pulse signal that we discovered was approximately three days earlier than Dahlia's recorded event. It emerged from roughly the same section of the sky, and though it was weaker, it relayed much of the same information—that is, the code seemed quite similar.

We told our superiors about it and were instructed to remain silent.

So we did as we were told.

I had grown up in bureaucracy. It was liberating in a sense. Sometimes I did not envy the people in positions above mine. They had to make decisions, and decisions can be weighty and dangerous things.

After we sent the snippet of the pulse that we had recorded up the chain of command, we forgot about it. Perhaps, on my drive home to my flat, I wondered about the origins of the pulse, but I did not wonder long. By the time I was home and seated comfortably in front of my dinner, the pulse was a long-forgotten memory.

---

* Pushchino is a small town in Moscow Oblast, just on the outskirts of Moscow proper. It was home to a massive research center for the Academy of Sciences. One of those sciences was astronomy, and the site had a radio telescope array.

† "RT-22" means, essentially, radio telescope, twenty-two meters in diameter. RT-22s are used to scan the skies for millimeter and centimeter radio waves.

That was it: the sum total of my involvement in the Pulse affair.

I was told several days later that my superiors had been made very un-comfortable with the data we had sent to them. There were rumors that it was a weapon, possibly designed by the Americans. I knew better, of course. This was a signal from the deepest reaches of space. It was not a weapon and it was not anything man-made.

When the Elevation began and word of Dr. Dahlia Mitchell made the newspapers in Russia, I grinned to myself. My wife, she saw my smile and asked me what I knew of the situation. I told her only that I was laughing to myself at the fact that the Americans were always claiming to discover this or that when, surely, there were others in the world who had picked up the same thing.

**11**

HISTORICAL EDITED TRANSCRIPT FROM A CONVERSATION RECORDED IN
WHITE HOUSE CHIEF OF STAFF GLENN OWEN'S OFFICE
BETWEEN HIMSELF AND:
NATIONAL SECURITY ADVISOR KANISHA PRESTON
PRESS SECRETARY PER AKERSON
DIRECTOR OF NATIONAL INTELLIGENCE LT. GEN. NADJA CHEN
DEPUTY DIRECTOR OF SCIENCE AND TECHNOLOGY IAN BROXON
RECORDED AT WHITE HOUSE ON 10.27.2023

KANISHA PRESTON: Astrophysicists see radio wave signals from space all the time, but not like this. This pulse is a thousand times larger than anything that's been picked up before. It is incredibly powerful.

GLENN OWEN: As in technologically superior?

KANISHA PRESTON: As in way beyond anything we're capable of creating right now.

LT. GEN. CHEN: Do we know what it says?

DEPUTY DIRECTOR IAN BROXON: No. But my people tell me the mathematics used to encrypt the data in this pulse is beyond advanced.

LT. GEN. CHEN: I'd like authorization to alert the Joint Chiefs of Staff. We—

GLENN OWEN: We need verification on this. It could be a fluke. Worse, it could be a hoax. I know there's a suggestion we just detected a message from an . . . *extraterrestrial intelligence*, but until we know what that says, we shouldn't make any decisions. If we start ringing the bell on this and it turns out to be bogus, we're going to be pilloried.

LT. GEN. CHEN: And if the Pulse isn't bogus and we're late to the party? How do we know the Chinese don't already have it?

KANISHA PRESTON: We don't. The Russians do, though.

LT. GEN. CHEN: Exactly.

GLENN OWEN: Deputy Director, please start from the beginning.

DEPUTY DIRECTOR IAN BROXON: One of our TAO operators, Jon Hurtado, was handed the drive by an astrophysicist at Santa Cruz. Dr. Dahlia Mitchell. Something of a dark matter expert. Apparently she reconfigured a radio telescope array to run some experiments and discovered this pulse. I'm not sure she understood what it was but she knew enough to share it with her ex-boyfriend.

LT. GEN. CHEN: And there's no evidence she gave it to anyone other than Hurtado?

DEPUTY DIRECTOR IAN BROXON: Not at this juncture.

PER AKERSON: Was she alone?

DEPUTY DIRECTOR IAN BROXON: There was a graduate student working a late shift. Clark Watts.

PER AKERSON: Has the FBI talked to either of them?

DEPUTY DIRECTOR IAN BROXON: Yes.

GLENN OWEN: Okay. So, in the meantime, we figure out what we've got. If it proves to be what everyone thinks it is, we tell the President. We disclose this the wrong way, we could have big problems. Any thoughts? There's not exactly a manual for this sort of thing, is there?

LT. GEN. CHEN: There is, actually. Majestic. 1947.

GLENN OWEN: Oh, come on. Those dinosaurs? None of that is relevant anymore.

LT. GEN. CHEN: I wouldn't be so quick to dismiss them. They have protocols for this.

PER AKERSON: You're kidding, right? Majestic is ancient history.

KANISHA PRESTON: Look, I just have to point out that if this is real, it's coming from a much more advanced intelligence—one that may have already infiltrated all of our systems. Chances are, it's a million moves ahead of us.

GLENN OWEN: So we bring in the President's science advisors, communications people, and the NSA. Deputy Director, do you have anyone you can recommend to decode this data?

DEPUTY DIRECTOR IAN BROXON: I know one person, but . . .

GLENN OWEN: Why the hesitation?

DEPUTY DIRECTOR IAN BROXON: He's a handful. Dr. Xavier Faber.

GLENN OWEN: Bring him in.

THE TASK FORCE

12

XAVIER FABER, PHD, COMPUTATIONAL LINGUIST AND FORMER MEMBER OF THE DISCLOSURE TASK FORCE

NEAR BAYFIELD, CO

AUGUST 8, 2025

Rumors have dogged Xavier Faber's life and career for several decades.

He first came to public attention when he single-handedly proved the dynamic optimality conjecture, a computer-programming question from Sleator and Tarjan's 1985 binary search tree paper that had been quite difficult—some argued impossible—to solve. The dynamic optimality conjecture is a concept proposed by two computer scientists, Daniel Sleator and Robert Tarjan, in the mid-1980s. The two invented different data structures, ways to organize information in computer systems, including the "splay tree" (a self-adjusting binary search tree designed to retrieve items from a computer's memory more easily). In Sleator and Tarjan's binary search tree paper, they wondered if a splay tree was dynamically optimal—that is, if splay trees can perform as well as any other search tree algorithm. It couldn't be proven that they do—until Xavier came along.

At the time, Xavier was a twenty-two-year-old graduate student in mathematics at the University of Pennsylvania. He was something of a rabble-rouser—known to work on the quad lawn while blasting industrial rock music like Ministry from his dorm room windows.

Xavier's illuminating ideas led him to MIT and then NASA, where he worked on several aborted Mars mission programs—aborted largely because Xavier was considered too difficult. He fought with his colleagues, his superiors, even the janitorial staff (once resulting in a physical altercation that saw him get ten stitches in the ER). Xavier was fired after only a year at NASA and retreated to the woods outside of Halifax, Nova Scotia, where he proceeded to develop machine-learning tools that he sold to various and sundry tech corporations. While this supported his rather unorthodox lifestyle—embarking on several annual adventures where he'd travel to a random spot on a map with only a single set of clothes and a cheap cell phone and attempt to stay for a month regardless of the language barriers—Xavier's real passion was Skinwalker, the little-known multi-paradigm programming language he'd created himself. And it was Skinwalker that brought Xavier into the orbit of the Disclosure Task Force.

These days, Xavier lives on a ranch in Southern Colorado, where he raises alpacas and tweaks his green home—a solar-powered oasis in the middle of the western United States' largest energy gaps. He is married to a biochemist named Yamuna Chakravorty and they have two adopted children, eight and ten.

Given his history and current off-the-grid existence, it should come as little surprise that Xavier was difficult to track down. After finding no way to contact him directly, I traveled to Denver and rented a car before utilizing several faded physical maps to find a small ghost town near his home. I camped there for two days on the advice of a local rancher that Xavier passed through the town on his weekly forays "down mountain" to scavenge car batteries from an abandoned car lot near a defunct rural airport. I flagged him down in the middle of a dirt road, and when he pulled his battered Jeep over to talk to me, he rolled down his window, and said: "Ten minutes. And if I'm not curious about why you're here after those ten minutes, then I'll drop you off at the nearest intersection."

I accepted and had persuaded him to talk within five minutes. I hate to be too self-congratulatory, but I'm a good journalist: I know how to get a source to open up. With Xavier, it took only one name: Dahlia Mitchell. He invited me back to his home, made me a dinner of trout (which he'd caught himself), Israeli salad, and jalapeño cornbread. After the meal, we sat out on his porch and stared up at the stars. With all the lights out in a two-hundred-mile radius of his cabin, we could make out just about every star in the vast Milky Way.

Here's what everyone asks me first: When did you really know?

I don't have an answer for that.

Wish I did.

You gotta understand how it all happened, at least for me. I was sitting in my cabin in Nova Scotia, just another Thursday afternoon, when a black chopper flies low over the trees and lands in a field about half a mile away. They didn't try to hide. They'd come for me.

I wasn't a survivalist but I didn't take too politely to unannounced strangers.

Assuming they were there to jam me on some of the software I'd been developing for a few of our country's less savory friends, I grabbed a sledgehammer and went to town on my hard drives.* Had all twenty-seven of them busted to dust by the time the knock on the front door came. I answered it to find a guy with no neck and biceps the size of my thighs holding an HK416.

He noticed the sledgehammer in my hands, asked me if I was Dr. Xavier Faber. I nodded and he said I needed to go to the chopper with him.

That was extent of that. Flight time was roughly four hours. None of the soldiers who escorted me spoke to me. Several times, they bantered into mics on channels I wasn't privy to, but for the most part they slept. I couldn't close my eyes. My mind was racing. Why? Here's the thing: I knew people didn't want to talk to me because I'd written a few suspicious programs—programs they'd rather not have floating around the dark web. If they wanted me to spill on some of my contacts, they'd have made a more ostentatious show of force, try to prove to me that talking was my best and only option. The muscle wasn't there to make statements; however, they were there because they needed something I hadn't provided yet. Their handlers wanted my brain, not my products.

We landed at an army base and jumped into a waiting train of SUVs, exactly the way you imagined it all looked. Glenn Owen, our illustrious White House chief of staff at the time, beamed when I climbed into the second SUV. He sat between two Secret Service agents. We made small talk. I'd seen him on TV and complimented his running of Ballard's campaign. Though I never really had an interest in politics, her win as an Independent certainly caught my attention. I knew Glenn played an outsized role in keeping

---

* There's a popular conception that you can delete the contents of a hard drive by waving a strong magnet over it. It's an idea shown in movies and on TV. According to Xavier, however, it's wrong. To be effective, you'd need a seriously strong magnet—not the sort of thing people have at home. Even more effective, he says, is just smashing the hard drive into tiny pieces.

President Ballard focused on what mattered to the voters: jobs, security, low taxes, the usual stuff.

"You haven't exactly been recommended," Glenn said.

"Let me guess: Broxon?"

Glenn nodded. "He's worried we won't have a short enough leash for you."

"He would be."

That was the extent of our conversation. I wanted to ask about why I was there, who'd really brought me in—'cause Broxon wasn't a powerful enough person to have me tracked down for a meeting—but I knew I wouldn't get the answers I was looking for.

We met at the White House. Cabinet Room. Door closed, and I found myself face-to-face with a collection of some of the smartest people in the United States. I knew a few of them.

Dr. Neil Roberts, an exobiologist I'd worked with at NASA. He was mid-fifties and had published a few revolutionary papers about how life could survive in both the outer reaches of empty space and beneath the thick ice of Triton, Neptune's largest moon.[*] Like all such thought experiments, it was compelling stuff but, ultimately, hardly seemed useful in the grand scheme of things.

I knew Dr. Sergei Mikoyan well. He was a linguist and spoke something like twenty-five languages. The man was a legend for some work he'd helped develop around machine learning—helping researchers teach computers how to differentiate between languages. I wasn't part of any of the projects he'd been involved in, but I'd read his work and it was brilliant.

The woman next to Mikoyan I didn't know. When Glenn made the introductions, he said she was Soledad Venegas, a particle physicist. Soledad was young, maybe five years older than me, in her mid-thirties. Had short hair and big hoop earrings that resembled an atom with five orbiting electrons. A nice touch.

Dr. Andrea Cisco was an astrophysicist at the University of Washington. Was well-known for her work on gravitational waves, though the few times I'd met her—at MIT conferences—she came across as harried and graced

---

[*] There's long been conjecture that life may exist beneath the ice on Triton, one of Neptune's fourteen moons. If it exists, it would most likely be microscopic.

with even fewer social skills than most astrophysicists. She didn't even look up at me when I was introduced.

Those were the scientists. The other people in the room were with the administration. We had Kanisha Preston, national security advisor; Terry Quinn, the White House's lawyer; and Lieutenant General Chen, the secretary of defense.

I took a seat and made a little jab at Dr. Neil Roberts. That's my style.

"So, has NASA found any alien bugs, Bob?"

He frowned and said, "Not since you were fired."

Touché.

Glenn handed out custom tablet computers, one for each of us. They ran GNU/Linux with custom hardware and pretty intense security—hardwired kill switches for Wi-Fi, camera, GPS, and cellular data. These were new and had nothing on them but a single data file. We opened them and took a look.

If you've ever been hiking—like not day hiking but a days-long trek into some remote wilderness—you'll know the feeling that I got the first time I saw the Pulse. It was like climbing through a primordial forest, having to slash your way through dense undergrowth for days on end. Exhausted, bloodied, bruised, feeling like you've been pummeled within an inch of your life, you drag your broken body to the summit of some windswept peak and then look out over . . . the most gorgeous landscape you've ever seen. Lush valleys ringed by deep-green forests, little cobalt-blue lakes nestled at the base of soaring, snowcapped mountains. The air is crisp and pungent with pine. The sky is cloudless, the clearest blue you've ever seen.

That was how the Pulse looked on that tablet.

I'd spent a career navigating the turbulent waters of poorly written computer languages and badly designed code—through the inky swamps of Objective-C and the minefield of C++. At that point, even my own language, Skinwalker,[*] was clean but flawed. All computer-programming languages have one insurmountable issue: they're written for and designed by human

---

[*] Xavier told me that the Skinwalker name was something of an inside joke. It is a reference to a late 1980s paranormal case involving a location in Utah known as the Skinwalker Ranch. Originally named the Sherman Ranch, it was, according to its owner and several paranormal investigators who decamped there in the 1990s, the site of some very odd goings-on involving UFOs and "skinwalkers"—shape-shifting witches of an evil disposition derived from Navajo folklore. Xavier had read about the ranch and thought the Skinwalker name was "really cool, really metal."

beings. I know there are exceptions, but most are inherently damaged, because our minds aren't capable of anticipating all the potential problems down the road. That's reasonable.

The code at the heart of the Pulse was incomparable.

That was why the brainiacs and me were in the Cabinet Room. The government was befuddled by it. Even though I'd only seen it for several minutes, I had no idea what the code was designed to do or who had made it. Though I'll admit I had some guesses.

Glenn gave us the background on the code.

We got the story on who picked it up and where, but even though the thing was a mystery, one thing was clear: the government wanted this code broken, and fast. If it was from a foreign power, they wanted to know which. If it was natural—which seemed absolutely insane—they needed to understand how it was created.

Glenn asked, "Is it a new sort of cyberweapon? Some sort of Stuxnet* that got out of the bag early? Or is this actually a message from outer space?"

I was first to speak. "It's not a weapon. Too complex."

Roberts, of course, rebutted me. "I wouldn't be so quick. I've seen some incredibly complex malware, Dr. Faber."

"You're confusing complex and complicated," I replied.

Glenn cleared his throat and stopped our banter.

"Okay. Look, let's switch it up. If this data is from out there, maybe it's some sort of natural event," he said. "What's your read on that idea?"

I said, "This is intentional and it's vast."

Dr. Sergei Mikoyan asked: "How do we know this isn't something randomly triggered, like an alarm?"

"You're not seeing it for what it is," I said.

Dr. Roberts, always the joker, said, "Remind me again why you lost your position at NASA." He laughed hard. No one else did.

Dr. Venegas was next: "What exactly are you arguing, Xavier?"

It'd hit me a few seconds earlier, just before Dr. Roberts and I had our verbal tussle. Dr. Mikoyan's question about randomness, entirely wrong, still

---

* Stuxnet is a reference to an incredibly advanced computer worm engineered by the computer scientists in the US and Israel. It was unleashed in 2010 to target Iran's attempts at uranium enrichment by infecting and destroying their centrifuges.

got me thinking. The Pulse was perfect. So that'd mean the creator of the Pulse was brilliant and far more technologically adept than any of the folks sitting around that table. And that suggested something very bad.

"You want to know what I'm getting at?" I asked the room before pointing at the Pulse Code swirling across my tablet. "I'm telling you that this says we're doomed. This isn't from here. It is from a culture, potentially a civilization, far more advanced than our own. Why would they reach out to us? What could we possibly gain from having contact with them?"

Dr. Roberts, our resident optimist, suggested: "An exchange of ideas."

I told him I needed to see the rest of the Pulse.

Kanisha spoke up. "You've got all we've got."

"That's a problem," I said. "I hope you have every radio telescope tuned to wherever in the sky this came from."

"We're working on that," Glenn said.

"Better work fast."

I was getting frustrated. No one at the table was following where I was going. We'd all just been hit with the same information, but I'd expected more from them. You don't just dump the greatest discovery in human history in a bunch of scientists' laps and then sit back and wait until they have the answer.

Kanisha could read my irritation. "Tell us why, Xavier."

"This is just the first pulse," I said. "There will be others."

Everyone was quiet after that.

Glenn stood. "How do you know that?"

"I don't," I said, "not one hundred percent. But what we can tell from this thing already, it's got some repeater sequences in it. Think of them like little timers. You wouldn't add them if this was a one-off. If it doesn't take, so to speak, then they'll be sending it again. Maybe even if it does take."

We mulled it over. Not all of us convinced.

"So we prepare for that eventuality," Glenn said. "If this is what Dr. Faber suggests it is, we'll need to inform the President. You all have the rest of the night to pull together a brief. I'll be back in the morning to get it. We'll provide all the coffee and tea and meals. Just have something ready."

The room cleared out, leaving the scientists behind. We looked at each other and, after a second of uncomfortable silence, got down to work.

Giving you the blow-by-blow details of what happened that night would be incredibly dull. All you really need to know is that we drank a shit-ton of coffee, scribbling across eight hundred sheets of poster paper, had some real knock-down arguments, and came to a conclusion. It was just after dawn when Glenn reappeared. He looked as though he'd gotten even less sleep then we had. Adjusting his tie, he closed the door and sat with a sigh.

"So, what am I going to tell President Ballard about this thing?"

Kanisha did most of the talking, at least at first.

"We're convinced this is from an outside intelligence," Kanisha said. "It has none of the hallmarks of what we're capable of here on Earth. You need to tell the President that we've picked up an alien communication and—"

I had to interrupt her there.

"I'm not convinced it's a message," I said. "We're still debating that point, but in my mind this thing is more of a transmission. It isn't something we can respond to. It's something we get and have to deal with."

Glenn was disappointed. Despite the fact that we'd just told him that humanity had just received its first proof of intelligence beyond our own planet, he wasn't pleased that we couldn't neatly wrap this thing up.

"Deal with it how?" he asked me, but looked at Kanisha.

"We need to decode it," Dr. Cisco said, "but we don't have the tools here to do that. We need to establish a working group, get more people involved in this thing, and figure out exactly what this mess—I mean trans-mission—is. Once we have it deciphered, then we'll know what threat, if any, it poses."

Glenn ground his teeth, mulling it all over.

"So you want me to tell the President that we've just definitely inter-cepted an alien broadcast but we have no idea what it says or what it means. And if I'm hearing any of this correctly, it might even be something that should have us concerned. Dr. Xavier Faber, is this pulse some sort of signal for an invasion?"

I said, "I think that's a possibility."

"I can't go and tell the President any of this until I know what that Pulse Code actually is," he said. "Is this a recipe for intergalactic cornbread or does it contain battle plans for a million spaceships hovering off in the distance somewhere? Maybe—just throwing this out there—it means nothing. Could it be that at the end of the day you will decipher it and find that it's the last word of some civilization that died two million years ago?"

We had no real answer.

But I had an idea.

"Sir," I said. Dr. Neil Roberts looked at me funny, 'cause he'd never seen me use that word to anyone. "Dr. Cisco's right. We need to form a committee or a task force, or whatever you want to call it, and decode this thing. We need to do that yesterday. You give us the resources to do it, we can keep the whole process on the down-low, and we can give you an answer in one week's time."

I have no idea why I suggested a week. Seeing how complex the Pulse Code was, it might likely have taken years to crack. But a week is what came to mind, and it's what I said. The other PhDs looked at me like I was insane.

"Fine," Glenn said, "but the Pulse Code stays here, on the tablets, in the White House. As of right now, you all are the task force. Go home, get whatever you need, and then get back here tomorrow. Your one week starts at midnight tonight. Anything that comes up while you're breaking the code, the very second you see something that concerns you, no matter how trivial it might appear, you let me know. I don't need to tell any of us this, but if a single digit of the Pulse Code leaks outside of your working group, then you will be remanded to the custody of whatever branch of government I can think of that will hold you the longest. You understand? This thing gets out before we have a lock on it, and you will never be heard from again."

Glenn left and sent in several of his advisors and support staff to start making the logistical plans. I had nothing to go back to in Nova Scotia, at least not for a week, so I'd camp out at a hotel nearby and await the return of my colleagues.

But, as you probably already know, that was the last time we saw Dr. Cisco.

She died, tragically, in a car accident on her way home.

Or that's what we were told.

**13**

Today started with the worst headache.

Like, the worst.

I was in the shower and it just came on suddenly, crawling over my head with needle fingers from the nape of my neck to my temples and then settling down behind my eyes. I've never had an aural migraine before, but as I stepped out of the shower, everything was pulsing. The lights in the bathroom, the sunlight through the window—it was dimming and brightening in waves. I got back into bed, texted a colleague at work that I'd be late, and then curled into a ball.

I woke up an hour later feeling kind of better. But not by much.

Can't imagine what people who have these sorts of migraines all the time have to go through. I took two Vicodin and drove down to campus. Frank was in LA for a conference and I didn't have a class until after lunch, so I hunkered down in my office convinced I'd have time to go over some paperwork, catch up on the ever-growing pile of email, and maybe, just maybe, read through a couple journal articles I've been dying to get to. Sadly, none of that was to be. The Pulse was waiting.

It was one of those Christmas morning feelings.

I could barely stand the anticipation of seeing it again.

After the initial excitement of discovery and handing it off to Jon, I've tried to keep myself focused on the dull realities of life—work, exer-

cise, eating, sleeping, and checking out the cute barista at the café near campus. But I can't. There is no normal in the world after the Pulse. I've been replaying my conversation with Jon, when I handed him the drive, over and over in my head. Tweaking every word, rolling them around to divine hidden meanings. The truth is, even then I was downplaying the importance of it. But I knew—I knew intrinsically—in each and every cell of my body that the Pulse Code was bigger than any other discovery.

Again, me and the melodrama.

Me dismissing things like the discovery that the Earth is round (it is, all you doubters) or the creation of penicillin or the invention of telecommunication seems flippant. What about the wheel? How about fire? Or calculus?

They're all steps forward. The cataclysms, wars, man's inhumanity to man—they're all horrible branches on the same tree of history. But the Pulse isn't like that. It chops down the tree. When people know about the Pulse, when humanity understands that we are no longer alone in the universe, everything will change.

I'm serious.

And me, I was trained to be rational above all else. To weigh and study and calculate and to make all my decisions based on evidence. With that rationality comes an understanding: Discovery must be leavened with a healthy skepticism. Science simply doesn't work if scientists are losing their minds at each and every potential breakthrough. I know that. And yet I also know that the Pulse isn't like finding a new star or black hole. It's not even akin to determining the source of dark matter. All that stuff, it just falls by the wayside. And this is me, Ms. Dark Matter Is the Best Thing Ever, talking.

This is bigger than a cure for cancer. (It might even lead us to one.)

This is bigger than conquering death.

Me writing this now, so soon, feels . . . I should be embarrassed by it. I should have kicked the Pulse Code over to Conrad* or Ishikawa† and

---

* Dr. Conrad Naha, an astrophysicist at the California Institute of Technology. An expert on binary stars, he went missing during the Colorado EMP attack.

† Dr. Sunjin Ishikawa, an astronomer with Pennsylvania State University. She died of a ruptured aorta in the early stages of the Elevation.

then sat back and let them tell me how important it is. Maybe they'd find something I'd missed. But I didn't and they won't. I gave it to Jon rather than another astrophysicist or an astronomer because I knew they wouldn't jump on it the same.

Not like this. Not with this energy.

Being an astronomer, I understood they would be as critical as possible but they'd take their time and crunch the numbers and then . . . then they'd do what they were trained to do: Move it up the ladder if it was important, if it was real. Up the ladder, they'd recheck the calculations, rerun the numbers, and see what was reproducible. There would be peer-reviewed articles and the machine would work properly. At the end, maybe two or three months from now, possibly even longer, the information would make its way to the officials who need to know. Then the public might find out. Or might not.

The might not part is important.

I'm not a conspiracy theorist.

I hate that stuff.

I don't believe that there are hundreds of thousands if not millions of people willing to lie to keep an illusion alive. September 11 wasn't an inside job. Norway exists. Climate change is real. What looks like conspiracy is really just individual failings magnified by the size of the apparatus around them: people make mistakes, the universe is random, things break for no reason, brains hiccup without explanation, emotions go off the rails. Fact is it's a wonder any system runs smoothly.

Just look at the DMV.

I'm not a conspiracy theorist but I still think that if I'd sent the Pulse Code through the proper channels, there's a very good chance it would be lost. Or unrecognized. Do you know how many undiscovered species of animals are sitting in museums right now? Seriously, this is nuts: every year an enterprising young zoologist runs the DNA on a stuffed crocodile or jaguar sitting on a dusty shelf for the past 150 years and realizes it's a new species.

Conspiracy?

No, just an oversight, a technical blunder, a jealous curator, a mis-

labeled sample, a janitorial error, a filing mistake, or the most logical answer of all: it was just another crocodile or jaguar when it was
killed, didn't look any different than any of the other millions everyone
has seen before, and it was put on a shelf because no one cared. And
probably no one cares still.

The Pulse Code could just as easily wind up lost in a digital ar-
chive on a forgotten hard drive. One mistake, one oversight, one jealous colleague, one miscalculation, and the Pulse could be forgotten.
I'm not going to take a chance of that happening. Not knowing what I
know about it. Not feeling what I feel.

So my afternoon was spent poring over the details again.

And just like every time I look at the Pulse, I got more and more
excited. I missed my lecture start time, showed up late, and delivered
a dull presentation on gravitational waves. One of my students actually commented on how tired I looked.

After class, I left a message for Jon.

I need to know what he's heard.

Jon, I know you check your email every two minutes!

I just . . . I need to know that I've done the right thing. That the
people he gave the Pulse Code to are taking it seriously and they're
going to freak out as much as I am. I need to know that I'm not crazy
and that I didn't break protocol just because I'm convinced the world
is going to change.

—

Tonight the headache came back, worse than before.

Like really, really bad.

I took another two Vicodin but they barely helped. The aural part of
the headache was the same. The lights in the room pulsated. Each bulb
was like a strobe: the light rippled out and waxed and waned with a
clear rhythm. I couldn't help but study it even as my head throbbed,
my ears threatening to explode. The space between the light waves
was uniform. Which seemed weirdly impossible.

I sat in my kitchen, trying to keep my eyes open, watching as the waves spread out across the room, wall to wall. They actually went through the walls.

And each wave that hit me, I could feel it.

Each wave of light that hit me pushed me backwards. Not hard; lightly, as though the light waves . . . this, of course, is impossible, but it was like they were moving through a liquid. Not air. I chalked it up to the migraine distorting my sense of perception.

The headache stopped ten minutes ago.

The pain just ebbed away, uncurling its needle fingers from my brain and retreating back to the nape of my neck before it sunk under the surface again. I know the pain will return. No amount of Vicodin will shake it loose. Surely it's stress. The Pulse discovery and my lack of sleep, the excitement of digging into the information—it's overwhelmed me.

After the headache retreated, I took another shower.

I was scared to.

—

The headache is gone but my brain . . .

I can tell it's not the same as it was a day ago.

Something has been altered. Imperceptible, maybe.

The thing is I can still see the light waves.

14

EDITED TRANSCRIPT FROM THE FIRST UNOFFICIAL
DISCLOSURE TASK FORCE MEETING
PRESENT: NATIONAL SECURITY ADVISOR KANISHA PRESTON, DR. XAVIER
FABER, DR. NEIL ROBERTS, DR. SOLEDAD VENEGAS, AND DR. SERGEI MIKOYAN
RECORDED IN WHITE HOUSE ON 10.30.2023

Though they were brought in for their expert opinion on the Pulse, the experts assembled at the White House to meet with Kanisha Preston were to become the members of the Disclosure Task Force, the group charged with writing the message President Ballard would communicate to the world about first contact. In addition to Dr. Xavier Faber, the Task Force's experts consisted of:

Dr. Neil Roberts—*An exobiologist with NASA, Dr. Neil Roberts (forty at the time) had a long-running dispute with Dr. Xavier Faber about alien-human communication. Unsurprisingly, they came from different sides of how to interpret the Pulse Code. Where Roberts saw a hopeful future in communication with an alien intelligence, Xavier saw the potential for Earth to be attacked by a more technologically advanced species. Given his disposition, Dr. Neil Roberts soon became the Task Force's cheerleader.*

Dr. Sergei Mikoyan—*A leading authority on computational linguistics, Dr. Sergei Mikoyan (fifty-six at the time) was brought to the Task Force from his post as a computer language lecturer at King's College, London. More a philosopher than a scientist, Dr. Sergei Mikoyan was the team's empathetic core: he believed the Pulse represented a bridge between two cultures, an opportunity for humanity to reach its highest potential.*

Dr. Soledad Venegas—*Dr. Soledad Venegas (thirty-two at the time) was a Yale-based particle physicist and fell in the middle of Dr. Mikoyan and Dr. Neil Roberts in her approach to the Pulse. She was neither the dreamer Dr. Sergei Mikoyan was nor the idealist Dr. Neil Roberts was; in her mind, the origins of the Pulse were not nearly as important as the mind-boggling science behind its creation.*

KANISHA PRESTON: Okay. Update time. Seems Dr. Cisco had an accident. Car accident on the way home while she was out. Drugs in her system, maybe stress. Went off the road and was dead by the time she got to the hospital.

DR. NEIL ROBERTS: Jesus. She had a family . . .

KANISHA PRESTON: We're on lockdown now. No one leaves the building. From now on we sleep, eat—everything—under watch. Can't risk anyone else getting hurt.

DR. XAVIER FABER: Or anyone else potentially leaking any of this.

KANISHA PRESTON: I think we all take offense to that suggestion, Dr. Faber. This was a tragic accident and the timing is unsettling, but it happens. There are no tea leaves to read here. We need to continue on and hopefully we can find someone with Dr. Cisco's expertise. In the meantime, Dr. Mikoyan, you were going to be giving us an update?

DR. SERGEI MIKOYAN: We think the Ascendant have—

KANISHA PRESTON: The what?

DR. SERGEI MIKOYAN: Sorry, that's in the notes we sent late last night. I assume you haven't gotten to those yet. That's okay. We weren't comfortable calling the originators of the Pulse "them" or "the others." It seemed a bit silly and it got confusing quickly. So we had to give them a name. Dr. Xavier Faber calls them the Ascendant and that kind of stuck for now. We don't have to use it officially.

DR. XAVIER FABER: It's a good name. It's sexy.

KANISHA PRESTON: What're you inferring with the name?

DR. XAVIER FABER: Pretty obvious, really.

KANISHA PRESTON: Humor me.

DR. XAVIER FABER: Well, we already know that the intelligence that created the Pulse is far more advanced than we are. Studying the code, we also now know that they're somewhat like us. I don't mean we've learned anything about what they look like or what sorts of space cars they drive. We don't have the faintest idea and the Pulse doesn't contain any of that information. What we do know, however, is that they get how we think. They know how our minds operate. This Pulse Code, the data embedded in it the way it was written, is singled out for us. This wasn't some blast to the whole galaxy. We were meant to see it. And so, thinking about what to call this intelligence, I figured "the Ascendant" sounded about right. They're like us but to the nth degree.

DR. NEIL ROBERTS: And he's not speaking for all of us. Just so you know that.

KANISHA PRESTON: I'm sure he's not. Dr. Faber, you just told me that you are certain, or seem certain, that this pulse was written for and directed at us. Why? How can you be sure it wasn't just some shout-out into the stars?

DR. XAVIER FABER: The way it's written. I know you're going to be disappointed to hear that we don't actually know what the code does yet—

KANISHA PRESTON: I am.

DR. SOLEDAD VENEGAS: We don't know a lot of things about the code still. The truth is it might not do anything, but we can save that discussion for—

DR. XAVIER FABER: It does something. Of course it does something. You see what I have to deal with in here? Listen, it's quite simple. Our minds function logically. Mathematics and physics, all of it is linked to concepts of how the universe functions. The way we determine that is via patterns. That's what our brains evolved to search for. Patterns. But our patterns, the ones we understand and look for, might not be the same patterns other minds seek out. You got me?

DR. SERGEI MIKOYAN: What Dr. Faber is saying is that our concept of reality is built upon certain undeniable facts—time, space, motion, gravity, et cetera—and all these truths are founded upon patterns. Patterns that are distinct to us as a species.

DR. XAVIER FABER: So this Pulse Code was written by the Ascendant to tap directly into our pattern-finding brains. It wasn't designed to affect dogs or whales. I said it was a Trojan horse first time we met. First time we talked about this. I still think that's the case here. And that means that it could contain one of two things: either it's a weapon designed to eliminate us, like specially formulated weed killer, or it's a gift, maybe plans to build a cold-fusion reactor or the perfect toaster that gets bagels just the right shade of rusty brown.

KANISHA PRESTON: And which do you think it is?

DR. XAVIER FABER: I'm sure you can guess.

KANISHA PRESTON: Dr. Mikoyan?

DR. SERGEI MIKOYAN: I think it is likely a gift. The way that I see it, this pulse was beamed to us from very far away. It was not packaged in anything harmful, as far as we can determine. It has not wreaked havoc with our computers. And the code, in my estimation, speaks the loudest. It was designed carefully, beautifully, and to be accessed simply, given the technology that exists in our world at this time—

DR. XAVIER FABER: All of that could be said of a weapon. Like a Trojan horse.[*]

---

[*] A Trojan horse, sometimes called simply a Trojan, is a kind of computer virus that is disguised by its creator as a piece of legitimate or innocuous software. By definition, a Trojan virus is always malicious.

DR. NEIL ROBERTS: I'm with Dr. Mikoyan on this.

DR. XAVIER FABER: Big surprise there.

DR. NEIL ROBERTS: If it truly were a weapon as Dr. Faber implies, I find it hard to believe they'd beam it out so randomly. If it were a weapon, it would be sent widely. They would want as many Earth-based radio telescopes as possible to pick it up, not just by a low-level academic in California. Don't forget, from what we've been told, Dr. Mitchell *stumbled* upon the Pulse. She didn't even know what she had at first. That doesn't sound like a weapon to me.

DR. SOLEDAD VENEGAS: I'm closer to Dr. Faber in my thinking. While I agree with Dr. Roberts that it is unusual that the Pulse was sent in this manner, looking at the code itself, I don't see any evidence that it is meant to contain anything more than digits. If this code was a gift, it wasn't coded properly or perhaps the code broke down over time. What none of my colleagues have mentioned is that this thing appears to be very old. Ancient, even.

KANISHA PRESTON: Ancient? How so?

DR. SOLEDAD VENEGAS: We can't determine when it was actually sent. The data is too thin on where it originated and the speed at which it traveled. In many ways it seems to have simply appeared and then vanished as though it didn't actually traverse space at all.

KANISHA PRESTON: So it's not from space?

DR. XAVIER FABER: That's not what we're saying. It's complicated, but we'll get to that side of this in a little bit. Dr. Venegas was making a point that makes me look good, so let's get back to it.

DR. SOLEDAD VENEGAS: The code itself, the feel of the language, suggests it was written very, very early in our history. Like most anything, languages evolve over time: diversifying, getting more and more complicated, and, at the same time, becoming easier to navigate and use. If you trace all languages back, you'll likely end up with the ur-language—the original tongue from which all the others derive. Now, it's still very much speculation, but this proto-human language might consist of certain root words, sounds, that nearly all human languages have. Even though we're at a very early stage, I see some similarity between the Pulse Code and this theoretical ur-language. The fact is the Pulse Code is designed for us to *absorb it*. It is designed for the human mind. I realize that sounds odd and I'm not quite getting at what I mean, but this is like art. It's very hard to define what art is and even harder to always distinguish good from bad art. When we see something we like, something that touches the human condition, it's appealing, even if it's a splotch of paint on an otherwise empty frame or a bit of softly twisted driftwood. There's an aesthetic. The code appeals to us.

KANISHA PRESTON: Okay. Dr. Faber, you're biting your tongue . . .

DR. XAVIER FABER: Soledad's spot-on. It appeals to us. This code wants us to accept it, to bring it in, to study it and copy it and see it. But I think that doesn't even matter in the long run. The Pulse hit our planet for a reason. Maybe the radio telescopes picked it up—certainly Dr. Mitchell's did—but that wasn't the end goal. This thing is like solar radiation washing over the planet, washing over all of us. We're looking at it as a code, using math to try and crack it, but—and this is going to sound a bit crazy—I don't think that is what it was intended for originally.

DR. NEIL ROBERTS: Here is where he goes off the rails entirely.

DR. XAVIER FABER: I think the Pulse Code is a program.

KANISHA PRESTON: Explain.

DR. XAVIER FABER: It's meant for us. Not to decode, not to puzzle over or send a return telegram. It's designed for us physically. I think this thing is like a virus and we've all just been infected with it.

 **15**

A little more than forty-eight hours after I'd found the Pulse, something changed.

The migraine was one thing. Painful, strange, but it was short-lived and, despite my seeing waves of light, it made sense. I looked online and saw a huge uptick in the number of people reporting similar symptoms: migraine-like manifestations after I'd intercepted the signal. Scary. What the hell does it mean? I saw there were dozens and dozens of threads on multiple forums devoted entirely to people seeing radiating waves when they had migraines. Some were pretty sketchy, but in a weird way it gave me comfort.

But that was before. That was early.

How fast this stuff changes . . .

Today I woke up and knew, just knew, there was more going on.

Once, I heard a podcast about a man who'd felt a tumor in his brain three months before it was actually picked up on an MRI scan. Nuts, right? When he was asked how he knew there was something there, he said he'd felt a change. It wasn't anything he could put his finger on, exactly. The way this man described it, there was an itching . . . a tickle just on the inside of his right ear. He tried to get at it with a Q-tip, which was a big mistake. He dug deep enough that he ruptured his eardrum. Ouch. Outside of the pain, which was intense, there was the fact that he had a nagging ringing in his ear for months after. The itching, the tickle—it didn't go away.

Two doctors later, he had the scan. They found the tumor. It was removed and he recovered successfully. When he woke after surgery, he knew right away that it had been successful. The itch was gone. The tickle vanished.

The story was impressive but anecdotal, of course.

All the best stories are.

Maybe the tumor was resting on a nerve. I'm obviously not that kind of doctor, I don't know. But what I understand is that this man felt something was off. Like in a very general way. And indeed it was. Just took the doctors a few extra months to find it.

There's something off in my head too.

It's not an itch. Or a tickle. There is a reverberation in my head. That's really the one way I can properly describe it: a pulsating, the same way that the light emerged in waves when I had my migraines, but inside. It sounds insane. It sounds like there's part of me that's losing my grip, but I can actually feel it.

Deep in. Growing there.

When I was a kid, Dad brought Nico and me to a lake in Germany, a place where people would swim in the summers. It wasn't very large, but when a slight breeze picked up, little waves would form on the water and splash so gently onto the shore. Nico and I would lay there, our legs in the water, our backs on the muddy sand. Arms over our faces, we'd let the little waves lull us to sleep. The way those waves felt, brushing against my skin, is the same sensation I've got right now in my head.

It doesn't make sense, but there's no pain, there's no discomfort. You know the way you can feel your heartbeat when you're still? The way your whole body ticks with each pulse of the muscle? That's the feeling. It's natural. It's strange but normal, in a way; a new normal—a changed situation.

I'm writing this down at Nico's house.

Big brother won out this time.

I drove over two hours ago for dinner. The boys were laughing and having a great time telling me about their science projects. I really wanted to listen, to be the good aunt who gives advice and helps guide them. I've always had this dream that when they're grown-up and young twentysomethings trying to figure the world out, they'll lean on me. They'll call and we'll go out to coffee when they are in town and I can be a shoulder for them. Work problems, romance issues, troubles with friends. I really want that to be my role for them, but . . . I couldn't listen over dinner.

I just . . . I couldn't focus.

Tonight, the waves inside my head were distracting me. Another migraine was coming, the needle fingers uncurling from the nape of my neck again, ready to march across my head leaving their trail of pain.

Like always, my brother could see something was wrong.

I told Nico I just needed to take a little break, to lie down and rest in a quiet, dark room for a little bit.

That is where I am right now.

And the light waves are here again.

They're sliding down from the corner of the room, right at the intersection of the walls and the ceiling. Light waves that are radiating out, slowly, pulsing across the space between the corner and me.

It is stunning. Beautiful.

No, they're not light.

They're . . . they're gravitational waves.

This is impossible . . .

 **16**

NICO MITCHELL, DAHLIA'S BROTHER

SAN FRANCISCO, CA

AUGUST 22, 2025

While Dahlia Mitchell was perhaps the most famous of the Elevated, Nico, her brother, did not lose any additional family members to the Elevation.

He still lives in San Francisco with his wife, Valerie, and two sons, both in middle school. Nico trained as an architect but eventually found work in marketing. He and Valerie started their own advertising company roughly five years before the Elevation. It was both successful and fulfilling.

He misses having a nine-to-five job.

Nico and Valerie run two bed-and-breakfasts in the city. They cater to business travelers and tourists, though there haven't been many people passing through recently. During the off-seasons, Nico helps with reconstruction projects downtown, while Valerie tutors neighborhood kids.

Taller than I'd expected, Nico is thin, in his mid-forties, with graying hair and clear-framed glasses. He walks with a slight limp and has a bright smile. Nico gives me a tour of the house before showing the room where Dahlia stayed the night she first started to see gravitational waves . . .

I found her in here a few minutes after she'd left the table.

I was worried about her. The months leading up to that night were tough. My sister was struggling. She didn't want to tell me; she was always closed up, you know? Dahlia had this drive, this self-determination thing. I suspect it was because of our mother . . . well, how it ended for our mother . . .

Things were tough at work for her. She felt like she wasn't being taken seriously. Her asshole boss was giving her a hard time about her research. I'll be the first to admit that I never really understood what she was looking for out there, but she was resolute in trying to find it. That sort of single-mindedness took a toll on her. It would take a toll on anyone.

I knew about the painkillers.

She was a classic case. A back injury when she fell during one of her runs. Doctor prescribed opioids and kept refilling the prescription. I can't tell you how many times Dahlia told me she was done with them. But every time I got a chance, I'd look in her medicine cabinet or even dig into her purse. I'm her brother, after all.

She always had the pills.

So that night, dinner at my house, when I walked into the guest room and found her . . . acting crazy, I assumed it was the drugs. That wasn't just me being presumptuous either. Dahlia fell over when I walked in, knocked her purse to the floor. The pills scattered around the room and we ended up picking them up out of the cracks in the baseboards for weeks afterwards. Had to lock the door so the boys wouldn't wander in and accidentally find one.

When I walked into the room, Dahlia was talking about waves.

She was seeing them emanating from the ceiling and rippling across the empty space between her and the wall. She described them like they were waves of light but she told me they were gravitational waves.

I had to look that up later. Based on what I found, gravitational waves are invisible. Takes an incredibly expensive and complicated machine the size of a football field to detect them. And that didn't happen until just a few years before the Elevation. These were concepts from theoretical physics, not the kind of thing you can suddenly start seeing. But Dahlia was seeing them the same way you and I see a sunset.

She was stunned, fascinated.

You can only imagine how much it meant to her. It was like she was seeing the face of God or suddenly getting the answer to the universe's biggest question. Awe. That was the expression on Dahlia's face. Seeing the pills scattered all over her room, I assumed it was drug induced. She was tripping and had some revelation. I will tell you that I didn't see anything. There was some dust in the air but not a single wave or light or gravity.

Then she passed out.

Looking back on it now, after everything that happened, I was scared. It wasn't just her health. I could handle her being a little bruised, maybe sick, but her mental state—the fact that she was seeing these things—really unnerved me. Valerie too. You have to understand, when you've got a parent who suffered from mental illness, a parent who committed suicide, every weird thought you have or gesture you make takes on added significance.

Medical workup at the hospital was normal, at first.

All the blood tests, all the scans—they came back with normal levels. She was high from the opioids. But we expected that. Everything else, however, was as expected. No cancer, no chronic illness. So that left the mental end of things. When Dahlia woke up the next morning, she had a meeting with several psychiatrists. That didn't give us anything either. The docs came away talking about retinal migraines, schizoaffective disorder, the usual list of potential problems. And when they found out our family history, things got twice as complicated.

When Dahlia was feeling better, I went in with a cup of coffee and a Danish.

She had a fifth-floor room that overlooked the parking lot, and just beyond it, if you squinted hard enough, you could make out the ocean. When I came in, Dahlia was out of bed and sitting by the window.

She sipped her coffee and asked me, "How bad is it?"

I told her it was bad. "They think you're nuts."

I knew I shouldn't have said the words the second they came out of my mouth. After what happened to our mom, we were both sensitive to jokes about mental illness. Still, I couldn't help myself.

"Am I?" Dahlia asked.

"No," I lied. "Just the migraines, like you expected."

"You know the pills I've been taking?"

"Yeah," I said. "I wanted to talk to you about—"

"They're not working anymore. They have no effect."

Dahlia had been prescribed pain meds. She got hooked on them pretty quick. The way she described it, they took the edge off her. Chilled her out a bit. But her dose doubled all the time.

I was worried.

So when she told me they weren't working like they used to, I told her maybe that wasn't a bad thing.

Dahlia wanted to go home.

I told her they'd send her home just as soon as the doctors had reviewed the last round of tests. She was antsy to go. Dahlia didn't mention the Pulse but told me work was piling up, regardless of what her boss thought of her research. I asked her to tell me a little more about what she was working on, but she didn't answer.

She was staring off into the middle distance between us.

Eyes focused on . . . nothing.

Dahlia said, "I can see the waves again. They're stronger now."

She reached out to touch one of them. At least, that's what I assume she was doing. Dahlia carefully stretched out her fingers, gently trying to pluck something invisible from the air the same way you'd pinch a dust mote.

I don't know if she got it.

But she began seizing a few seconds later.

**17**

EDITED TRANSCRIPT FROM A PHONE CALL BETWEEN
DR. XAVIER FABER AND KANISHA PRESTON
(RECORDED BY DR. XAVIER FABER, TRANSCRIBED BY KEITH THOMAS)
RECORDED ON 11.4.2023

KANISHA PRESTON: Hello?

DR. XAVIER FABER: National Security Advisor Preston? Sorry to wake you. It's Xavier Faber with the group. We've, uh, we've found something . . .

KANISHA PRESTON: Okay . . .

DR. XAVIER FABER: A Trojan horse. I think that this code is a Trojan horse program designed to hack human DNA. I don't know what the outcome is supposed to be, but I know that this signal, the Pulse, wasn't a message. It's a package. This thing was just delivered to each and every one of us.

KANISHA PRESTON: Hacking human DNA?

DR. XAVIER FABER: It's incredibly complicated. Dr. Roberts has some ideas, of course, but . . . We've never seen anything like this.

KANISHA PRESTON: How? How would that even work?

DR. XAVIER FABER: You're the doctor. I imagine it'd be done the same way scientists manipulate DNA now. DNA can be edited with biotechnology. Damaged genes can be removed or repaired. We're only a generation away from editing someone's DNA to repair the genes associated with inherited macro-degeneration. If this code hacks human DNA, then it does roughly the same thing. Only, instead of repair genes, it alters them . . .

KANISHA PRESTON: What would be the goal of altering human DNA? Why would an alien intelligence want to do that? Why not just . . . *invade*?

DR. XAVIER FABER: Best we can think, it's an attempt at reading us. That sounds stupid when I hear myself saying it out loud, but that's our best guess. It could be that the Pulse Code is linked back up with some sort of receiver and they basically just scanned our whole genetic code. But . . .

KANISHA PRESTON: But?

DR. XAVIER FABER: Here's the thing that I'm most worried about: even if we crack this code, figure out exactly how it works and what it does, we're behind the eight ball. The Pulse already hit the Earth. If the Pulse does something bad, we've all already been exposed.

THE ELEVATION

18

PRESIDENT VANESSA BALLARD

DETROIT, MI

SEPTEMBER 18, 2025

Flying into Detroit, my plane passed low over a city that has completely surrendered itself to the vicissitudes of nature. No other American city has embraced the Finality and turned what most view as catastrophe into opportunity. I wouldn't call the people who fly in from across the country to visit Detroit "damage porn" tourists, though for a while this was the impression people had of them: posing in front of derelict and overgrown buildings for social media selfies, touring the waste-water treatment plant lakes by kayak. The city had seen this sort of thing before, of course. Pre-Elevation, there were movies filmed in Detroit just to capture that urban decay. That was different; that was piggy-backed on the pain and suffering of other people. Now the people are gone. The city is empty.

What was, at its heyday, a sprawling metropolis of 1.8 million has dwindled to just over 15,000 people—the same size as Bend, Oregon, or the sunken city of New Orleans. One of those 15,000 is our last president.

She resides in the Field House in Palmer Woods. It's a well-known architectural wonder from the 1950s with a broad sloping roof. Dubbed "the butterfly house" for its unique shape, the house looks out onto an empty neighborhood. All the houses, outside of one directly across the street where the Secret Service has an office, are unoccupied. I notice several of them have trees growing from their roofs and none have windows; this is a testament to the looting that engulfed much of the country in the hours just following the Finality.

Long hair graying, President Ballard, now in her mid-sixties, still looks

119

every bit as presidential as she did during her first campaign. Near the living room windows looking out over her backyard, we sit in comfortable leather armchairs and drink tea. President Ballard has become quite health conscious and takes great pride in growing, drying, and brewing her own teas. She enjoys them herself and gives them to friends, family, and the occasional visitor.

I remember when I was first told about the Pulse.

It was Glenn. We were in the Oval Office corridor, moving from one meeting to another. When Glenn had something serious to tell me, something he knew I might have a big reaction to, he slowed down and wanted to make eye contact.

So I slowed and he talked.

He told me that National Security Advisor Preston had received a communication about the interception of an unusual signal. Was this, quote, unquote, "unusual signal" a problem or merely a curiosity? I asked.

He indicated it was a problem.

Then he told me that a radio telescope in California picked up a signal coming from outside our galaxy. That this pulse—this was the first time I heard the word in relation to this event—was sent by an intelligence alien to our planet. Even more, this pulse contained a code. A code they were working to break.

I think my first reaction was befuddlement.

It certainly wasn't excitement, though that came later.

Glenn was never shy about sharing his thoughts. He repeated how the Pulse was picked up, adding that only a few people, all inside the NSA, had seen the code and then ended with his take.

"It's real," he said. "I've had a committee, working alongside Kanisha, sorting this whole thing out. They're the best brains in astronomy, computer science, linguists, and physics, and they tell me that this is very much a message from outer space. What we have, Mrs. President, is potentially monumental."

I had never seen Glenn that . . . solemn.

And yet hopeful.

There was a light in his eyes when he told me about the Pulse. Of course, we shared an interest in the stars—me from my father and my upbringing, Glenn from his philosophy days. Remember, despite Glenn Owen's fiery career on Capitol Hill, his polarizing reputation as an arch-politician, he was a philosopher first. This was a man who'd written several books on nihilism that became cult classics with edgy intellectuals. The idea that there was other life in the universe and that it had reached out to us during my administration, well . . . We both knew that this could be a defining moment. Monumental indeed.

But I wasn't going to cancel all my meetings that day because of it. Half the world was still in turmoil. Grinding war in the Middle East, terrorism ripping Southeast Asia to shreds, and climate change making everything worse. Back home, the divisions, as you recall, were worse than ever. We had racial strife that had exploded overnight on social media, an economy that had been stabilized but was still weak, a surge in methamphetamine addiction, and more gun violence issues than we'd seen in forty years*—and that's coming from a dyed-in-the-wool Second Amendment supporter. That isn't even touching on my own life and my husband's health. Hard to balance all that, for sure.

Even though my mind was spinning at the thought of an upcoming liaison with an alien race, I had important things to do first.

So I thanked Glenn for telling me, asked him to keep me in the loop, and suggested he pull together his team and make them official. A task force, brought together to figure out what the message from space was and how we were going to handle it. And I needed them to give me some answers soon: I had a duty to tell the American public, certainly the science sector, what was going on.

"It's called Disclosure," Glenn said. "Public acknowledgment that the United States government has been in contact with or has awareness of contact with an extraterrestrial intelligence. It's a big step, Mrs. President. We've never made it before because we've never had a reason to."

I asked him if he thought this team, this task force, could draft this Disclosure message. Would they be capable? Would they be willing?

---

* And it spiked even more with anti-Elevation violence, but there were a number of violent standoffs between sovereign citizens—convinced the government was using the Elevation to claim land, weapons, and wealth—and law enforcement. Towards the last days of December 2023, just before Christmas, the murder rate in the United States reached an astonishing 25 per 100,000. It was a very dangerous time to be alive. Perhaps the most dangerous time in US history.

He said he thought so and I told him to get it done.

The whole conversation lasted maybe three minutes. Thinking about that now, considering everything that happened after, it makes me laugh. But that's how history works. The most important moments are sometimes wrapped in the smallest, most insignificant of packages. Three minutes and a decision was made that would chart our course, not just for the United States, but also for the entire globe. Of course, hindsight is what it is. I would have made changes; I would have put aside some of the partisan differences that came up later.

Glenn and I didn't speak about the matter for a couple of days. We likely wouldn't have talked again about the Pulse if it hadn't been for what happened to David.

I know that a lot of this made the papers. His Parkinson's diagnosis was public knowledge pretty early on. The pundits, left and right, exploited it when they could. Almost always, using his health to attack me. Some suggested it made me weak, that I was struggling emotionally and therefore unfit, and others dared to link it to conspiracy theories about our marriage being a sham. The fact that we'd never had children was some sort of red flag for them. How could a woman be an effective president if she was denying her basic biology? I actually heard people say that.

What wasn't in the press was the fact that David's illness was getting worse.

Harvey Stimson, the White House physician, came to me that same week and told me that he was concerned. This was . . . well, the timing was difficult.

I would have done anything for my husband. I told him multiple times that I would gladly give up the presidency if it meant giving him a better life, a better chance at healing.

There'd been many scientific breakthroughs in treating Parkinson's—the discovery of the PINK1 gene,* some novel stem cell therapies—and I was hopeful, genuinely hopeful, that we'd find a cure in David's lifetime. Of

---

* The PINK1 gene provides the body with instructions for a protein called "PTEN induce putative kinase 1." While the protein isn't fully understood, it provides a protective function and PINK1 mutations likely play a role in Parkinson's development.

course, I anticipated it might get worse with the stress of being in office. David and I discussed it at length before I even ran. He was my rock . . .

President Ballard pauses here and looks out the window at the backyard. There are birds fluttering about several feeders she's set up, and in the distance black smoke curls up over the treetops and into the pale sky.

That's not a house fire, though we've seen plenty of those.

They're burning refuse. Mostly leaves, branches. They've got a clever composting system that uses ash. It's highly alkaline and counteracts the acidic soil in their gardens; they grow tomatoes for the whole neighborhood. Delicious and big as apples. You'll have to try a couple of them on your way out.

Going back, I was saying that David's health had taken a bit of a hit right when the Pulse was found. Or at least when Glenn first told me about it. Dr. Stimson caught me that evening and told me David was exhibiting some worrying symptoms: a tremor in his right hand, speech changes, trouble sleeping. I told him I was aware of the changes. I also mentioned that David was complaining of some new pain at the base of his spine. Stimson wasn't sure what that could be but told me he'd look into it.

Sure enough, the night I was told of the Pulse . . . it began.

David woke up in the middle of the night. He'd gone to bed early, around ten. I was up working in the Treaty Room until midnight and was very quiet when I came in. He was tossing, turning, and mumbling something. I was exhausted and I fell asleep despite the noise and turmoil. I woke up at two thirty and David wasn't in the bed.

He was standing in the corner, staring up at the ceiling.

When I asked him what he was doing, he said, "They're up there."

"Who's up there?"

David turned to me and his face was wet with tears, his eyes red from crying, and he said, "Don't you hear them?" I shook my head. There was no noise I could make out. David said, "I can't believe they're here. Never thought I'd ever see them . . . And she . . . she looks so sweet."

I assumed David was dreaming. Walking in his sleep.

But he was awake. We had the Secret Service scan the ceilings, give the room a once-over with their equipment. They didn't find anything, of course.

I called Dr. Stimson and he rushed over. The exam was normal. Eyesight, hearing, motor reflexes—all of it normal. Dr. Stimson wrote it up as a sleep disturbance. David slept fine the rest of the night but I lay awake staring at the corner of the ceiling. I never heard anything, never saw anything, but it haunted me. Seeing him like that. The things he said, it sounded like . . . like he really heard . . . I don't know.

Days passed. The Disclosure Task Force got to work.

I spoke briefly with Kanisha Preston and she told me she was confident the team would have the Pulse Code cracked within forty-eight hours. She also let me know that their initial analysis suggested the code was likely a program. However, it wasn't anything that would have run on our machines. She couldn't rule out that it was a weapon. That was the last thing I needed, some intergalactic bomb being beamed to our planet from a trillion miles away.

They kept working and I focused on domestic matters.

You'll remember this was right around the time of the train accident in Elizabeth, New Jersey.* I got the call maybe ten minutes after it happened. Two trains, filled with morning commuters, collided at full speed. Eighty-six lives lost. Worst rail disaster since 1876. After the FBI and local police ruled out terrorism, it was clear that it was driver error. What we had was radio communications and the black box from both of the trains. It was when those audiotapes, the one from the conductor of the northbound train, hit the media that people began freaking out.

The driver was hallucinating.

Just thinking about those tapes, the things he said, gives me chills to this day. He claimed he was seeing "the lost ones" on the tracks in front of him. He was speeding up to reach them.

The lost ones. End of the day, everyone wrote it up as delusion. The man was in his late fifties, smoked, ate too much red meat, and likely had a stroke. An autopsy was inconclusive, considering most of his body had been reduced to ash in the ensuing fire. Here's what the media didn't know, what

---

* While the Elizabeth rail accident was horrifying and tragic, in the aftermath of the Finality several additional mass-casualty incidents would become associated with the Elevation. The plant explosion in Little Rock, Arkansas, the sinking of the *New Waratah* in Lake Michigan, and the Evergreen Building collapse in Salem, Oregon.

I'm going to tell you: the conductor talked about the "lost ones" but he also named them. The police kept that from the press and amazingly, for once, they were successful. I think it was done for privacy reasons, protecting family members, but . . . well, there's a twist to that.

What the driver said on that tape was: "There's the lost ones . . . The lost ones come back . . . Ronald, Suzanne, and Little Curtis . . ." Took investigators several months to link those names to anything more than just rambling. The lost ones—the conductor knew them. I was dismayed when I heard it.

Ronald, Suzanne, and Little Curtis were three of his classmates at his elementary school in Pennington, New Jersey. The three went missing in 1974 after taking a bus downtown on their way to a movie. The kids were never found and police suspected a serial killer who'd been operating in the area in the mid- to late '70s might have abducted them. Nothing much came of that. Case still open, as they say. At the time of the crash, it was a spooky footnote in the investigation.

A spooky footnote; I wish that was all it was.

Three days after the accident, while the funerals were being held for the victims of the accident, David had another . . . attack. We were in the bowling alley at the White House. It's one lane, in the basement just under the North Portico, and refurnished a few times by previous presidents. I wasn't much for playing, but David enjoyed it. We had fun; it was great to see him laugh.

When I brought up the Parkinson's, David was dismissive.

"I'm feeling fine," he said. "Don't stress about me. Seriously. It's just old age making things worse. College football injuries sneaking up on me. What the hell happened to that hopeful woman who told me that we'd be creating a better world together once we reached the White House?"

I told him she'd wised up.

"Bullshit," he said. "Look, I'll bowl a perfect strike just to prove it."

He winked at me, very cute. Then he turned, bowling ball in hand, positioned himself, focused on the pins. David pulled his arm back, ready to move, when . . . he didn't. He stood there, frozen in that position like a statue. And then—crash—the bowling ball falls from his hand, slams down against the wood of the lane, and rolls off into the gutter. David hasn't moved; he's staring down at the pins.

I got up, concerned.

He—he was bleeding from his nose, and he kept repeating, "Why are they here? Why are they here?"

I asked him who he was talking about.

He said, "My mother . . . my baby brother . . ."

I wanted to break down right there and then. My husband, the First Gentleman of the United States, was staring at a wall and telling me he was seeing his dead mother and his baby brother, Jacob, who'd died when David was only three or four years old. Then David collapsed. His legs just fell out from under him.

I cradled him as the blood kept streaming from his nose and called for help.

A helicopter took him to Walter Reed.

That, for me, was the start of what we came to call the Elevation. Of course, at the time it seemed a random event, a factor of David's illness. But when it began to happen other places, when the tragedy in Elizabeth was linked to what was going on nationwide—when there was no denying it was real—that was when everything changed. The Disclosure Task Force became much more than just a committee determined to help us navigate the waters of telling the world aliens were real: they became our lifeline to a new, radically different future.

A future where Dahlia Mitchell was our guiding light.

19

KANISHA PRESTON: We're recording...

DR. NEIL ROBERTS: All righty. President Ballard has approved the creation of a Disclosure Task Force and a Disclosure document. This document will essentially be our message to the globe about what we know and we what believe are the next steps in this historical moment. Here's what we know, and feel free, Dr. Faber, to interrupt me at any point to disagree or make a snarky remark—

DR. XAVIER FABER: Don't worry. I'm always ready.

DR. NEIL ROBERTS: So. Here's what we know: Approximately three days ago, astronomer Dr. Dahlia Mitchell of the University of California, Santa Cruz, intercepted a signal from deep space. To be specific, this was a pulse from the Bullet Cluster. She recorded part of it. We have studied the data contained in the Pulse and determined it is of extra-terrestrial origin and designed by an intelligence far superior to our own. (pause) How am I doing so far?

DR. SERGEI MIKOYAN: You're doing excellent.

DR. XAVIER FABER: Mediocre, but keep going.

DR. NEIL ROBERTS: This pulse is the very first verifiable contact humanity has received from an outside culture. While we have the code embedded in the Pulse, we have no answers as to the culture—

DR. XAVIER FABER: The Ascendant.

DR. NEIL ROBERTS: Right: we have no answers about the Ascendant, their location, their society, their biological makeup, their—

DR. XAVIER FABER: We get it. We don't know shit all about them and likely won't ever. Let's keep focused on what we do know. Which is . . . ?

DR. NEIL ROBERTS: We know they have beamed this pulse at our planet and that it contains a program, essentially. Here is where things get a bit more complicated. The program inside the Pulse Code is designed to hack, for want of a better word, our DNA. The code functions like a chemical mutagen, but one we've never before encountered. Look, this is all very, very early, but as far as we can tell, it works something like this: the code alters the base pairs that make up the DNA chain.* Perhaps it's stripping down nucleotides, incorporating changes that are imperceptible to the DNA replication apparatus. I suspect the changes include insertion of additional base pairs. Possibly many, many base pairs. For what purpose, we're still unsure.

DR. SERGEI MIKOYAN: I don't care for the use of the word "hack." That sounds malicious and we still have not determined if the code is a bad or good program. We know that the Pulse was spread across the globe and that means it likely encountered each and every person on the planet. If it is active—and that is still a big if—we need to assume it is doing something at this very moment.

DR. XAVIER FABER: I think "hack" is an excellent word because it hints at the severity of this thing. I know Drs. Mikoyan and Roberts have ruled out the possibility.

DR. SOLEDAD VENEGAS: To sum up, we are tasked with creating this Disclosure document. It will be presented to President Ballard. She will decide how she wants to present it, but, considering the importance

---

* DNA base pairs are standard nucleobase pairing with hydrogen bonds: A (adenine) with T (thymine) and C (cytosine) with G (guanine). This bonding gives DNA its distinctive double-helix structure.

of this situation, we all assume she'll want to do it in as public a forum as possible.

KANISHA PRESTON: The President is less worried about optics than she is about ensuring that this is accurate. Last thing anyone wants is panic. We don't want to tell the world that we've been in touch with an alien intelligence that wants to help us evolve when they really want to eat us.

DR. NEIL ROBERTS: That's certainly not going to be an issue.

DR. XAVIER FABER: I don't know . . . I've heard human tastes delicious.

KANISHA PRESTON: The other thing we'll need to focus on is what comes next. We tell the world we've received this code. That means we're not alone in the universe. But so what? Do we try and reach back? What do we say? I need you to come up with those ideas. I also need you to make some hypothetical leaps: tell me what you think we know about this intelligence, what the code tells you about their motives.

DR. XAVIER FABER: We need to talk to Dr. Dahlia Mitchell. The reports, the interviews with her—they're too surface-level. I need more detail. Specifically, I need to know what she thought she was seeing, what she thought she'd found.

DR. SERGEI MIKOYAN: And the interviews didn't answer this?

DR. XAVIER FABER: Sergei, what the Feds have asked her so far are just verbal bait and switch, attempts to catch her lying, to reveal she set the whole thing up. Dahlia's a scientist; she needs to be questioned by her peers. If we want to know what happened when she found this thing, we need to hear it directly from her. So, can we bring her in?

KANISHA PRESTON: I don't see why not.

DR. NEIL ROBERTS: I do have a larger concern. I'm worried we're already too late in terms of alerting the public. If we are correct that this pulse has reached every man, woman, and child on the planet, then we can also assume that, whatever it was intended to do, it's started. Regardless of whether we call it hacking human DNA or not, the Pulse was designed to interact with us. Outside of tuning every radio telescope on Earth to the Bullet Cluster, we need to focus on ourselves. We need to scan the news for each and every story about a potential society-wide affliction . . .

KANISHA PRESTON: What are you suggesting, Dr. Roberts?

DR. XAVIER FABER: He's finally come around to my side on this. If the Pulse Code is hacking human DNA, what's it programmed to do? We need to know what's going on out there. My guess: the shit's about to hit the fan.

**20**

AUTHOR'S NOTE

Xavier was right about "the shit" but wrong on the timing.

It had already hit the fan. However, most people hadn't noticed.

That's because when the Elevation spread, the results were subtle. It began with a few scattered cases, nothing to raise alarms. And unlike a virulent disease like Ebola or a norovirus, the symptoms differed for most people.

They were also, almost always, mental in origin.

While the media picked up on a few wild incidents that spread across social media, the first cases of the Elevation that I could track down weren't as dramatic. For me, the inaugural case was the elderly woman doing donuts in Cheyenne, Wyoming.

I spoke to Thomas Franklin Bess, a forty-six-year-old fireman who was one of the first to be called to the scene. He was a firefighter for twenty-one years and he still speaks of his work with reverence. No longer able to work due to a back injury, Thomas spends his time working as a handyman, driving around the largely empty neighborhoods in this sprawling suburb and fixing the few remaining residents' toilets and sinks.

Thomas and his crew were called out to an intersection where an accident had been reported. Only, it wasn't an accident. When the engine arrived, they were waved down by a few people on their cells, including a young woman who claimed her mother was "going crazy."

Sure enough, there was a red sedan doing donuts in the middle of the intersection. Donuts. Round and round.

Thomas motioned for the old woman behind the wheel to slow down and stop the vehicle. She didn't listen. She just stared straight ahead, mumbling to herself. Round and round she went, with the wheel turned at a perfect angle to keep the car in its rotation but missing the curbs and everything. The firefighters couldn't just let her block traffic until the sedan ran out of gas, so they dragged a tire spike strip from the engine, threw it down in front of the car, and, pop, the elderly woman ran over it and the tires instantly deflated.

When the firefighters pulled her out of the sedan, she was mumbling about how she could hear the grinding of the Earth under the street. "There's a well under here," she said. At the time Thomas didn't think much of it. The woman was clearly unhinged. She was escorted to a waiting ambulance and taken off to the nearest hospital.

A couple of days later, that very same intersection collapsed. At first Thomas assumed it was a sinkhole. That happened from time to time. But it wasn't a sinkhole, at least not a natural one. Two cars went into a thirty-foot-deep pit, a void that engineers said was caused by an old well, one that had been abandoned but never properly sealed up. Thomas was struck by how eerie the whole thing seemed.

"I thought the woman was prophetic," he told me. "Well, until I heard about the others just like her."

The old well that swallowed up two cars made the local news; the old lady doing donuts did not. But she was the tip of a very unnerving spear. In the very hours that followed Thomas's encounter with the elderly woman, I was able to stitch together a series of social media posts about incidents with similar unpredictable, inexplicable circumstances. It seemed that over the course of a single week, a large portion of the world's population suddenly started to go . . . weird.

There was the strange death of a young man, Orlando Macintyre, known to local police as a breeder of pit-fighting dogs. Orlando dropped out of school after ninth grade and was described by his mother as being "troubled and very slow to learn." Two hours after Thomas's encounter in Cheyenne, Orlando's body was found in a barren field near Dayton, Ohio. The cause of Orlando's death was never determined, but authorities suspected drugs played a role. What was unusual was the fact that Orlando was discovered gripping a scrap of paper in his left hand—a scrap of paper that contained a complicated mathematical formula that a professor at Bowling Green State University determined was a partial proof—or solution—for the Hodge conjecture.[*]

That same day, in Mesquite, Texas, a mother of three named Francine Sharpless drove her minivan into a crowded farmers market. Before detonating the homemade explosive in the trunk, she shouted to startled witnesses: "I'm going to free you now!"

These are just two of dozens of similar cases. And these are the cases for a single given day in the United States. I found thousands of identical events in countries across the globe. There was the oil tanker that ran aground in Denmark, the train derailment in Singapore, and the fires that burned down most of Athens.

These are, of course, the bigger events.

I also found hundreds of instances in the records of many smaller, more personal accounts of transformation. I'm certain that most of these testimonies would have been lost in the barrage of second-by-second updates and new posts. Many of these posts were of drawings—pen, crayon, pencil, charcoal, paint, digital; they ran the gamut—all done in a feverish, almost art brut[†] fashion. If you were to create a video of these pieces, having each of them appear on-screen for a few seconds, you would immediately notice the similarities: cascading colors, overlapping circles, radiating lines. Each and every one of them was an illustration of something people aren't supposed to see. Gravitational waves, infrared colors, and, in a few cases, even having what the comic books would call "superpowers."

People like Carter Loisel.

---

[*] The Hodge conjecture is an unsolved problem in algebraic geometry that was first presented by mathematician Sir William Vallance Douglas Hodge in 1950. The person who proves or disproves the conjecture will be awarded $1 million by the Clay Mathematics Institute.

[†] The term "art brut" frequently refers to "outsider art" or art made by people without any artistic training. Most often, it is associated with art by the mentally ill. That certainly is the connotation here, as much of the art created by the Elevated that I've seen is very reminiscent of work by schizophrenic artists like Adolf Wölfli.

**21**

ADELE FRANCE, MD, EMERGENCY MEDICINE PHYSICIAN
CHICAGO, IL
JANUARY 3, 2026

Adele France is in her early thirties.

Two of her three siblings died due to Elevation-related causes.

Like the rest of the world, she was caught off guard by the changes that suddenly spread through the population. Being on the front lines of the medical emergency—and scientific mystery—that followed, she witnessed firsthand how families were left confused and frightened in the wake of the Elevation. Her own family was one of those: looking up everything they could on the Internet, calling their doctors incessantly, hitting every ER and urgent care center that would accept their insurance (sometimes even those that wouldn't), and emptying the shelves of their local pharmacies. Of course, none of that helped.

The Elevation wasn't a disease doctors knew how to treat.

Today, Adele lives in Chicago, but when she was a medical resident, she lived in Oklahoma. She tells me she enjoyed the wide-open spaces and the sky that seemed to never stop. It was there that she saw her first Elevated human.

I was a resident when the first case came in.

This was in rural Oklahoma. There's this loan repayment plan for medical students if you choose to do part or all of your residency at a rural hospital. I didn't come from money and I certainly wasn't looking forward to the idea of paying off student loans for the next forty years. So I jumped at the opportunity and took a job in Boise City.

With the political turmoil over health care, the place was really struggling. I'd say something like seventy percent of my patients were on government assistance. That's probably low. Most of the stuff we saw on a day-to-day basis was your typical flus and injuries. A lot of farm equipment injuries.

Most days we'd be sitting around waiting for something, anything, more exciting than a baby with a sore throat or a farmer with a sprained ankle. Never in a million years would I have guessed that something would be one of the first Elevated.

It was maybe six o'clock, late in the summer. I remember the shadows were really long and I was standing outside with a friend who was a nurse. She was on her smoke break and I was just stretching, getting a last few rays of the sun. An old woman drove up in this ancient station wagon. She was in quite a state, frantic, honking the horn and waving her arms like the world was ending.

I ran over there and she rolled down the window.

"It's my grandson," she was yelling. "He's gotten real bad!"

There was a boy in the car, sitting in the back seat. I remember clear as day how he looked. The boy was sitting there, legs crossed, about seven or eight years old, and he turned and looked over at me. Just as cool and collected as he could be. The look in his eyes . . . I have no way to really explain just how much it affected me. This is going to sound silly—certainly sounds that way in my head as I'm saying it—but the little boy's gaze was *too knowing*.

That's the best way for me to describe it, though even that doesn't get at the effect his look had on me. I had sat beside my grandfather as he passed away. I was in college then and hadn't had any real experience with death outside of pets, really, so I was a wreck. He was sitting on a couch, wrapped up in blankets, and listening to some gentle music. I held his hand and stared into his eyes; my mom and dad were sitting right beside him on the couch.

We'd been there twelve hours, just waiting, watching, comforting as we could. His breathing was the first to go. It went from strained, long inhalations to ragged, lateral breaths—shallower and shallower. The sun had just come up and I remember the light in the room was so soft, almost hazy. I held my grandfather's hand tightly as his breathing slowed even more. Finally, it just kind of stopped and he turned to me and looked at me, staring me directly in the eyes, and . . . he smiled. And died. But at that last second, that very last moment, looking into his pupils, wide and dilated and dark as the depths of the ocean, I felt like I was seeing his soul—a soul rich with so much wisdom, so much experience. Those milliseconds were overflowing. In them, I felt a massive wave, a tsunami, of knowledge wash over me. Subsume me. It was like gravity had reversed and I was launched out into the vastness of space, a tiny fragment lost in the entirety of the cosmos . . . That may be putting it a bit too poetically, but the feeling was real.

And it wasn't frightening. It was just . . . awe.

I had the exact same feeling, the same sensation of being overwhelmed by an almost impossible force, when I looked into that little boy's eyes. I froze. I hadn't done that since I was in med school. It didn't last long; I snapped out of it and got the boy out of the car as his grandmother screamed and yelled.

Naturally, I'd assumed something had happened to the boy. Maybe he was sick or there had been an accident. He didn't have a mark on him. He wasn't hot to the touch, wasn't pale. Seemed completely fine at that moment. Anyway, I brought him into the ER and had the nurses do a workup. I talked to the grandmother to get a history and figure out what exactly was going on.

The grandmother, sixty-five at the oldest, was clearly panicked. It took her a while to calm down, but when she did, she confirmed that the little boy hadn't been injured. He wasn't sick—not with a virus or an infection. What was happening, according to her, was that the boy wasn't himself anymore. He'd changed.

"Changed how?" I asked.

"He's saying things, telling me things, that he shouldn't know."

I didn't understand what that meant, but I put a note in the chart that we needed to get a psychological evaluation and have a social worker come by to chat with the grandmother as well. I asked about the things the boy was saying.

"He says he can see inside things . . ."

"Like . . . like what?" I asked.

"People, mostly," she said.

The way this boy's grandmother said it gave me chills. The first thing my clinical brain thought was that the boy either had a particularly detailed imagination or possibly was suffering from schizophrenia. It's rare to see in kids, though. Especially little kids. I don't know the rates off the top of my head, but schizophrenia in children under twelve is almost unheard-of.

The boy's vitals were all normal. His blood results came back normal too. Nothing elevated, nothing of concern. Before we went ahead with scans, I had our psychologist come down and talk to the boy with me. Just to see exactly what it was that he was telling the grandmother—exactly what it was that had her so concerned. A lot of times kids clam up. That's expected. They're in an unfamiliar place, talking to people they don't know and don't necessarily trust. In all honesty, that's a positive thing. That's something a well-adjusted kid does. Think of it more like a hardwired survival instinct.

This boy didn't clam up.

If anything, he was too relaxed. Too talkative.

The first thing this boy said when we sat down across from him in this cramped exam room was "You have metal in your ankle. The left one." He said that to the psychologist and she laughed, nervous, and asked him how he knew that. The little boy said he could see it, plain as he could see the glasses on my face. The psychologist said that as a kid she'd fractured her ankle, tore some ligaments and a tendon, and had several surgeries. There were metal plates put in. Small, but there.

"How do you know that?" the psychologist asked the boy.

She was jumping the gun. I think the comment, the first words out of the little guy's mouth, threw her off. There's a whole procedure to these things, how to ask questions without setting up expectations. Psychology is a dangerous game: you have to know the rules and play it right, otherwise you really can't get at the truth of what you're looking for. Anyway, I think we were both stunned, confused, and she wanted to jump directly to the matter at hand.

"I didn't know it. I see it," the boy said.

So I asked him what else he could see.

The boy leaned forward and stared at me like he was scanning a page for a particular word. It was unnerving, him looking me over. Took maybe thirty seconds, and then he leaned back in his chair and said, "I see three things. First, you have a tattoo on your backside, just above your butt crack.

It looks like a bird but it's all artistic looking. Second, you have a surgery. I don't know what it was for, but the doctors made a small cut on the right side of your belly. There's a part missing in there. A part of your guts that most people have but that's not inside you."

"The appendix?" the psychologist asked.

The boy shrugged. "I don't know what it's called," he said, "but it's like this little squiggle that comes off the bigger part of the guts. Most people, it kind of looks like a little tail that's tucked in. She doesn't have one."

"She" being me.

I didn't say anything. There's this cliché about being at a loss for words, but it's true. It can happen. Most clichés are like that; the reason they're overused is because they're so . . . real, some sort of common currency among humans, shared experience. Anyway, I couldn't reply. The psychologist said, "You mentioned three things. What is the third?"

The boy smiled and turned away shyly.

"Go on," the psychologist said, "it's okay to tell us."

He laughed and looked at me and said, "You've got a little plastic *T* in your . . . in your vagina." He was talking about my birth control. My IUD looks like a little *T*, of course. Placed in the uterus, it knocks around and prevents unwanted pregnancy. I'd had it implanted only a few weeks earlier. Now, I suppose it's possible the boy was somehow familiar with an IUD. Maybe someone in his family had one or he'd seen a commercial or I don't know. But the other stuff—the tattoo and, even more, the fact that I'd had my appendix taken out . . . it was mind-blowing. And at the same time it was too much to believe. I figured the boy was being coached.

So I wrote it down and we did the scans.

X-ray first. Found nothing abnormal. Here's where we faced some trouble: there was technically nothing wrong with the boy. What his grandmother was complaining about was unusual, yes, but not dangerous. Technically, there was no threat to his life. Running tests under these circumstances was both expensive and unwarranted.

At the same time, whatever was going on with the boy was distressing the grandmother. When I told her that everything looked okay, she was upset. She insisted that she wouldn't leave the hospital until we'd figured out what was wrong with her grandson. When I suggested that there was nothing wrong, she looked at me like I'd lost my mind. The boy's grandmother stood up, walked over to the door to the examination room, opened it, and said, "Come. Let me show you."

We went into the exam room where her grandson was and she took his hand. Then she asked if we could walk through the waiting room. Like I said at the outset, this was a small town. Despite that, there were actually five people in the waiting room at the time. Three had come in while we'd been talking to the boy and we hadn't yet had time to do a workup on any of them.

The boy's grandmother took the boy by the hand and led him past each of the people in the waiting room. It was weird for a few moments, the boy standing there, staring at these sick people, and the psychologist and grandmother and me watching. The first patient, an older woman, began asking us what we were doing, when the boy said, "She has black stuff in her lungs, sticky and thick. It's making her cough and the air doesn't get down in deep like it should."*

The older woman nodded and said, "Yeah ... he knows ... how's he know?"

But we'd already moved over a few chairs to a man with a moustache who was slumped over and fast asleep. He reeked of alcohol and we'd had him pass through several times before complaining of pain and looking for opioids.

The boy stared at the sleeping man a bit longer than he had at me or the psychologist or the older woman. Then he turned to his grandmother and said, "He has lumps all over the inside of his body. They're going to kill him, aren't they?"

Of course, we didn't know then that the boy was the first.

His name was Carter Loisel and we also didn't know that there was another patient, a young woman with kidney stones, who'd been filming the whole thing on her cell phone. She uploaded the video to her social media sites a few minutes before she was brought back for treatment.

By the time she was out two hours later, the Net had blown up.

That little boy was the face of the Elevation.†

At least, until the others showed up.

---

* What the boy described seeing was most likely COPD, a condition commonly attributed to smoking though genetically acquired in some cases, encompassing emphysema and chronic bronchitis.

† Sadly, Carter Loisel passed away from an Elevation-related cerebral aneurysm five months after his ER encounter.

**22**

KIARA MCCAIN, MD, MPH, NEUROSCIENTIST AND EPIDEMIOLOGIST
AUSTIN, TX
JANUARY 15, 2026

My flight to Austin was a rough one.

The plane passed through several storms, and the turbulence had a handful of people on the flight vomiting. I picked up my rental car and made my way downtown, over the Congress Avenue Bridge, where a nightly display of emerging bats used to charm thousands of tourists, to the Perry-Castañeda Library on the University of Texas at Austin campus. It is a large, white stone building with low-slung ceilings. Inside, the architecture is clean—a lot of light, woodwork, and earthy tones.

I meet with Dr. McCain in a vestibule on the third floor.

As the Elevation first spread across the globe, medical professionals were still scrambling not only to explain what was going on with the people turning up in their emergency rooms but also to determine if these bizarre cases were linked. Dr. McCain emerged as an early proponent of the theory that what physicians were seeing was indeed novel—that it wasn't a chemical exposure issue or a viral outbreak; that the changes manifesting in the brains of the affected were "built-in"; they were due to physical changes—alterations in the very substance of the brain itself.

Though she left her medical practice three years ago, Dr. McCain continues to occasionally consult on cases for the state of Texas. Today, her passions are her children—she has five, aged three to fourteen—and watercolor painting. Dr. McCain is African American and tall, with chunky glasses and a tight ponytail.

We called it the Elevation.

I believe the name came from a researcher in Nevada, someone on Lance Guttman and Raj Cheema's[*] team. I think it was something of a joke at first. They saw some of the people that had been coming into the ERs, claiming ridiculous abilities, and kidded that maybe these people were the next step in human evolution. They were Elevated.

The name, the idea, it stuck.

A lot of us think of the little boy who had, quote, unquote, "X-ray vision," the old woman driving in circles who could hear a well beneath the street, but they were only the more media friendly of that first wave.

This was happening in every city and town in the United States.

Parents were walking into emergency rooms with children who were seeing things, hearing things, feeling things they couldn't—magnetic radiation, ultraviolet colors, the ultrasonic songs of mice.[†]

There were videos popping up online by the dozens.

I received thousands of case reports in just twenty-four hours. Somehow my office became the in-box: doctors, researchers—they saw something they couldn't explain and sent it in here. The high school girl endlessly scribbling mathematical formulas on her classroom whiteboard; the pilot who'd tried to fly his plane through a mountain; the older gentleman, a former pastry chef, who woke up one morning and started lecturing his nursing home staff in quantum mechanics; and the middle-aged woman who carefully cut the flesh off her thigh to manipulate the tendons inside and watch the muscles dance.

They all appeared random, just instances of mental unbalance. It all happened so quickly, no one could see the bigger picture. With the medical system overwhelmed, this stuff looked at first like a case of mass hysteria.

Only, no one's ever seen mass hysteria on this scale.

---

* Drs. Lance Guttman and Raj Cheema are neuroscientists at the University of Nevada, Reno. Both were involved in Dr. McCain's early work on identifying Elevated patients. Neither was willing to speak with me for this project.

† This story always fascinated me. Dr. McCain couldn't actually recall where she'd heard it, but I was able to track down the source—a case in Wichita, Kansas. Apparently, a fifteen-year-old girl in the city's suburbs came into the ER reporting an unusual form of tinnitus, an almost incessant squeaking in her ears; turns out, she was hearing the ultrasonic battle and mating cries of field mice. All mice, I learned, make calls—some quite complicated—but most are of such a high register that we can't actually hear them, much like dog whistles.

What could cause millions of people, thousands of miles apart, to suddenly wake up one day with itching inside their heads and the ability to sense things the rest of us can't? No one could say, but the first step in solving the cause of the Elevation was admitting that it existed in the first place.

I'm not one to toot my own horn; I was raised Presbyterian. But I think I was the first to see the pattern, the thing that connected each and every one of these cases. Now, I might have had the idea but I didn't do the work, the on-the-ground work, required to make it real. That came down to the partnering physicians and neuroscientists who really dug into the data, the statisticians who crunched the numbers at the CDC and gave us our graphs, our smoking guns.

In a majority of the most severe cases, the patients had MRI scans of their brains. The doctors were looking for brain bleeds, evidence of strokes, injuries, multiple sclerosis, dementia, infections—the list goes on and on. When we compared those scans—at least the first batch that came in, a few hundred or so—it was impossible to see any correlation: there was nothing immediately obvious.

You ever get that gut hunch? You just know something is wrong?

I had that looking over those scans.

I knew there was a connection between the cases that I wasn't seeing— that no one was seeing. I promised myself I wouldn't leave my office, wouldn't sleep, until I found that connection. Eighteen hours, six caffeine-filled energy drinks, a package of chocolate coconut cookies, and seven bathroom breaks later, I saw it. It had been staring me in the face the whole time. All of us, we'd missed it.

Every brain was smaller than it should have been.

Not a lot smaller, but noticeable.

The average adult human's brain weighs 1,300 to 1,400 grams and is roughly 15 centimeters in length. There are variations, of course, but you'd be shocked by the consistency. The brain of each of these individuals was 12 centimeters in length—every single one of them. We could estimate the weight based on the dimensions, but in the few who had passed away, we found they weighed 1,100 grams. Exactly. How's that for a ringer?

Now, you're going to say that this makes no sense. But I'm telling you that the Elevated—these people who suddenly had the ability to outthink, outsee, and out-hear the rest of humanity—had *smaller* brains then the rest of us.

That is counterintuitive, correct?

Big chunk of the medical establishment, mostly the older-school neuro-scientists and neurosurgeons, nearly had a heart attack after hearing what I'd found. It flew in the face of hundreds of years of anatomy and what we know about the human brain. But it was real. The brains of the Elevated were smaller, more compact, because they were using more of their minds. Again, that's heresy to say: the brain isn't supposed to work like that.

The human brain has been the same weight, same dimensions, for about the past 2 million years. Then, precipitously, in a matter of days, it changes. It transforms, it becomes even more plastic—that's the term we use—and shifts into a subtle new form, a form capable of incredible feats of sensation and logic. I mean, we saw much more after with people like Dahlia Mitchell.

My first question on seeing those scans, realizing what it likely meant, was simple: How does something like this happen? Is it a virus? Is it from environmental contamination? Is it genetic? There had to be some causal relationship between the affected people, the Elevated. It was only a matter of figuring out what.

What happened next, I had nothing to do with.

I didn't make any recommendations, though if I had, I'm sure no one would have listened to me anyway. Who was I? Just another doctor strug-gling to figure out a problem affecting the whole country; another voice in the crowd. I might have gotten the ball rolling but . . . well, I never would have foreseen it.

Terrible what people do when they get scared, isn't it?

# 23

AUTHOR'S NOTE

The Elevation spread like wildfire.

That's a cliché, but it feels quite apropos for this event.

The number of cases exploded within the first six days. From a few dozen the day after Dahlia discovered the Pulse to several thousand two days after that. This was just in the United States, according to databased medical insurance forms and hospital intake records. There were other countries where the numbers were mind-boggling. The medical system was inundated and quickly overwhelmed.

What seemed like a chaotic, scrambled display of symptoms at first soon gave way to a clear pattern. For some, the Elevation was a thing of wonder akin to a religious awakening. For others, it was a nightmare. And, like all processes that alter the human body, it didn't always end successfully.

Many grew sickened. Many more died.

The Elevation changed the affected in stages. These stages were not strictly defined and frequently bled into each other. And like any biological process, it could be messy. The stages, as documented by the CDC in November of 2023, were as follows:

Phase 1—The Elevated experienced visions, heard voices, and saw visible manifestations of normally invisible processes—like gravitational waves—or long-dead relatives. Many of the initial symptoms of the Elevation appeared similar to schizophrenic disturbances and were accompanied by nosebleeds.

Phase 2—With heightened cognitive abilities, some Elevated became savants overnight. They could calculate new forms of mathematics, develop innovative computer algorithms, uncover unseen biological processes, and create unimaginable works of art.

Phase 3—As the Elevation took over more than neurological functions, the first deaths occurred. The process was simply too much for their bodies to handle. Those who survived could perceive another, unearthly world overlapping our own. This was not another planet but another reality inhabited, it was assumed, by the Ascendant.

Phase 4—During the final stage of the Elevation, the affected simply vanished. This happened within milliseconds (and will be discussed in more detail later). It is believed, though never proven, that the Elevated had actually shed their limiting human forms and moved into the Ascendant's plane of existence.

As to why only some people—roughly 30 percent of the population—were affected by the Elevation, researchers can't confirm, but there are theories: First is genetics. Scientists suspected those who were Elevated had a particular gene—perhaps one related to language acquisition, as many of those affected were bilingual. Second was psychological makeup: sociologists studying those who became Elevated determined that they demonstrated more altruistic attributes than the general population. These suggestions, however, were only hypotheses; it would, one researcher told me, take several decades until science fully understood the Elevation.

One thing was clear, however: once begun, the Elevation could not be stopped. While the human body naturally attempted to prevent or stall the Elevation's progress, it ultimately had to accept the change; those whose bodies would not simply died.

During this time, there were, at first, many different, competing theories. Perhaps it was some virus—that was a commonly accepted idea in the first few days—or even a terrorist drug that had been introduced into our environment via the water or air. These were quickly ruled out. Another suggestion emerged: that this was a genetic abnormality triggered into expressing itself now due to environmental pollution or a contaminant in the food supply. Again quickly ruled out. With each theory that was knocked down, a dozen new, more outlandish ones took its place.

What the general population didn't—couldn't—know was that the symptoms of the Elevation began shortly after Dahlia Mitchell had discovered the Pulse. That information wouldn't come out until after the Disclosure Task Force released their initial report one month after the Pulse was first recorded. And by that time the world had already been irrevocably altered . . .

24

SAI LAGHARI, OWNER OF THE NEW OLD WORLD WEBSITE

RALEIGH, NC

JANUARY 19, 2026

Though Sai Laghari was born in Pakistan, his parents—both mechanical engineers—emigrated to the United States when he was in elementary school.

Raised in St. Louis, Missouri, he was a run-of-the-mill student who loved stories about the Bermuda Triangle and the Loch Ness Monster. More than that, he loved the fact that these phenomena were "unaccepted" by modern science: they were taboo. While Sai hadn't shown any outstanding talent for programming in his youth, in college he proved a quick learner and adept coder.

After college, Sai found a job as an IT specialist at an accounting firm. But his passion was in web design. When he launched New Old World three years later, in 2021, he sensed "that this was going to be the site I'd be known for."

Sure enough, Sai's site would go on to change the course of history.

Originally, New Old World was something of a clearinghouse for obscure information: fringe news stories about UFO sightings and anomalous phenomena, opinion pieces on "damned data" (information unaccepted by the scientific and historical orthodoxy), and reviews of "forgotten" books that Sai had found intriguing. He wasn't personally invested in the stories that ran on his site but saw himself as something of a curator, giving "voice to the voiceless."

The site caught on and Sai was soon inundated with material sent in by readers. At first, he was careful in selecting what he featured on the site. In interviews, he claimed that he wanted to ensure that his readers weren't just getting "any random person's version of reality," but that changed, and he started

posting nearly everything he was sent. In fact, the more outrageous and per-
plexing the information was, the better. Denying that he did this to increase
his site's following (people who most frequented the site and habitually posted
in the forums quickly became its primary source of material), Sai said that he
came to the conclusion, after years of research and reading—he claims to have
read twenty-five thousand books—that only the most amateur of investigations
were dependable. Everything else, in his mind, had been corrupted by what he'd
termed "the treason of reason."

Sai had come to believe that all logical truths generated by the state (this
encompassed everything from government and academia to big business and
the military) or carried by the media (again, as broadly defined as possible)
weren't to be trusted—only folks whose ideas were generated as far from the
mainstream as possible. Sai liked to call these people's theories "naïve thinking"
or "outsider theories."

In the wake of the "fake news" tsunami of the late '10s, New Old World
quickly became a mainstay for conspiracy theorists. In time, it also became
the hub for wild speculations and alternate philosophies about the Elevation.

I meet Sai in his Raleigh, North Carolina, home. He and his wife, Ginger, a
former nurse, have set up quite a welcoming spread—sweet tea, sandwiches,
and pastries—on his back porch. Though their kids are grown, Sai and Ginger
have a pool and several neighborhood kids splash around in it as we talk. Sai
is short and has his dark hair slicked back in a tight ponytail.

Yeah, so, Carter Loisel . . .

I heard about the kid the same way most of the world did: social media.

This is going to sound lazily cliché, but my aunt forwarded an email
chain about it. My aunt Stella would send along just about anything that
appeared in her in-box. So you can forgive me for not taking the Carter thing
seriously at first. I actually almost deleted it.

First time I watched the video of Carter Loisel diagnosing patients in the
waiting room of some desert town in the middle of the middle of nowhere,
I got chills. Honest-to-God chills. Right up the lengths of my arms and the
back of my neck.

And then more people sent it to me.

Contacts out in the world. Folks who know what I do, the sort of information that I disseminate—they started hitting me up left and right with questions about the video. Did I think it was legit? Hell yes. Did I think it had something to do with government mind control programs? Certainly might. Was this kid possibly the result of an alien/human hybrid breeding program?* I was open to that possibility.

You have to understand, we were all just stabbing in the dark at this thing. It was so early in the outbreak that there was a novelty to it. It left people stupefied 'cause they weren't jaded yet by all the brouhaha and nonsense that followed. I say that facetiously, of course. What followed was, as we all know, the greatest "false flag" operation† to ever befall our country, if not the world as a whole.

Accompanying the video was a brief note about how each of the kid's diagnoses were verified. Whoever put the thing together—and I later learned it sort of snowballed online with multiple people adding bits and pieces—added X-rays and test results. Those documents were what sealed the deal for me.

Slam dunk.

See, I was trained as an EMT, and while I would never say I'm as knowledgeable as a doctor about medical issues, I know enough that I could tell the results of those tests were legitimate. Even more, what Carter was say-

---

* An oldie but a goodie in terms of conspiracy theorizing, the alien/human hybrid concept has its roots in the alien abduction movement that began in the 1960s. While UFOs had been witnessed buzzing about the skies in the 1940s and '50s, in the '60s and '70s they made contact—allegedly abducting humans from their cars, beds, even backyards, for all manner of bizarre experiments. Many skeptical researchers have linked these reported abduction scenarios—almost always recounted while the subject is under hypnosis in a psychotherapist's office—with ancient stories of night hags and succubi. And, as in those tales, the aliens frequently steal men's sperm and women's eggs; the resulting offspring are alien/human hybrids, insanely brilliant, physically powerful, and almost always malicious.

† A key conspiracy theory concept, a "false flag" operation is one in which a government or corporate actor (whoever happens to be in power) carries out what at first appears to be a terrorist or antigovernment/anticorporate action, from a bombing to a school shooting. This event is then used to generate support for the government/corporation against the various forces allied against it. To those in the know (the conspiracy theorists), the false flag event was actually carried out by government/corporation to engender goodwill and sympathy. An example: a man suffering from mental illness who was not legally supposed to own an assault rifle uses the rifle to massacre people in a mall. In the wake of the massacre, politicians call on the government to pass stricter gun control laws. Digging into minute details of the massacre, conspiracy theorists would "discover" evidence that the massacre was a fake—and the victims crisis actors—designed by the government to curtail Second Amendment rights.

ing was legitimate too. Here we had a bona fide case of a human being, and a young human being at that, seeing illness in a body like a goddamned scanning machine would.

It was incredible.

I immediately placed the video at the top of my website and surrounded it with as many exclamation points as possible. Then I made a reaction video that I posted on several streaming sites and I followed that up with a commentary video. At our peak, the New Old World site got 15,000 unique visitors an hour. This was before the video, so I knew that once I jumped on something, I could give it the push it would need to hit the TV news channels and the press.

Within two hours of me posting the video of the "Carter Incident," as some idiot reporter down in Miami dubbed it, it became the biggest-trending news item of the decade. It felt good to be, essentially, the guy at ground zero for that moment. I took advantage of it immediately and linked the Carter Incident video to most of the other important items that I had been hoping to promote. Gave them all a serious boost too. Little did I know how interconnected they'd all be . . .

You looked at me a bit funny when I said it was the greatest false flag operation in the history of the world. I know it sounds a bit like an exaggeration when I say it that way, but neither of us can doubt the fact that our world has fundamentally changed. And not for the better, I might add.

I don't believe the Elevation was real.

What Carter did on that video—it was genuine. The boy was seeing inside people. He was diagnosing illness, and, as we all know, that was only the start. Before he "Elevated," as they say, he had seen a great many more things than just a handful of tumors and broken organs. Carter was the first Elevated person we, as a country, ever saw. The first one *they* decided to present to us.

"They" being the government, of course.

I have some moles inside one of the companies that helped roll out the whole Disclosure program to the public. He sent me several incriminating emails that clearly showed that, not only did the government know about Carter well before that doctor found him, but that they'd had evidence of other, quote, unquote, "Elevated" people long before they chose to let the proverbial cat out of the bag. Naturally, I can't give you a name or put you in touch with this individual, because, well, we all know what would happen— even now, so long after it all went down.

There are videos, you see.*

I can't reveal my sources, like I said. But I have it in writing from knowl- edgeable authorities that there are people who are kept confined in the sub- basement of a New Mexican army facility who are like Carter.

Only, the thing that makes them different is on the outside.

You understand?

That boy could see inside people and his gift is invisible. These others, they're not so lucky. They've been twisted and modified, reshaped by some- thing into mutations. I heard there's a girl with two spines . . .

Freaky, right?

Here's what I want you to go home thinking about: The Elevation, this thing that spread across the globe in a matter of hours—could it really have been random? Nothing like that ever happened before in the history of man- kind without a little help, a little prodding. My guess is that the Elevation was really just a whole smattering of different things: mental illness, some genetic abnormalities, some poisonings, and toss in a whole heap of crisis actors. You do that, mix it together, and edit it slickly with big-money Holly- wood effects, and you've got a winning formula for an instant plague.

Why would the government want to do that?

Well, duh, it's pretty obvious to me.

All about control, people. Always has been, always will be.

If the Feds can say we're being transformed by some weird new disease, then they can lock us up, take our guns, claim our property, all in the name of protecting us. Right? Not like they haven't done that numerous other times: the AIDS crisis in the 1990s,† the supposed crack cocaine epidemic . . .

---

* I assume that Sai is referencing the very same videos that Dr. Frank Kjelgaard claimed to have seen. They come up several times in the story of the Elevation.

† As the AIDS crisis exploded in the late 1980s, a number of conspiracy theory pamphlets, papers, and newsletters began to circulate that claimed that HIV was created in a US government lab. This bioengineered disease—a Frankensteinian patchwork of monkey virus and polio—was de- signed as a weapon of war and unleashed on the gay community by conservative government doctors.

When I ask Sai about the government's eventual explanation for the Elevation—that it was the result of the Pulse Code Dahlia Mitchell had discovered—he laughs uproariously.

My God, that explanation, well . . .

It actually didn't change anything I'd believed before. In fact, it just hammered home the truth of the matter. How can you spin a story like this and get people to buy it? Here's the way it works and I'm telling you this for free, understand? This is brilliant, absolutely unbeatable stuff, and I want to make sure that when you write it all up, I'm the one credited. Okay. Okay.

Here it goes: Our beloved government is engaged in the biggest false flag operation in the history of the world. They're convincing the entire population of the United States, and eventually the freaking globe, that there is something called the Elevation making some people crazy, some people insanely brilliant, and others . . . well, others are just dying from it. That's the sales pitch and it helps explain why folks like Carter Loisel and all the others are acting the way they are.

So people are going to freak out and the government is going to step in and say, "We have this under control. You all are safe." The end result of that move is to strip us of our freedoms, of course. Make us a slave nation, as they say. Kinda like what the Kims did in North Korea.

But then there are people—people like me—standing up and saying, "This doesn't pass the sniff test!" Other folks follow my lead. They start asking questions. They start rocking the proverbial boat. That's when the government spin doctors, the ad masters behind this whole thing, come up with the best lie ever told: "It wasn't us; it was the aliens!"

Yeah, right!

The aliens we never see, the aliens we never talk to, the aliens that we know nothing at all about. It was them. Best part is that everyone bought it hook, line, and sinker. Clever, I'll give them that. Very clever. It gets even better when we hit the Finality. If you honestly thought that all those billions of people just stepped over into another world, well, I've got a bridge in Arizona I want to sell you . . .

25

PRESIDENT VANESSA BALLARD

DETROIT, MI

SEPTEMBER 18, 2025

Moving outside as dusk falls, I follow President Ballard to a nearby park.

It's a rectangle of grass, very flat, with no trees, and surrounded by several abandoned big-box stores that stand empty, sentinels to this quiet city. Trees sprout from the rooftops of the stores; their shattered windows reveal thick underbrush growing inside. We walk to the center of the park and President Ballard points out a flock of passing egrets, large white birds that drift overhead. She tells me that they have a rookery in a canal nearby. And the park we're standing in? It doesn't appear on any maps, because five years ago it wasn't a park but a parking lot.

We stay at the park until night falls and bats stream out of the buildings.

On our way back to President Ballard's home, she comments on the fact that when she was in office the world seemed very small. Nearly every point on Earth had been visited, the skies conquered and subdued. True adventure lay in the stars or, most importantly, inside the minds of men. But now . . . now the world had suddenly reverted; it was as though our advancements had been erased and the wheels of progress reset. For her, the idea promised great things. The world was open again.

In a way, human history itself had been Elevated . . .

The Elevation.

What a thing . . .

When the first cases began rolling in, I started hearing about it. Like just about everyone else in the country, I saw the video of the boy.

Then the next one came in . . .

And then the next.

I spent my time on the plane back to DC watching videos, reading posts, about what, even then, in the earliest hours of the Elevation, was looking like a wave. It was inexplicable and strange. There was a video of a schoolteacher in the South somewhere who had a breakdown in the middle of her lecture on root numbers. This poor woman's nose was bleeding heavily, but she was staring up at the ceiling and cooing to a baby that only she could see. Unnerving.

Of course, it got me thinking about David.

When we got back to the White House, I called Dr. Stimson and asked if he'd seen the videos. He said he had and wasn't in a position to make a judgment call about what they meant. Being rational above all else, he suggested it was a case of mass panic; perhaps there was a triggering video or image that had set all these people off.* Times when there've been mass panic events, it's usually because of a society-wide stress, an unconscious anxiety that explodes in strange behaviors.

In college I read a history of the "dancing plagues" that broke out across medieval Europe, mostly in France and Germany. People suddenly got up and danced, some of them until they lost consciousness or even died of dehydration. In the medieval mind-set it looked like the work of demons and devils.†

Whatever the Elevation was, I knew it wasn't that.

David hadn't had an attack since the incident in the bowling alley. The

---

* I encountered this idea several times during my conversations with researchers. The idea of a "triggering" image is one that's been popular culturally since the advent of photography and motion pictures. The concept is certainly believable: a particular image or series of images can hypnotize or somehow similarly alter a person's behavior. While it is true that certain flashing images can cause seizures in people, the so-called weaponized image or film has been a long-standing MacGuffin in a manner of media—the movie that kills, the recording that activates a "Manchurian candidate," the photograph that hypnotizes. However, according to people I spoke with at the FBI, no such image or film has ever surfaced. Neurologists tell me that it is simply a myth—a concept that just seems so good, it must be true.

† Incredibly, the dancing plagues were very real. Essentially moral panics—like satanic ritual abuse outbreaks in the US, laughing waves in Nigeria, and the "vanishing penis" panics in Korea—the dancing plagues were, as President Ballard described, eruptions of uncontrolled dancing. They were often triggered by passing preachers or astronomical events (a comet in the sky, for example) and were less about disease or illness than rigid moral codes that crippled the population. Folks who lived in constant fear found instant relief in suddenly dancing. They lost control for the first time in their lives and it felt . . . amazing. So they kept doing it.

folks at Walter Reed did a full workup and found nothing. He came back the next morning, smiling and happy and seemingly unaware of what he'd experienced the night before. No, he didn't have another attack. Not like the first. But the changes, the transformation, began nearly as soon as he got back.

We were in a cabinet meeting with the secretaries of transportation and energy. Things had gotten a bit heated as we were arguing about emissions. I wanted more regulation; my Republican secretary of transportation wanted less. The usual back and forth, but it was civil.

David had been quiet the whole meeting, when he raised his hand, interrupting the conversation, and pointed to one of the windows overlooking the Rose Garden. He pointed and said, "Watch. Three . . . two . . . one . . ."

Wham! A crow slammed into the glass, startling everyone sitting around the table. The bird fell and twitched outside as Secret Service agents ran over to inspect it. The secretaries of transportation and energy seemed nervous; one of them remarked that it was a shrewd distraction. I just watched David's face, his eyes, and I could see . . . I don't know how to describe it, but there was something different in his expression. It wasn't malevolent—far from it; it was . . . it was as though I was looking at David but David was *gone* . . . I expected that the Parkinson's would rob him of his dignity but not his personality. This was clearly a transformation.

After the meeting, I asked David to talk to Dr. Stimson again.

He took my hand and told me not to worry.

Then he said, "What is going to happen is inevitable. Trying to stop it is like that mythological king who steps into the ocean and tries to stop the tide from coming in. He drowns. The Elevation is going to overwhelm us all. We can't fight it. We need to accept it and hang on for the ride. I need you to be strong, Vanessa. I love you with every cell of this body. I will see you again."

His nose bled again, blood running out so fast that it spattered all over his shoes and my suit.* He fainted and I, thankfully, was able to catch him before he cracked his skull open on the edge of a desk.

---

* Doctors determined that the nosebleeds many of the Elevated suffered from were a direct result of increased breathing rates. As you might expect, seeing gravitational waves or long-dead relatives would cause most people to be anxious. That anxiety led to increased respiratory rates, the drying out of nasal passages, and an increasing incidence of nosebleed. Regardless of the mechanism, the effect was startling.

I stayed up all night with him at Walter Reed.

When he got to the hospital, his organs were already shutting down. They called it a cascade. He went from walking around, talking, to being on life support in a matter of minutes. I made sure that word of his condition didn't get out. The press was told that he was hospitalized for breathing problems and that an update would be forthcoming soon.

That night was one of the longest, most difficult nights.

And this was before the Elevation had really taken off.

Before the Finality.

While I was at the hospital, I got an alert that there was a data breach at the White House. Someone had hacked into David's medical records a few hours before he was taken to the hospital. The breach only got worse the deeper we looked.

It wasn't just David's medical records . . .

**26**

EDITED TRANSCRIPT OF CONVERSATION RECORDED BY
WHITE HOUSE COUNSEL TERRY QUINN
RECORDED AT THE WHITE HOUSE ON 11.7.2023

TERRY QUINN: Have a seat.

GLENN OWEN: What's worrying you, Terry? You have that expression on your face, the one you get when someone's made you upset.

TERRY QUINN: Per . . .

PER AKERSON: The President's concerned we have a mole in the White House.

GLENN OWEN: A mole? That's so old-fashioned. I think today they say "sleeper" or "plant." *Of course* there are moles. This is the White House; the place has more leaks than a Chinese market. I don't understand the concern.

TERRY QUINN: Bigger than leaks. The President is concerned that there is someone on her staff that is aligned with a group whose interests aren't aligned with our own. I'm being cryptic, but—

GLENN OWEN: Hang on, is this some sort of interview? Like you don't trust me? Did President Ballard tell you to corner me, poke me, and see if I squeak? Jesus, Terry, you've known me twenty years. And, Per, shit, man, we've been drinking together just as long. I'm an open book. Everything I've ever done is readily available for you to read through. Just ask.

TERRY QUINN: We don't suspect you of anything, Glenn. But we need you to be vigilant. You noticed anything funny going?

GLENN OWEN: You gotta be kidding. Noticed anything funny? Everything in this madhouse is funny. Seriously, though, what are you talking about and why haven't I been brought into the loop yet?

PER AKERSON: We only just found out, too, Glenn. President Ballard updated us just a few minutes before you came in.

GLENN OWEN: So it was your idea to grill me? You two knuckleheads came up with that idea all on your own, huh? Well, you both suck at it. I didn't answer any questions, just gave you a little pushback, and you both rolled over, legs spread, tails quivering. Terry, lock the door. Tell me what the fuck's going on.

TERRY QUINN: We know that someone inside the White House hacked into the First Gentleman's medical records. We suspect it's the same person who's been accessing the Disclosure Task Force files and the Pulse Code. Beyond that, there aren't many more details.

GLENN OWEN: No idea where this stuff's been going? It hasn't been showing up online, some data dump into the deep web? A conspiracy theory hub like that New World place? Or some hacker clearinghouse?

PER AKERSON: There's no evidence of any of the information showing up online, deep or surface web. We think whoever is accessing this stuff is either saving it up or sending it to someone in particular.

GLENN OWEN: Okay, okay. We need to get a handle on this stat. Bring Kanisha in and tell her. Lieutenant General Chen as well. How's the President handling it? I mean, the fact that David's information's been compromised.

TERRY QUINN: She doesn't like it. She's worried it's bigger than that.

GLENN OWEN: Bigger how?

PER AKERSON: We've heard some disturbing rumors about Dr. Cisco.

GLENN OWEN: The Dr. Cisco formerly of the Disclosure Task Force who flew home and died in a car accident? Please tell me you two aren't trafficking in conspiracy theories now. You're going to make me sick.

TERRY QUINN: They're only rumors . . .

GLENN OWEN: But the President thinks there could be a connection, right? She's got it in her head that the person hacking into the First Gentleman's records and the Disclosure files is . . . what? Responsible for causing the death of Dr. Cisco? And why? Why would they kill her? Why not Dr. Xavier Faber? He's certainly the one asking for it. No, guys, this is silly. Let me talk to her. In the meantime, we've got much bigger fish to fry. You saw the video of the boy?

PER AKERSON: Yes. Social media's blowing up with this stuff. Doctors are freaking out, saying maybe the tap water's been laced with LSD.[*] There's a wave of this stuff coming, Glenn. I already told Terry, already told the President, but I think we're going to have to buckle in for a wild ride . . .

GLENN OWEN: All right, so let's just focus on one thing at a time. Per, keep an eye on whatever mania's sweeping the country. Terry, let me know if we hear anything more about this mole. I'll see if I can get to the bottom of these Dr. Cisco murder rumors . . . God help us . . .

---

[*] The LSD in tap water idea isn't as far-fetched as it might seem. Per, or the doctors he's referencing here, might be thinking of the small French village of Pont-Saint-Esprit. In 1951, Pont-Saint-Esprit experienced a very unique and quite terrifying mass poisoning of some kind. Two hundred and fifty people in the village awoke on August 15, 1951, suffering from horrifying hallucinations and violent illness. Four people died. An initial investigation suggested that the cause was ergot (a fungus) poisoning due to improperly stored rye grain. But others thought something like mercury poisoning was more likely. With an event as strange and unique as this one, conspiracy theories were bound to sprout up—in particular, one that claimed the entire event was a mass LSD dosing, part of the CIA's clandestine MKNAOMI behavior modification program. An American soldier stationed in the South of France at the time of the outbreak claimed to have been involved in the LSD dosing scheme. He was branded a liar and dismissed.

**27**

CARLA FRANKLIN, INVESTIGATIVE REPORTER
SEATTLE, WA
FEBRUARY 21, 2026

A Pulitzer Prize–winning journalist, Carla Franklin began her career in the mid-1990s, covering politics for the New York Times.

After breaking a story on corruption in Steven Meyer's New York senatorial run, she wrote a bestselling book on campaign finance corruption. While she wasn't a well-known figure outside of DC circles, she quickly became one when, during the height of the Elevation, she published an investigative series now dubbed the "Pulse Gate," the apparent cover-up of the suspicious deaths of a handful of physicists and astronomers associated with the Pulse Code data—people who'd gotten the information from Dr. Cisco.

While her investigation brought these cases to light, it did not assign blame. Nor did it determine what group or groups (if there were any) were behind the supposed "murders" of these scientists.

Today, Carla lives in Seattle. She teaches writing workshops and writes poetry. Having grown tired of what she calls "the rigid formalism of journalism," she enjoys crafting experimental poetry—mostly of the "concrete" variety (the careful arrangement of words and images to create typographical effects).

Wiry, with one leg always bouncing, Carla, now in her mid-fifties, has red hair that she keeps quite short. We meet in her home office, where several cats lounge on the windowsill and watch a busy bird feeder in the backyard.

I first heard about the death of Dr. Andrea Cisco at a cocktail party.

You'd be amazed how many stories are broken when people are drinking.

This was a black-tie affair I was dragged to by my editor. The world was going nuts around us: the whole Elevation thing had just exploded across the front pages of every real and semi-real news outfit. People were going insane about it, thought it was the end of the world. And here we were, sipping drinks at some rich dude's mansion. I guess you can only cover breaking news for so long.

Everyone needs a break, right?

It was late. I'd honestly had too much to drink and just wanted a fresh scene. So I stepped out onto the balcony overlooking the bay. I'd taken in a few lungfuls of sea air and listened to a few sweet minutes of traffic when Austin Franks* walked out, breathless and sweating like he'd run up about twenty flights of stairs to find me. Turns out, he pretty much had, but with his bulk, three flights were as good as twenty.

"You wouldn't believe how long I've been trying to track you down," he said, settling on a bench and wiping the sweat from his face with the end of his tie. "Did you get the files I sent you? The ones about Dr. Cisco."

I hadn't. If I had, they were buried somewhere on my desk or my in-box.

"You do know about the insanity happening out there, right?"

I pointed out to the ocean but meant the larger world.

"Yeah," he said, "of course."

"So this is more important than that?" I asked.

He nodded cryptically, almost like he'd been expecting this.

Austin Franks was exactly the kind of guy you'd expect a dramatic "spy" performance from. Every month he had a new lead that would "change everything I thought I knew" or "shock me to my core." I was fooled a couple times, I'll admit. He said he had dirt on the CEO of a weapons manufacturer sneaking guns to the Taliban. It was a dead end. Second time I just should have known better, but by then Alan had a lock on my particular areas of interest: toppling high-ranking misogynists, exposing graft in Russia. He was able to wrap them all together in a particularly salacious tidbit, and I wound up chasing my tail for near three weeks.

---

* "Austin Franks" was a pseudonym used by Walter Gottsegen, a muckraking journalist associated with a number of online news digests of questionable newsworthiness. He frequently allied himself with fans of the New Old World site and propagated unsubstantiated rumors of conspiracies within the Ballard White House—in particular, a long-running suggestion that David Ballard wasn't suffering from Parkinson's but an undisclosed mental illness.

This time, however, he wasn't his usual rambunctious self. He was more subdued, outright concerned. I figured it was just a new angle he was milking. The whole distressed whistle-blower thing.

"I sent these files to you two weeks ago in an email. They were encrypted. But I'm not surprised you didn't see them."

He went on to suggest that my computer was compromised—everyone's was—and that talking to me was the best option. "I just need to tell you what I've discovered and then maybe you can start connecting the dots for me."

I wasn't in the mood to hear another wild-eyed theory and tried to shut him down then and there. I reminded him that both the leads he'd sent me before didn't pan out. But this time he was genuinely scared.

So I listened, and that's how it started.

The way Austin presented the story, Dr. Cisco died in a car accident on her way home from a rushed conference in Washington, DC. She'd flown back, called her family from the airport, and checked in briefly at work before sending a cryptic email to a colleague about an "anomalous code" she'd been asked to analyze. A code she called "Pulse radio." The email hinted obliquely at the fact that she had a copy of this code on her person and she might have sent part of it to several associates she'd trusted.

While the afternoon was clear and sunny, it had rained several hours earlier and the roads were slick. Drivers reported seeing Dr. Cisco's car weaving across lanes on Route 40 as though she were drunk. Minutes later her car collided with a concrete barrier. Paramedics arrived at the scene eight minutes after the crash. Dr. Cisco was unresponsive at the time. She was pronounced dead en route to the hospital. Tragic story; nothing particularly new and nothing worth acting like a spy who came in from the cold for.

But obviously there was more to it.

Before he could tell me the rest, Austin pulled me aside and we walked across the patio down near a row of hedges where the sound of traffic was louder. He eyed the building behind us, looking at the windows and people passing by inside. He said, "Coroner ruled the death as accidental. Said something along the lines of Cisco likely being overtired, maybe from travel, and that she fell asleep at the wheel. Case closed. But I know someone who worked in the hospital where she was taken. They did blood work and found she'd been drugged. Here, I have the results."

Austin pulled a folded piece of yellow paper from his back pocket and pressed it into my hand. I told him I wasn't sure what I could do with this information. I'm not a biochemist. I'm also not a coroner.*

Austin just shook his head and then, even more softly, said, "Cisco's not the first. There are others, at least three that I'm aware of—two here in the States and one in England. All three of them astrophysicists; all three of them died in . . . unexpected accidents. And just like Cisco, all three had been sent this anomalous code, Pulse radio, to analyze. I haven't seen the code; I don't know who sent it or what it relates to. That's why I need your help, Carla. That's why I need someone with your expertise to come in and see the patterns, the associations, I can't."

Sure, Austin's demeanor had me concerned, but everything he was telling me was so vague. Deaths made to look like accidents, a mystery code—it was all too much to believe. And I didn't want to wind up with the journalists who'd chased the GEC-Marconi conspiracy theories† to their early retirements.

Still, Austin seemed certain, and there were tangible, in a sense, clues: the deaths, the anomalous code, and the paper he'd handed me. Despite every neuron in my body telling me to just walk away, I told Austin I'd look into it. He seemed instantaneously relieved. And that made me feel even worse.

So I did what I do.

---

* Carla provided me with the results that Austin gave her. While that original crinkled note didn't survive the ensuing years, a photocopy of it did. I showed the note to a coroner and, sure enough, it seemed quite clear that Dr. Cisco had a significant amount of a powerful sleep aid in her system. Did this mean she was drugged? Well, not in and of itself. But the coroner that I spoke with also mentioned that Dr. Cisco had a high dose of fentanyl on board—a particularly dangerous combination. It's a huge red flag.

† The GEC-Marconi theories relate to a string of "mysterious" deaths in the early 1980s. Between 1982 and 1990, over two dozen computer scientists working in Britain on classified defense projects (including US projects) died in what reporters categorized as unusual ways: bizarre accidents, unexpected suicides, etc. When one looks over the list of deceased scientists and their sometimes decidedly strange causes of death—carbon monoxide poisoning, sexual misadventure, drunk driving, jumping off bridges, and even one scientist who attached wires to his chest and then pushed the other ends into an electrical socket—it is easy to imagine that these were actually murders. Those who attempted to find a link between the deaths and, even more, lay blame on some nefarious agency—the Russians, the US, the mob—could never pinpoint a perpetrator. The case was soon forgotten.

I began an earnest investigation into this whole thing while the world was going nuts over the Elevation and every editor in town wanted scoops on what was causing people to suddenly be able to see ultraviolet light or hear the creepy ultrasonic calls of insects. You were there, of course. I'm sure you read all those headlines. Some of the worst were online. I remember all the disgusting sites . . . There was one in particular: a, uh, New Order . . .

New Old World?

Yes, that's it. They peddled some of the more repulsive stories about what was causing the Elevation. I think the worst was an article claiming it had something to do with single mothers who worked more than one job . . . I don't . . . Anyway, let's not rehash that hot garbage. Even though I never fell in with any of those fake news blowhards, the Pulse Gate stuff was as close to a true, dyed-in-the-wool conspiracy as I'd ever seen. Someone killed those scientists, and it had everything to do with the Pulse and the Disclosure Task Force.

Dr. Cisco was murdered and it was done to cover up the fact that she'd leaked the Pulse Code to several of her colleagues. I can't speak to her mind-set. Maybe she saw it as an opportunity to get a leg up on everyone, a chance to publish before the fray. Or maybe it was money. Everyone she talked to about this is dead. They either died in the Elevation or were murdered.

You being a writer, all the research you've been doing, I'm sure you already know who was behind the hit on the scientists. But you don't know the details like I do. Your readers, they think they know how this went down, but really they don't.

You want me to tell you whodunit?

You'd love that, right? Have that scoop in your book.

I told Carla that, sure, that would be huge. But I also told her that I wasn't there to solve every twist and turn in this mystery. I was there to tell a story about how humanity was transformed, how the Finality left the United States crippled and how that led to the state we find ourselves in today: a less-than-whole country trying to rebuild itself.

I told Carla that if she were to trust me with the information, I would present it in the best light possible. I would frame it as her tale—unverified, of course, but true to however she wanted to present it. She agreed and said the following:

Took me three solid weeks of digging.

I'm talking three solid weeks of little sleep, no food, and an occasional lap swim just to process some of the more convoluted angles in the story. But I did it. I got to the bottom of what happened and who was involved and then I gave it to my editor. She was delighted and frightened about what I'd found. Then, of course, it was shut down. The paper threw out the story. My editor told me they'd done some of their own digging; the ombudsmen found inconsistencies in my work. She accused me of being sloppy. Of failing to see errors and buying a bogus story hook, line, and sinker 'cause I clearly had an agenda.

My reporting ended up being only about the deaths.

I linked them as well as I could, but by the time the editorial shears had butchered my story, it looked like just another conspiracy rant about weird demises. Pulse Gate was just a catchphrase, a couple buzzwords for the on-line nutjobs to throw around like Molotov cocktails anytime they suspected something the government was telling them wasn't exactly kosher.

So the story died.

I considered resurrecting it as an online post or even a book, but by the time that was possible, the Elevation had already wrecked the landscape. Truth is, during the years that followed the Finality, no one would have cared; they were all too busy picking up the pieces of their lives.

The Twelve did it. They're the killers.

It started, as far as I was able to determine, in the 1960s with a group called Majestic 12. Originally they were set up as a consulting group—some military people, some scientists—analyzing data related to the UFO phenomenon. That didn't go very far. Folks in the government didn't really care, and, for the most part, everything they looked at was easy to debunk. There were no spaceships entering our skies, no string-bean–looking aliens were abducting weirdos, and no one ever got an implant that wasn't some random chunk of cartilage. The Majestic 12 that all the UFO fanatics talk about? It ended as soon as it began, late 1960s.[*]

---

[*] Carla does a pretty good job here of succinctly summing up the history of Majestic 12 but I'll add this additional note: the entire existence of Majestic 12 was in doubt the moment they appeared on the UFO scene. The whole concept of the Majestic 12 group first emerged in the early 1980s through a series of documents mailed to a UFO believer and researcher. Those founda-

But life is circular, right?

Majestic 12's corpse was resurrected in the 1980s as a disinformation tool. Turns out the government had a use for the UFO fruitcakes. Experimental aircraft, war games, advanced technology—the UFO community was a good smoke screen for that. It worked, and so it continued: there was a very public dump of faked Majestic 12 material in the late '80s* and into the 2000s and beyond. Continued long enough to become a meme in and of itself. Then a joke . . .

However, a core group of the CIA agents creating the disinformation campaign at the heart of Majestic 12 went in a very different direction. There were originally three of them, but the most important figure was a man named Simon Household.[†] I don't know if that was his real name, but that's what he was called. If you do some digging, you'll come across a few biographical sketches of Simon; I wouldn't trust any of them but print them if you want.[‡]

This group, the core team, was called the Twelve.

And they were an assassination squad.

At last tally, as of about six years ago, I counted eight murders—or suspicious deaths, as they say—associated with the Twelve. These individuals died in car accidents, of drug overdoses . . . A few of them were killed in seemingly random crimes like muggings. The one thing that connected all these people was, *boom*, the fact that they were researching signals from outer space. In the 1990s, there was an Italian physicist who claimed to have

---

tional documents had long been considered fakes, crafted either by other believers or as part of a government disinformation campaign. What is most interesting here is that my research suggests that while Majestic 12 did exist—in both the early incarnation and, later, as just the Twelve—the documents were indeed fake. So something of a double-blind.

* These 1988 documents were mailed to various people in the UFO community: writers, researchers, and troublemakers. The documents detailed the discovery of a downed intergalactic spacecraft, complete with little alien bodies on board. Some UFO researchers used the documents as proof of larger conspiracy theories, and antigovernment advocates looking for more ammo bandied them about.

† He'd come up before under the name Simon Grieg.

‡ To wit: Simon, aged forty-nine at the time of the Elevation, was raised in Portland, Oregon. He lost his parents to cancer at a young age and joined the military after high school. A quick learner with a brilliant mind for strategy, Simon excelled as a soldier. His skills soon caught the attention of Majestic 12 agents, who groomed him for his eventual role as the head of the secretive organization.

picked up an unusual fast radio burst. He died in a plane crash and all his data, *poof,* went missing. The same thing happened to Dr. Cisco: she sent some colleagues information about the Pulse Code and she died. The people she gave the code to also died, all in accidents or as a result of suicide.

Far as I could determine, Simon and the Twelve set it up.

They made it happen. I don't know if they've got a little band of merry killer elves or a few of those gray aliens I hear so much about working for them, but they got these jobs done quick and clean. Then they vanish like ghosts protecting the world from . . . ? I have no idea, honestly. That's the thing I could never figure. The Twelve has this reach; they have some important secrets they want safeguarded.

I never figured out what those were, however.

Simon Household and the Twelve killed those scientists to stop them from looking at the Pulse Code or sending it to anyone else. The million-dollar question, of course, is: Why? And that, my friend, I've got no answers for.

 **28**

A day after I was discharged from the hospital, the White House called.

Forty-eight hours of being watched by nurses and drugged by doctors, and I was almost ready to pull my hair out. I wanted to go home, but everyone—even me—agreed that I shouldn't be alone. First time for everything, right?

So I went to Nico's place.

The doctors had diagnosed me with a psychotic break and chalked it up to stress and excitement. I didn't tell them about the Pulse, just that I'd been working insanely long hours and staring at impossibly distant objects. Somehow, when they found out what I do for a living, they weren't surprised that I went little nuts and claimed to see gravitational waves.

They took away my painkillers and gave me sedatives.

I slept for about fifteen hours. When I woke up, I was in Nico's guest room and beyond thirsty, in a way I haven't been since college. Valerie was in the kitchen reading when I stumbled in looking for a glass of water. She sat me at the table and gave me a pitcher of cucumber water she'd prepped for a party that evening. I drank until my throat stopped burning and then told her how embarrassed I was about the fainting incident. I hoped that the boys weren't too scared.

Valerie was sweet.

She assured me they were fine, that the whole scene wasn't that bad. Yeah, right. Their aunt passed out on the floor, babbling about seeing waves of light emerging from the walls, pharmaceuticals scattered all around her. The poor boys are probably scarred for life.

What an aunt I turned out to be . . .

As I sat there, downing glasses of water and trying to keep my head from spinning, I realized something. That's not quite right: it wasn't a realization. It was more like an awareness. It felt like a muscle had relaxed inside my head. A clutch eased. I imagined my mind like an engine, and at that second, sitting there in the kitchen, I shifted from second to fourth gear. That's stupid sounding, but it felt like a sudden charge, a ramping up of my thoughts.

There were numbers, letters, formulas, algorithms, all flooding in.

I needed to write them down.

And fast.

Valerie gave me a few pads of lined paper and some pencils and pens from the boys' art cabinet and I got to work right there in the kitchen. I was at it for an hour, just letting the stuff flow out of my head, breaking pencil lead after pencil lead, lost in my own world, before someone broke me from my reverie.

"Dahlia?"

I looked up to see Jon standing there.

He was so out of place that at first I didn't recognize him. He was also wearing a suit and he looked handsome. He hadn't shaved, which was natural, and I remember telling him to just grow a beard, but he liked that in-between stage, that indecisiveness. That should have been a red flag from the start. But he was too damn cute then and he's still too damn cute now.

Anyway, he was there and he looked pretty concerned.

"I heard about what happened," he said. "You okay?"

I told him I was fine and that it was good to see him.

"So, what . . . what do they think it was?"

Valerie stepped out of the room and let Jon and me have some privacy. I sat with him on a window seat overlooking my brother's backyard, where a wooden playground turned dark brown in the drizzle.

Jon took my hand; he really was worried. His hands were so warm. It felt good, comforting.

"They aren't sure," I said. "Could be it's just a mental break from stress. Sometimes people see things with a bad migraine. Flashing lights that undulate. It's nothing really unusual. In my case, I was seeing things that—"

"Gravitational waves," Jon said. "I heard."

"Right," I laughed. "I'm just shocked I wasn't seeing dark matter. That would make more sense, don't you think?"

Jon didn't reply. He told me that he'd sent the data I'd given him up the chain of command just like we'd discussed. Then he lowered his voice. Just as I'd expected, there was agreement that this was something special—something from outside our universe. While Jon didn't have the details on what the next steps were, he did know one thing was certain.

"They're taking it very seriously," he said, "and they want to talk to you."

"Who's 'they'?"

"There's a committee tasked by the President to look into this."

"So they want to interview me? I, uh, I'm not exactly in the best place right now. I'm not even home. I suppose I could do a video call or—"

Jon said, "I'm here to pick you up, Dahlia. They need you in DC tonight."

"Me?"

"You did discover this thing."

"But I've already been interviewed. For hours, Jon. I told them everything that I knew, what happened and how it happened . . . gave them my analysis and the raw data. What more could they want from me?"

"You talked to agents. These are scientists. People like you."

I was going to ask what the urgency was, but I knew. I knew how big this thing was and I was happy they were taking it seriously. Still, the thought of hopping on a flight to talk to some bureaucratic suits wasn't exactly the first thing on my mind. I had to finish what I was working on. I had to . . . the urge was . . . I couldn't even believe I was taking the time to talk to Jon.

"What is this?" Jon asked, looking over the papers and my scribbles.

"I don't know yet," I replied, "but I think it's important."

Jon just nodded and then kissed my forehead.

"We need to leave in about twenty minutes," he said.

A half hour later I said goodbye to Nico, Valerie, and the boys and then climbed into Jon's SUV for a quiet drive to the airport. I wrote the whole way, my mind possessed by the numbers I was writing down. They made no sense as they came out, just on automatic. I figured that when I'd put them all together, I would know what I was saying, what I was trying to get out.

On the flight, just after the plane leveled off and the stewards began pushing their trolley of drinks down the aisle, Jon told me what was happening outside my head.

Then I saw it.

There was Wi-Fi on the plane and I watched a few minutes of news on my cell phone. The coverage was breathless—panicked, even. Most of the video that the networks were running was pulled from social media. There were these handheld videos made with cell phones of people freaking out in doctors' waiting rooms. I saw a video clip, really short, just a few seconds long, of a man using chalk to scribble mathematical formulas on a driveway. And then there was a clip of a young woman standing on the railing of a balcony; she was trying to reach out into the air above her and mumbled something about "she's so young . . . so young . . ." And then she fell. The video ended.*

I gasped, horrified, and shut my phone off. This thing, whatever it

---

* I was struck by Dahlia's description of this video and decided to track it down. As you can imagine, it was difficult. Sadly, there were many similar videos that were posted in the first few days of the Elevation. On October 29, 2023, fifteen people died in nearly identical circumstances: standing on rooftops or balcony railings, reaching out to touch something only they could see. The only clue to differentiate this instance was the fact that the woman Dahlia described said "she's so young . . ." With help from a video archivist at a now-defunct national news network that catered to airing more sensationalist material, I was able to find the video clip in question. The woman's name was Trisha Menzel and she was twenty-six years old. A copywriter at an engineering firm, she had been married two weeks before the Pulse arrived. At the time of her death, her wife claimed that Trisha had been seeing the ghost of a neighborhood friend who died in a car accident twenty years earlier.

was, was spreading fast, and it felt so uncomfortably similar to what I'd experienced.

"What are these people saying they're seeing?"

Jon said, "Ghosts, some of them. Others are seeing things that people aren't supposed to see, like ultraviolet colors, radiation—"

"Gravitational waves?"

Jon shrugged. "I haven't read of anyone else seeing those."

"You think I've got this thing, though?"

"I'm worried about that possibility," he said.

I told him that I felt fine. I wasn't seeing anything, wasn't hearing anything. But he motioned with his eyes to my hands. The whole time we'd been talking, with my gaze locked on his, I was writing. I'd scribbled out at least two additional pages of numbers and letters and formulas unconsciously.

We arrived in DC and were met by several Secret Service agents. They asked our names and we confirmed who we were. Then we were escorted to a van with blacked-out windows. It all felt like a spy show, like I was caught up in something that wasn't going to end well. Maybe it wasn't as heavy as that, but . . . I was anxious.

Who wouldn't be, right?

The agents didn't say where we were going.

We drove for about fifteen minutes, in complete silence, before the van pulled into a parking garage. There was another van. Only, this time the people standing outside it, waiting for us, were wearing hazmat suits. Seriously.

I asked Jon what this was all about.

He said he didn't know. I believed him.

I was ushered out of the van and one of the people in the hazmat suits, a woman, said, "Dr. Dahlia Mitchell, I'm with the Office of the Director of National Intelligence. Your presence has been requested at a meeting with the Disclosure Task Force. This meeting will be confidential. We're authorized to bring you there now."

I turned to Jon. He nodded. "It's okay."

"I'm going to see you after this, right?"

Jon said, "I'll be waiting."

I climbed into the second van, next to the people in hazmat suits. The driver was separated from us by a thick plexiglass window. The van drove but I couldn't see where: the windows were all too dark. No one spoke to me during the ride, so I kept working on my notes. They watched me as I scribbled, but they remained silent.

After about thirty minutes we arrived.

The doors opened and we were inside another parking garage, this time underground. The place was empty—no other cars. But there was a trailer, the kind you see at FEMA sites for researchers and medical staff, set up in the middle of the garage. It was lit up like Christmas. The people in the hazmat suits walked me across the empty garage to the trailer. The trailer door opened and a man stepped forward; he was wearing jeans and a hoodie. Seemed out of place.

He said, "My name's Xavier Faber. Good to meet you, Doc."

We shook hands as the people in the hazmat suits backed away towards the van. Then I climbed aboard and Xavier closed the door behind me. He locked it. The trailer was essentially one large office. There was a big oak table at the center, surrounded by eight chairs. In those chairs were four additional people.

None of them were wearing hazmat suits.

All were dressed casually.

"Welcome to the Disclosure team," Xavier said. "We have a lot of questions."

And so do I.

**29**

KANISHA PRESTON: Dr. Dahlia Mitchell, have a seat. We're all very eager to talk to you.

DAHLIA MITCHELL: The people in the protective suits, what, uh—

KANISHA PRESTON: You've heard about what they're calling the Elevation, right? Some people are quite concerned we're dealing with an outbreak, a pandemic of some sort.

DAHLIA MITCHELL: But not you all . . .

DR. XAVIER FABER: We're tough like that.

DR. SERGEI MIKOYAN: It's more complicated. It's not so much that we feel as though we're safe; it's more that we're not convinced that this is a virulent plague. We don't think it's a matter of contagion. The Elevation seems more . . . genetic. In our estimation, everyone on Earth has already been exposed.

DAHLIA MITCHELL: Exposed to what?

DR. SOLEDAD VENEGAS: The Pulse.

DR. NEIL ROBERTS: Excellent to have you here, Dr. Mitchell. As you've been told, we've been studying what you discovered. It's . . . well, I'm sure you know it's remarkable. We have a lot of questions, as you can imagine.

DAHLIA MITCHELL: What makes you think the Pulse is responsible for this . . .

DR. SOLEDAD VENEGAS: The Elevation. Our belief is that the Pulse Code contains something akin to a Trojan horse, the kind computers are infected with, and that it is designed to affect human DNA. We're not sure how.

DAHLIA MITCHELL: I think I know . . .

DR. XAVIER FABER: Okay. Wow. Um . . . we weren't expecting that. We'd hope you'd come in and tell us more details about how you found the Pulse, the original analysis you did, but . . . great. Tell us what you know.

DAHLIA MITCHELL: I've been writing. It came to me early this morning. Just flooded into my head, all these . . . answers. I've got it all here, all spread out over scrap paper. I think that if you take a look over it all, look at it closely, you'll see that it's the solution for the Pulse Code. Here . . .*

DR. XAVIER FABER: This is . . . this is extraordinary. How did you say you got it?

DAHLIA MITCHELL: I woke up this morning and I knew it. That sounds silly but it's true. I think you're right: the Elevation is the result of the Pulse. It is designed to alter human DNA, but that's only part of the process. It targets the brain and rewires it. Look here at this sheet . . . This is a biological program, like a genome editing tool designed to increase the neural connections in the prefrontal lobe of the human brain.

DR. SOLEDAD VENEGAS: But it doesn't affect everyone. Only a certain percentage of the population seems to be targeted. Perhaps it is self-limiting.

---

* I've seen photographs of the notes Dahlia wrote on those scraps of paper. They're impressive. I was, again, reminded of Art Brut. There was no single thread of thought in the notes—as far as I could follow them—but multiple concepts jostling for space on the page at the same time. The notes take up every available inch of blank space on the paper; some are written in tight, exacting lettering, while others are big, sweeping, and barely controlled. If these notes were the product of a group of people passing the sheet back and forth, it would make sense. But the fact that they come from one hand, one mind, makes them all the more remarkable. They are, in many ways, emblematic of the Elevation itself: uncontainable, ineffable.

DAHLIA MITCHELL: I think it's only just beginning. This is the first wave, the early responders. I don't know why it's affecting the people it is now, but I suspect there will be many more later.

DR. NEIL ROBERTS: Dahlia, do you know why? Does this work you've been doing, this code, give you any insight into what exactly the Pulse is increasing neural connections for?

DAHLIA MITCHELL: No.

DR. XAVIER FABER: Dahlia, we've been tasked by President Ballard to draft a statement to the American public about the Pulse. We need to know what to tell the people before this thing blows up in our faces. Now, with the Elevation, our timeline has been supremely crunched. We need to give the President a message, a vision for how humanity should react and what steps we need to take. We need to have that message on her desk in twenty-four hours. We've already got a draft but . . . well, recent events have made it obsolete.

DAHLIA MITCHELL: Okay, what can I do?

KANISHA PRESTON: Tell us everything you know about the Pulse. You're Elevated, Dahlia. And I'm guessing you have insight the rest of us don't.

30

We finally left the quarantine room.

Our work is done. Our report is written.

What to tell the world about the Ascendant and how to say it.

It feels like we've been held in solitary for the past two days.

There's no way to classify it other than quarantine if you're kept isolated both physically and emotionally. While we were able to talk to each other, we had no idea what was going on outside of our little wing of government hell. Did the world end? Did we go to war? Did Christ return? We had no idea. Stepping out of those barracks was like emerging from a cave after a year in darkness. We were all in shock, blinking too much and laughing inappropriately. It was just so good to breathe real air, feel the sun on our skin, and hear unmuffled sounds!

Didn't mean we were entirely free, of course.

And I couldn't call Nico or get on my cell to see what had happened since we'd been isolated, but at least we had new faces in front of us. The first were soldiers. Guys with bushy beards and wraparound sunglasses ushered us from the barracks into a blacked-out bus. We rode it in silence, trying to see the outside world through the heavily tinted windows. We went on the highway and then took side roads. All I saw were the flashes of passing cars and the blur of trees.

While we drove, I became reflective.

It's too melodramatic, like my usual, to say that I was in a chrysa-

lis while we were in quarantine. But I did go in as one person and I came out as another. The itching, the tickle, that I'd felt inside my head when the migraines started has vanished. I don't see the gravitational waves either.

I feel comfortable—normal in a way.

Something I haven't felt in a long time.

But my mind is hungry. It's famished. That sounds weird to say, but I need information. Over the last week, my senses have been in overdrive: I hear everything louder and I taste everything stronger. My sense of smell, of touch, my sight—it's all enhanced and sharper.

Even though I look the same on the outside, I doubt I'd recognize myself if I sat down and had a conversation with Nico or even Jon. My responses would be different from before. The emotions would be more intense, and yet my analysis of them, running like a constant commentary track at the back of my head, would be even more critical than it was prior to being put in quarantine. I feel like more than one person.

This is the Elevation, and I know that if a surgeon were to cut open my brain and unfold the cerebral matter, she'd find a whole new landscape has grown inside my head. This is what the Pulse was designed to do.

This is what they wanted.

—

Our destination was a nondescript building in what I assumed was a suburban office park near DC. You know: ugly.

It had a massive parking lot that was populated by light poles and some recently planted scrawny trees. Leaving the bus, we were led by the armed men towards a glass-and-stone building.

"SEALs, I think," Xavier said, motioning to the bearded guys.

"That make you feel better?" I asked.

"Just saying," he said. "Means that this is all still hush-hush."

"I didn't think it'd change," I said. "Gonna be hush-hush from here out."

We entered the building and took an elevator to the third floor. The place hadn't been completed yet. There was the empty shell of what would one day be an office, but the ceilings, the flooring, the lights—none of that was in; just windows, concrete, and dangling electrical cables that hung vine-like from the non-ceiling. The floor itself was massive, like an airport hangar. We made our way into it, and at the center there was a single four-walled conference room.

It looked like a movie set, something whipped up overnight.

Which it probably was . . .

We were ushered inside to find a large oak table, leather office chairs—eight of them—standing lamps, even a potted plant and a water cooler. There were digital whiteboards on two of the walls and several mounted flat-screen monitors. We settled in and the soldiers, or Navy SEALs, gave us bottled water and packets of graham crackers. We ate and drank in silence as the men filed out.

The snacking and silence lasted for about fifteen minutes.

I think we were all just so happy to be someplace new that we didn't want to break the magic of the moment and ruin it with questions. Maybe not. Maybe we were all just so exhausted that we knew if we said something—like "So, what happens next?" or "Nice place here. Hope we stay awhile"—that it would sound embarrassingly stupid. So we ate in silence.

Then there was a knock at the door.

We all looked at each other and then Dr. Venegas said, "Come in."

The door opened and a man in a black suit and baseball cap entered. He took off his cap, wiped the sweat from his forehead, and then sat down with a huff in an empty chair at the head of the table. He grabbed a bottle of water, downed it, and then looked us over, nodding to himself. Then he laughed.

"This is the crew?" he asked, not really looking for an answer.

"Who are you?" Xavier said.

"My name is Glenn Owen," he said. "I'm going to introduce you to the President of the United States."

Holy shit.

31

AUTHOR'S NOTE

Each country dealt with the Elevation in their own way.

This, of course, was before anyone had made the connection between the Elevation and the Pulse. The government realized something was wrong, but President Ballard and the Disclosure Task Force hadn't made any recommendations. Truth is, they were still mum on the events shaking the world being anything but a viral outbreak of strange proportions.

While there were scientists like Dr. Jan de Schloten[*] already suggesting that the Elevation had an unlikely origin—his conjecture was that the Elevation had not evolved but was created, either in a government lab or a private facility. He was one of the first to speak about this sort of idea publicly—beyond the stuff Sai Laghari and his followers trotted out on his website and in the site's forums.

That isn't to say that all countries followed similar paths in their response to the Elevation, but no two were quite the same. The European block, for example, severely curtailed travel to and from the EU. France and Germany worked together to contain populations of Elevated in a rural hamlet on the border between the two countries. Portugal locked its borders, and there were several outbreaks of violence in Italy, with several terrible incidents of mob violence in Venice. Norway and Finland were the first countries to close their airspace, even after it was determined that the Elevation was not communicable. The European Union countries wound up being, in the long

---

[*] Dr. Jan de Schloten was an Amsterdam-based coroner and virologist who became quite infamous after his research into the Elevation was uncovered.

run, those least prepared for the toll the Elevation took on their populations. Panic, as we know, is nearsighted. And many European leaders found it difficult to get out of the fight-or-flight mode. That's what hurt them the most in the end.

European media had a field day comparing the Elevated to AIDS or even, in a few remarkable instances, Ebola victims. There was, in fact, a commercial playing on UK radio that compared Elevation "sufferers" (that was the word they used) to people stricken with leprosy. Before the Internet went down in England, I saw a viral video of rural Britons, armed with shotguns and rifles, rounding up folks they thought had the Elevation and shoving them into the backs of vans. This sort of stuff played out all across the world, of course, but it was worse in the UK and northern Europe. And that was just the tip of the iceberg in terms of how barbaric things got.

The Drammen Incident laid bare the true fear.

What happened in this Norwegian city of over 50,000 people was ugly, very ugly. Thousands were gripped by a collective panic no one had seen since the Black Plague. Over the course of the Elevation, there were more non-Elevated people—folks suspected of being Elevated—murdered in Drammen than anywhere else on the globe. And it wasn't just lynch mobs turning on strangers, immigrants, the destitute, though that did happen first. It was neighbor turning on neighbor and, in many cases, family members assaulting their own kin. I was told by workers from a human rights commission who visited the city a few months after the Finality that they found a ghost town run by children.

In comparison to Europe, South America turned inward.

Countries like Brazil and Argentina rallied massive support to tend to their own people and provided logistics to bordering states to handle the swell of Elevated. This plan took a while to develop—the participating countries didn't exactly have the infrastructure in place to handle more than a small number of affected people—but when they had their systems up and running, they became shining examples of how to handle a global pandemic of this sort.

The people in charge of the Elevation response in South America realized very early on that the Elevation was not a communicable disease—that it was more like a mental condition that likely had a genetic component, like autism or dementia. While much of the rest of the globe was in a frenzy, treating the Elevation like cholera, the Brazilians and the Argentinians were carefully designing a systematic and well-funded response. They also knew quite early that there was no treatment for the Elevation. Just like autism, it was something that was likely chronic and had to be managed over time. So they set up "pop-up cities"* where the Elevated could be monitored carefully. I find it quite remarkable that the governments of these countries, in crises only a few months before, were able to rally so effectively.

They were real bright spots in otherwise very dark times.

That's the 20,000-foot view, of course. I studied more than fifty-six countries in detail. What I found was that those countries that had significant internal divides before the Elevation—places where inequality was widespread and quality-of-life scores were on the lower end—struggled the most in dealing with the outbreak. Countries like the United States, Russia, India, and Australia had substantial trouble righting the ship, so to speak. Oddly enough, countries that you might have assumed would close up and lock themselves in tight didn't. Japan and Israel come to mind in terms of countries that unexpectedly, at least in my mind, opened their borders even more. I've heard it said a few times—and I actually consider it true—that the Elevation effectively solved the Israeli-Palestinian conflict.

Think about that for a second . . .

The most curious case, however, was that of Indonesia. It's worth diving into what happened there in detail, as it speaks volumes about the world response to the Elevation as a whole.

The first widely publicized cases of what was to be called the Elevation appeared in the United States, Canada, Nigeria, China, and Uruguay during the week of October 22. The associated videos, articles, and medical reports went viral pretty quickly. When they spread across global social media platforms, people in other countries started to take notice. The response, essentially, was: "Hey, we've got some folks suffering from this same sort of thing too. We aren't able to explain what's going on, but now we can work together to figure it out." That's exactly how the CDC and the WHO were supposed

---

* Though the idea of a "pop-up city" is appealing in a fantastical sense, they more closely resembled tent cities—the sort of thing that governments would establish for refugees of foreign wars. Despite being temporary and out-of-the-way, these places could house thousands.

to function: everyone sharing what they know and helping each other find a solution. Of course, that's the ideal situation.

After those very first cases got serious publicity—a video of a little boy seeing inside people's bodies is effective in any language—the wildfire spread faster than anyone could have imagined. I spoke to several epidemiological experts—people who were in positions of power at the CDC—about those early days. They had it rough. A lot of them didn't sleep for days on end, watching as the Elevation took off, spreading faster than air travel. Before the Elevation, the only way plagues and other viral outbreaks spread quickly in the twenty-first century was due to sick people getting on planes. However, this . . . this was nearly instantaneous. It seemed that one day there were thirty cases across the world. The next there were 52,000. By November 1 every country reported at least two hundred cases of people with the Elevation.*

Indonesia, however, was an outlier.

By the time each and every country had reported at least 100,000 cases of the Elevation, Indonesia had only reported fifteen. Everyone knew that was impossible right from the start. The Indonesians were clearly fudging their numbers or, even worse, trying to keep a lid on whatever was happening inside the country.

With the Elevation spreading uncontrolled, it was a while before anyone checked back in with Indonesia officials. They simply had too much to deal with back at home. Those first two months were so solipsistic, in a word, that it was hard for any agency to look beyond its own borders. In the States, we were dealing with the emergency situation in Florida,† the disasters in Chicago and Minneapolis,‡ and the chaos in Phoenix.§ So it shouldn't come as much of

---

* The United States, France, and Brazil reported over 5,000 each.

† Miami had an incredibly large number of Elevated—10,600—and they overwhelmed the already stretched medical infrastructure.

‡ A generating station in suburban Chicago exploded, killing twenty-seven workers, when an Elevated man locked himself in the control room and proceeded to shut off every automatic system while ranting about "coronal blooms." The event in Minneapolis claimed the lives of six pedestrians: a man who died of a stroke while driving—later determined to be due to the Elevation—lost control of his vehicle and it plowed into a tourist group from Arizona.

§ Riots broke out in downtown Phoenix on November 16, the day after concerned social service officers forcibly removed a young girl diagnosed with the Elevation from her grandparents' apartment after complaints by neighbors. The riots lasted two days. Two people died and three buildings burned down in the chaos.

a surprise that when epidemiologists and public health experts finally turned their attention back to Indonesia, they were in for quite a surprise.

Three months after the Elevation had really spread wildly across the globe, experts were looking at insane incidence rates. There were approximately 78 million cases in the United States, 100 million cases in Mexico, 130 million cases across Europe, a staggering 215 million cases in China alone, and places like Iceland had an unthinkable 45 percent of their population affected by the Elevation. That's nearly half the population removed from public life and work. It's no wonder social structures crumbled and had to be propped up by international partners.

But in Indonesia there were only 3,200 cases.

This was in a population of roughly 270 million people. Countries to the east and west of it, like the Philippines, Thailand, and Papua New Guinea, were looking at incidence rates around 30 percent of their populations. There was simply no reason that Indonesia wasn't affected at the same rate as the rest of the world was.

It made no sense.

Sure, academics suggested ideas about genetic diversity and cultural peculiarities—that perhaps there truly weren't as many Indonesian Elevation cases because their understanding of the Elevation was different from that of the rest of the world. In the long run, it was flawed thinking. It should have come as no surprise that Indonesian officials would trot out these very same hypotheses every time someone from the international community pressed them on what was truly going on. Though there was a media blockade, word occasionally leaked out that there were indeed many more Elevation cases than the Indonesian government was letting on.

That is until Dr. de Schloten began publishing his papers.

It was inevitable that there would be a race in medical circles to understand the anatomy of the Elevation. With the condition spreading so quickly and taking such a heavy toll—at least 15 percent of the people affected by the Elevation died because their bodies couldn't tolerate the immense physical changes their brains were undergoing*—anatomists needed to find the

---

* Many people—like the driver in Minneapolis—suffered from strokes, aneurysms, and heart attacks. Some were felled by far rarer conditions like neurodegenerative disorders.

trigger, so to speak. They needed to determine where the physical changes that were taking place inside the brain were originating.

When they appeared, de Schloten's papers were incredibly illuminating. For the first time a physician was able to isolate several areas of the brain where the Elevation had the greatest effect. A better way to put it might be that these were areas where the brain had been most transformed. Right away, it was obvious that the pineal gland was heavily altered in folks who struggled with severe forms of the Elevation.[*] After that, the optical nerves and the fornix were highlighted.[†] But each and every brain was different in unpredictable ways. The only way to truly find correlations between them was to study a vast number.

This is where things got hairy with de Schloten.

He was a gregarious fellow and was happy to talk to the media—the kind of outspoken doctor who loved the limelight. There were suggestions at the time that he had gotten involved in Elevation research solely for the potential spotlight. The man was not the most rigorous of academicians. And yet, he had an access to the corpses of the Elevated that dwarfed that of even huge universities and public health systems. I think by his own count—and his data, when it was made available, backed these numbers up—he and a team of twelve technicians had autopsied over 2,152 bodies.

That's a lot of dead Elevated people.

For a while, the question of where they all came from was lost in the excitement over what de Schloten was publishing. Though a lot of doctors who worked on the Elevation wouldn't like to admit it, much of what we know today about the process came from de Schloten's work—sort of the

---

[*] The pineal gland is an endocrine gland located inside the brain that produces melatonin, a hormone that helps regulate sleep and wake cycles in the human body. It resembles a pine nut, hence the name. In ancient times the pineal gland was considered the "seat of the soul." Today, some religions and New Age adherents consider it to be the "third eye," allowing adepts to gaze inwardly to the soul or outwardly to other dimensions. In the Elevated the changes that marked the pineal gland hinted at tumor-like symptoms: visual disturbances, headaches, mental deterioration, and some dementia-like issues.

[†] More brain parts. The optical nerves are, like they sound, the nerves connecting the eyes to the brain. The fornix is a triangle of white matter between the hypothalamus and hippocampus. It is involved in recall memory. The combined changes in these structures—personality centers, visual interpretation, and memory—could account for a lot of what the Elevated were seeing.

way a few researchers used Nazi doctors' data after World War II.* They may not have asked too many questions about the experiments they'd gleaned the information from, but they used it nonetheless.

When the question of procurement finally came to the fore, de Schloten's reputation came tumbling down in a matter of hours. An undercover reporter with a Danish outfit known for guerrilla reporting methods snuck into de Schloten's operation—the man had this massive morgue set up in a modernist building—and interviewed some of the techs and got access to the paperwork.

All the bodies that de Schloten was cutting up were from Indonesia.

When confronted on it, ever the politician, de Schloten claimed he wasn't sure exactly where the bodies had been obtained because he relied on a broker. Authorities in Holland raided his morgue and took possession of the corpses and the files. Every single one of those brains came from an Indonesian man, woman, or child. They'd been shipped in via military aircraft, and that meant that the Indonesian government was directly involved. Scandal ensued. Tense diplomatic talks began.

It was during those diplomatic talks with the Indonesian officials that the first videos were smuggled out of the country by people willing to risk their lives. The videos were, well, horrific. Turned out Indonesia had a bad Elevation problem, in line with the rest of the world. At least 30 percent of the population was affected, though there was evidence suggesting it was somewhere more along the lines of 35 percent to 38 percent.†

What happened there was a classic purge. When the Elevation started, old rivalries bloomed. The government saw it as an opportunity to wipe out its enemies: dissidents, criminals, immigrants, homosexuals, the infirm, and the "blasphemous." They instituted a killing machine, using fear and

---

* While little "useful" medical information came out of the Nazis' disgusting research experiments performed in concentration camps, there were endurance "tests" that were conducted at Dachau by Sigmund Rascher that many considered useful. Dozens of research articles have cited the data collected by Rascher, and this data was used in the development of things like survival suits for fishermen.

† The New York City–based international nongovernmental organization Human Rights Watch compiled an in-depth report on global Elevation rates in 2026. Using interviews with survivors and medical personnel, they were able to piece together very reliable estimates of Elevation incidence.

intimidation—and also bribes—to convince families and friends to turn over their Elevated loved ones to the state.

I've heard Indonesia officials argue that the program began with them trying to help the affected. They offered treatment and wanted the Elevated all in one place to make that easier. But it quickly got too chaotic as the numbers went up and up and up. Soon treatment became euthanasia as fears of contagion spread. At this time the country was effectively closed off. No outside information was getting in or out. And the Indonesian populace didn't know what Brazil and Argentina and the US knew: that this thing wasn't viral or transmissible. Locked in this awful echo chamber, what happened next happened swiftly.

By the end of the third month of the outbreak, Indonesia had murdered over 13 million of its people, though the true number will never likely be known. Some of those bodies wound up in Amsterdam with de Schloten. The rest of them were burned or dumped into the ocean to be eaten by sharks.

As I mentioned, the Indonesia story was useful for putting the whole Elevation and, eventually, the Finality into perspective. When humanity was faced with a process, a transformation that made us—forced us, really—to evolve into a new species, we panicked. A lot of people turned from something that we normally would have seen as good—a way forward in a world that had been beset by so much strife for so very, very long—and embraced an inner evil.

We, as a species, were given an opportunity to become something more than human, and most of us chose not to take it. All our religious convictions, all our talk about the betterment of mankind, all our faith in guidance from on high—it went out the window when we were faced with change on that scale.

Turns out that when the world we'd known our whole lives was transforming—not necessarily for ill, just being made different—we retreated to our least accepting, most fearful selves. Which may in fact give us a hint at the real reason why we got the Pulse when we did. A lot of people assumed the Pulse was sent to Earth because humanity had reached some sort of pinnacle—perhaps socially, scientifically, or technologically, or maybe all three. They wanted to believe we got the signal because we, humanity, were finally ready to join the larger universe—that we were now able to ascend some galactic ladder to our better, final forms.

I wish that were true.

But as the case of Indonesia proved, we were far from ready as a species. A few months back, I spoke to Viacheslav Kudryashev, a Roman Catholic professor of analytical philosophy at Notre Dame, who had an interesting take on the why of it all.* Like me, he was curious to know what caused the Ascendant to choose us: Was it because of our intelligence? Our technology?

For him, the answer was no.

All the interviews he's read, all the papers and research, all the conversations he's had, have led him to one disheartening conclusion: the Pulse Code arrived on Earth when it did, not because we as a species had reached an apex of intelligence and beneficence, but—quite the reverse—because we'd bottomed out.

As Viacheslav told me, the first two decades of the twenty-first century saw humanity divided, a species at war with itself. We had embraced technology and it brought out the worst in us: social media gave every person on Earth access to a loudspeaker to shout from their corner of the globe, no matter how big or small. And the deafening voice that resulted was one filled with hate. Pain, embarrassment, rage, impotence, disgust—all these emotions were championed over love, respect, and altruism. The algorithms that determined the users were shown to be *skewed* negatively, posts about violence spread the fastest, and the anonymity of the Net allowed everyone to unleash their worst, most craven impulses. This led directly to inequality and war.

"The Ascendant didn't choose us because we were something special," Viacheslav told me, "They chose us because we'd forgotten that we mattered."

---

* Professor Kudryashev is perhaps best known for his incredibly controversial book about the Evangelical church's response to the Elevation, *Romans: How Hating Thy Neighbor Became Loving Yourself* (2025). I won't go into detail on the book's thesis—it seems pretty self-explanatory, given the title—but in one chapter near the end of the book he detailed how he saw social media as the primary driver of violence and inequality in the twenty-first century thus far.

⣿32

EDITED TRANSCRIPT FROM AN FBI INTERVIEW
WITH DR. ROBERT R. JACOBSEN

TAMPA FIELD OFFICE: RECORDING #001—FIELD AGENT S. SCHWEBLIN

NOVEMBER 26, 2023

This interview took place towards the tail end of the Elevation.

Dr. Jacobsen had been working with the Bureau as an independent consultant prior to and during the Elevation. When he himself became Elevated, he was subject to a barrage of tests and extensive, detailed interviews. The following excerpt is from a video documenting the last of these interviews.

In the videotape, of which I have a digital copy, Dr. R. R. Jacobsen, an older bald man, sits in a straight-back chair at a small table across from an FBI interviewer. They are in a nondescript room with a single door.

AGENT SCHWEBLIN: Dr. Jacobsen, can you state your name and profession?

R. R. JACOBSEN: At this moment, my name is Robert Jacobsen and I have been the Walser Chair of Psychiatry at the University of Rochester for the past five years. I've been practicing psychiatry for the past twenty-two years—though, as you can guess, that has changed recently.

AGENT SCHWEBLIN: And please explain how exactly that has changed?

R. R. JACOBSEN: I am no longer Robert Jacobsen. I am in the process of becoming something quite a bit more than he was.

AGENT SCHWEBLIN: What are you becoming?

195

R. R. JACOBSEN: I would say more than human, but that is incorrect. I am still human. My body is thoroughly human—at least, the bones and muscles and tendons of it. But my brain . . . my brain is no longer my own territory.

AGENT SCHWEBLIN: "Territory"?

R. R. JACOBSEN: You, the government, the people, the media—you've been assuming that the Elevation is an invasion. You're only partially correct. For millennia we've been looking up at the sky and envisioning a time when intergalactic invaders rode in on saucers to pillage our planet and enslave us or, even less likely, befriend us and invite us to join some sort of outer space kibbutz. That's not the way this works. The Earth will be terraformed, transformed, but it won't be from without . . . We're being invaded *from within.*

    The intelligence behind the Pulse and the Elevation isn't interested in taking over our planet. That's too simple and too human in conception. Ever since we started walking on two legs, we've been beating each other about the head to claim what we want: land, sex, resources, money, souls. That is our way. That is not *their* way. It takes a lot of work to traverse the emptiness of space. So many resources. What if you could invade and transform a planet without even touching it?

AGENT SCHWEBLIN: So this is what they're doing?

R. R. JACOBSEN: In so many words. They're taking over our reality by transfiguring our minds. But here's the thing: when it first started and I was studying Dr. van Ranst's work on the early Elevation victims, the ones who didn't take, I figured that they were changing our brains to adapt us to a new reality—a reality that they inhabited. Does this make sense?

AGENT SCHWEBLIN: I think so, but please explain in more detail.

R. R. JACOBSEN: I was being optimistic, but there is no room at the table for optimism, as they say. There was some suggestion from the Disclosure committee that the intelligence behind the Pulse existed on a different plane of reality than we do. Maybe, some of us considered, the Elevation was their way of readying our minds to interpret this other reality the way you'd acclimate a climber to scale the highest peaks, slowly changing the quality of the air that they breathe so they can survive at those extreme heights. It made sense, the fact that people like Dahlia Mitchell could see gravitational waves, and that little boy . . . But I was wrong. The Elevation is misnamed: they aren't elevating us so that we can live with them. They're elevating humanity so that they can live inside our minds. That's the territory they're terraforming.

AGENT SCHWEBLIN: That's a disturbing theory, Dr. Jacobsen. What is your evidence to back that up? And let's say that your theory is correct: How would this intelligence make its way into our brains once they'd established a foothold?

R. R. JACOBSEN: Good questions. Speaking as Dr. Jacobsen, I would say that my evidence is entirely anecdotal. Yet I know it is true. I know it is true because it is happening inside my head at this very moment. The oldest joke in psychiatry is that the schizophrenic patient is actually seeing the reality the rest of us miss. The voices, the hallucinations, are glimpses behind the veil. Now, with the Elevation, it isn't a joke. There is no punch line but the end of the human race.

AGENT SCHWEBLIN: I'm not sure I'm convinced, Doctor. What about the second part of my question? How do they get inside once the mind is ready?

R. R. JACOBSEN: Dr. Jacobsen doesn't know the answer to that. I will tell you this: They aren't coming on space vehicles. They aren't going to teleport or shimmer in like some New Age angels. My brain is undergoing a transformation that can't be explained in our language, using our primordial understanding of biology and physics. The folding, the twisting, the shifting, the opening and closing of the flesh of my cerebellum—it isn't to make room for some sort of physical parasite. It also isn't a womb in which a new entity will grow. I am not an incubator, but my head has become an executable.

AGENT SCHWEBLIN: An "executable"?

R. R. JACOBSEN: Computer programming terminology. It means a program that is ready to be run. They are cleansing, folding, and manipulating our brains in a way that allows the gray matter to be activated. And when they are ready, at the Finality, the program they have implanted in the very fabric of our minds will run. When it runs, every Elevated human being on this Earth will vanish.

AGENT SCHWEBLIN: Vanish to where?

R. R. JACOBSEN: Not where. The place they came here from, it isn't a where. It isn't a when, either, but I think you've discovered that already. We're slipping in between. That's the best way I can describe it. I need you to understand—I need everyone on this planet to understand—that when the Elevated go—all two billion of us—it will be as though we were never here. There will be no forwarding address left behind, no way to reach us. In less than a thousandth of a millisecond, we will simply be gone. The rest of you will be left with questions that you can never answer.

AGENT SCHWEBLIN: The Finality? You keep using that phrase as if we're familiar with it. Should we be? What does it mean?

R. R. JACOBSEN: It's just you aren't familiar with it now. You will be. In just a short time it will be the only thing that anyone in this world talks about. Just this second, I conjured it into existence. A few months ago, you'd never heard of the Pulse, but it had been there all the time. A few weeks ago, the Elevation sounded like a sports drink. That is the way it will be with the Finality. You heard it today and it will be on everyone's lips tomorrow and even more the next day. For generations, people have talked about the death of humanity. Cataclysm. The Apocalypse. That is the Finality.

AGENT SCHWEBLIN: You're saying that when the Elevation ends, the world will end as well? And the intelligence behind the Pulse will make that happen?

R. R. JACOBSEN: The world will never end, at least not for a few more billion years. See how simple-minded and blinded we have been? No. The Finality isn't the end of the world. It is the end of humanity.

On the videotape, there is a sudden flash of light, and Dr. Jacobsen has moved to the other side of the room. One second, he is in his seat across from the interviewer. The next second he is standing near the door with a revolver—pulled from the guard stationed outside the door—pointed at his own head.

Dr. Jacobsen looks towards the camera, focusing on it and narrowing his eyes, before he nods once and then pulls the trigger.[*]

---

* It's important to mention that this was one of the only instances of presumed "teleportation" ever recorded. The forensic video experts I showed it to told me that the footage wasn't faked— that is, it wasn't edited for effect and Dr. Jacobsen's movements weren't the result of computer-generated enhancements to the image. That meant, as far as they were concerned, that it was real. I spoke to physicists and physicians, trying to get a bead on exactly what had happened. No one could properly explain it. An engineer at the University of Wyoming suggested that Dr. Jacobsen's sudden movement was due to sleight of hand—that the flash was generated by something on his person, some sort of explosive. That idea didn't wash with another expert I talked to at Stanford. She told me she thought that somehow—and her explanations were way over my head—Dr. Jacobsen had been "temporally displaced"; that is, he jumped through time and space. The whole incident, and the video of it, is something of a curiosity. Perhaps never to be explained. Honestly, I like that aspect of it: even at the end of time, some mysteries should remain.

33

FROM THE PERSONAL JOURNAL OF DAHLIA MITCHELL
ENTRY #325—11.26.2023

I woke up in the middle of the night and didn't know where I was. Not a good feeling. Not ever.

I looked around the room and saw it was a hotel room and remembered we'd been moved after we'd finished the Disclosure documents. I saw a bed, a window with sheer curtains, a television, and a flimsy dresser. There was a dull yellow glow of the hallway lights beneath the door. Outside, through the curtains, I saw streetlamps burning away in the darkness.

But that wasn't all I saw.

There was another room superimposed on top of the hotel room.

At first, I thought it was double vision and rubbed my eyes with my knuckles. Then, slowly, I opened them again. I saw the other room just as clearly as before.

It had plain walls that were the color of quartz. It was lighter than the hotel room I was in but I could see the source of the illumination. It seemed to be drifting down in a white haze from the ceiling. There was no furniture in this other room.

I sat up in bed.

It's hard for me to truly describe what I was seeing, other than that I was looking at an image laid over another image. Like I'd woken up inside a hologram. When Jon and I were first dating, we went to a movie; he has a thing for really bad comedies and I like seeing him

201

laugh. After the show, there was a guy promoting an augmented re-ality headset—an AR headset—in the lobby: the kind of bulky visor you wear to see computer graphics superimposed over the real world around you. The one we tried, there was a game where meteors came flying down at you through the ceiling. It was fun but . . . frankly, they got the look of meteors completely wrong.

The room I woke up in looked like an augmented reality setup.

I even reached up and felt my face, feeling totally silly, thinking someone might have slipped an AR headset on me. Of course, what I was seeing wasn't computer generated. It was real. It was right in front of me.

I tried to navigate the few feet between the bed and the window. It was difficult: I was walking in two places at once. Or at least that's how it looked. Here, in reality, my feet were on a bland carpet. There, in that other place, my feet felt as though they were in sand. It was warm. I tried to avoid a low coffee table but ended up slamming into it.

When I got to the window, I tried to reach out and touch the glass. In the hotel room, I was touching the wall: eggshell paint, slick under my touch. There was no glass in the other room's window; my fingers passed into air and I felt sunlight on my skin. But it was what I saw through that window that held me spellbound.

Even though the wall in the hotel room was blocking it, I could see a field beyond, tall grass waving slowly in the wind. There were mountains in the distance, and just at their base a city . . . It sparkled in the bright light.

And then it was gone.

Just—blink—vanished.

My vision slid back into the focus, the way two lenses line up when you look through binoculars. I was in the hotel room, and the other room, the other place, was gone. I sat back in the bed and replayed what I'd seen in my mind.

I could still feel the warmth of that sun on my arm.

It was so nice. Soft the way sunlight can feel.

I really don't want to tell anyone about this. The other Elevated, the ones who've made it this far, I'm sure they've been seeing it too. I don't know what to call it, but I think it is where they are from. It is where we are going.

It is nearly dawn now.

The sky is pink.

Traffic noises have started up outside. Cars are honking. I have ten meetings today. There are follow-up discussions with President Ballard's staff. There are reporters. There are scientists eager to take a crack at the Pulse Code and prove us wrong. They won't. They can't.

In an hour I'll go downstairs to the lobby and have weak coffee and a reheated croissant or a bowl of granola. I'll probably see Dr. Mikoyan down there; he gets up early and goes for long walks to think in the dawn air. We'll make small talk before a shuttle comes to pick us up.

I want to talk to Nico and see Jon.

I need to tell my big brother about this.

I need to share it with Jon, see his eyes go wide.

But even though we're out of quarantine, our communication is restricted. No visitors yet. I really want to tell someone about what I've been seeing, about the world to come. About how special it all is . . .

Ha. Writing that, I feel like a missionary. Like some believer who's just washed up on an unknown shore. And not scared of what's to come, not frightened about what I might find, but excited. Thrilled to be sharing the faith, this understanding that we're truly not alone, with the rest of the world—with the rest of the human race.

Maybe only some of us are chosen.

•••••••••••• ••••• •••• •••• ••••*DISCLOSURE*

34

AUTHOR'S NOTE

There were many concurrent events that shaped the course of the Elevation and how Disclosure happened.

One thread was the Elevation itself and the country's reaction to it; another was the Disclosure Task Force and their research, and a third, just as important, was the behind-the-scenes work at the White House in developing a Disclosure statement that President Ballard would deliver to the people of the United States.

This following section deals directly with what happened after Dahlia and the Disclosure Task Force turned their document in to the administration. What I found most interesting and enlightening was how President Ballard's people chose to spin the Disclosure message and in the process create a new narrative.

While the administration was pleased with what they'd been given—the level of detail, the science, the messaging—there was still the matter of selling it to the people. This is where the marketing executives came in . . .

■35

SARAH NAGATA, ADVERTISING "LEGEND,"
EDITED FROM AUDIO RECORDINGS MADE BY
WHITE HOUSE COUNSEL TERRY QUINN
RECORDED AT THE WHITE HOUSE ON 11.27.2023

Sarah Nagata, something of a marketing guru in the decade before the Elevation, was the brain behind the ill-fated Disclosure campaign.

Terry Quinn brought her in to head up the messaging around Disclosure—explaining to the American people, and the rest of the world, what the Pulse signal and the Elevation meant. Her job was to sell it, to spin it, and to make it work.

Today, Sarah and her wife are retired. They run a small farm in upstate New York. Sarah declined my interview requests, though she did tell me she "is still proud of [her] work with President Ballard's administration."

TERRY QUINN: Here's the question: How do we sell this to the public and not create more chaos than we already have? People are scared shitless by what's happening: this Elevation thing, and the fact that we're about to tell them that it's all due to an alien signal that we never warned them about . . . We're pouring gas onto a dumpster fire. There's no tactful way to do this, is there?

SARAH NAGATA: There's always a way. Sure, we're behind on this. Way behind. But now that I'm here, I've got a few ideas on how we're going to sell it. Did you know the idea of an engagement ring was a marketing ploy?

GLENN OWEN: No, I did not. Terry?

TERRY QUINN: Neither did I. Please tell us.

SARAH NAGATA: De Beers, the diamond company, hit a rough patch after the Great Depression. Surprise, surprise, after losing all their hard-earned money, no one wanted to spring for diamond rings. The company needed a way to get people back into the stores. How do you motivate people to spend? To believe in something that, before then, didn't actually exist? In the case of De Beers, you invent a tradition. Engagement rings. No men bought them before 1948; that's because they were the creation of some very clever marketing people. They made a tagline that is still used to this day: "A diamond is forever." And along with it, they crafted a custom: a man buys his love an engagement ring to symbolize his commitment. Three years after they launched the campaign, eight out of every ten brides had a diamond engagement ring. Now it's de rigueur. We need to do the same thing here: get the public to believe in something, in a concept that they will be sure always existed.

GLENN OWEN: That's a compelling pitch, but we're not hawking stones here. We're trying to get people to understand that, in the midst of what seems like chaos, history's greatest-ever event has just taken place.

PER AKERSON: First contact.

TERRY QUINN: We don't want the Ascendant to be seen as a threat. We know nothing about the Ascendant, and it doesn't seem like that's going to change anytime soon. These things, people—whatever you want to call them—sent this signal to our planet to spur on these changes, the Elevation. Who knows where it will lead? But for the time being, we're working on how to reverse it.

SARAH NAGATA: We need to separate those two right now.

GLENN OWEN: What? The Elevation and the Ascendant?

SARAH NAGATA: Exactly. Your goal is to come up with a compelling story about how you're addressing the Elevation. I'm going to help you spin it this way: We don't know the cause, but we're working on it. All indications suggest it's genetic, something these people were born with.* It is absolutely, unequivocally not contagious. You need every famous medical personality on TV, online, or otherwise to repeat that over and over again. Then say that doctors are spending every minute of every day developing a way to reverse the effects of the Elevation.

TERRY QUINN: And the Ascendant?

SARAH NAGATA: Give the Elevation stuff time to settle in. Let people get excited about the fact that the administration is taking their concerns seriously. Once they're feeling confident and secure, then take a week before you tell them about the Pulse. What happens next is going to be crucial.

PER AKERSON: You've got us on pins and needles . . .

SARAH NAGATA: The Pulse is a message of hope. It is an invitation.

GLENN OWEN: Let me stop you right there. You did read the ancillary reports, right? The stuff from the Disclosure Task Force? It clearly states that they don't consider the Pulse to be anything more than a carrier, a way of transmitting the code to our planet. The Ascendant—

SARAH NAGATA: And that doesn't work. Sorry to interrupt. Yes, of course I read the material. It was dry and very scientific. No one is going to read it outside of academic circles. If the last few years have taught us anything, it's that the public responds to emotion above all else. Even reason. We need an emotional message here. We need the Pulse to *mean* something.

---

* The idea that the Elevation was a genetic condition made complete sense, considering it was a case of genes being altered by the Pulse Code. However, it was not something that the sufferers were born with—not entirely, at least. While it seems as though there were people predisposed to becoming Elevated—oftentimes siblings would be affected, and in the case of twins 99 percent of the time both people were affected—the genetic predisposition theory hinged on the fact that the majority of people who were Elevated during the first wave had inheritable forms of mental illness in their medical histories. This wasn't enough, however, to convince researchers that the Elevation was truly genetic; it was much more likely that these people presented with symptoms sooner because they were more likely to be aware of symptoms, since they were used to taking medications or seeking help for changes in their perception or thinking.

TERRY QUINN: Like what?

SARAH NAGATA: This is just off the top of my head. Riffing. But I'd suggest it be an angle along these lines: The Ascendant have sent the Pulse to us—our planet out of the billions that crowd the universe—because we are special. Humanity is at a turning point. We are living on borrowed time, as they say. Our planet is recoiling from us after centuries of abuse, hitting back with brutal storms, crushing droughts, and overwhelming diseases. Now, more than ever, we need a powerful ally. For the past 2 million years, we've been the dominant force on this planet. That's changed now: the Ascendant aren't our creators; they aren't our big brothers; they aren't galactic bullies or interlopers. In my mind, they are emissaries inviting us to join something much, much bigger.* The Pulse Code is a test, an invitation to be part of the universe beyond our small backwater.

TERRY QUINN: Wow . . . Well, all right, then . . . Glenn?

GLENN OWEN: (slow clapping sound) It's sexy. It's powerful. I like the messaging and I like the angle. But where do we go next? I mean, we tell the world that this pulse exists, that it was sent by the Ascendant, and that we're now part of some . . . intergalactic commission. I get that, I like it, but I wonder what follows. You brought up the diamond angle, the invention of the engagement ring. How do we tap into that more directly?

SARAH NAGATA: With the Finality.

GLENN OWEN: Okay. Sounds kind of ominous.

SARAH NAGATA: It's serious. Sometimes people confuse seriousness with portentousness. It needs to be powerful. From what I read, from all the documents you gave me about the Pulse Code and the Disclosure Task Force's work, I think there is a general consensus that this event is building towards something bigger. I want to call that the Finality.

---

* Just as Dahlia saw herself as something of a missionary, bringing the Elevation to the world, numerous people imagined that the Ascendant were similar beings, tasked with carrying the message of the Elevation to our planet. What that message was or meant, however, was not something that could be determined right away. This aspect, the delayed solution to the mystery, was key to the marketing of Disclosure to the American public.

PER AKERSON: And what happens at this Finality?

SARAH NAGATA: Only the Ascendant know that.

GLENN OWEN: Now, that's risky. I don't know . . . Terry?

TERRY QUINN: I get where you're coming from, Sarah. I agree this thing, the Elevation, the Pulse . . . it's building to something. Obviously. But I'm not convinced that we get everyone riled up and expecting a miracle. You're talking about Rapture-style kind of stuff. That's dangerous.

SARAH NAGATA: Dangerous how?

PER AKERSON: Dangerous as in: What if it doesn't happen? What if the Pulse and the Elevation are it? What if the Elevation stuff stops tomorrow and all those people go back home as if nothing happened? Then we look like fools.

SARAH NAGATA: We all know it won't stop tomorrow.

GLENN OWEN: I thought we weren't going to bring the Elevation into this at all.

SARAH NAGATA: I said we weren't going to bring it in just yet. We bring it in at the Finality. Listen, Terry just described my concept as a religious thing. And that's exactly right. That's what we need right now. Religious terms are the only terms we have to encompass the depth of the emotional response people are going to have to this. To sell this thing, to give people the hope that they need to survive what's happening out there, we need it to be akin to a revival. That's what the Finality is about. It's the future to come, the gift . . .

PER AKERSON: Sounds like we'd be making up a lot of this from whole cloth.

SARAH NAGATA: We have to. There are no real answers in the Disclosure documents. The truth is simple and painful: No one knows why the Ascendant are doing this to us. We can't divine where they come from or what they are. Perhaps they're like us or maybe they're ten-foot-long slugs. Are they malevolent? Or, even more likely, are they just indifferent. But we can't tell the American people that. You want panic and terror? No. None of us do. We have to craft a story here, a message, one of hope and peace. This is an opportunity to unite people that will never, ever come again.

GLENN OWEN: You've got me sold. How long?

SARAH NAGATA: Get final approval from the President and my team can have a draft copy of the campaign in forty-eight hours.

**36**

GLENN OWEN, FORMER CHIEF OF STAFF
NEWPORT NEWS, VA
MARCH 4, 2026

Newport News, Virginia, is one of the few places on the East Coast that retains an uncanny semblance to its pre-Elevation condition.

There is a steady population, the vast majority from the surrounding states, of 100,000 people and all the sounds and sights one associates with a maritime city for the upwardly mobile and the established elites.

Glenn Owen moved here a year after the Finality. He tells me he was searching for a new life in an old place. He could have chosen something farther north, perhaps in Massachusetts or Rhode Island, but liked the charm of Newport News.

He's gone back to his roots and teaches philosophy courses to a group of several hundred former executives, bankers, lawyers, and people who worked in DC politics. Despite, or perhaps because of, the events related to the Ascendant, Glenn has found that his nihilism studies have captured a new audience.

The people who study under him have faced immense hardships, as have all of us, but they've also seen fortunes tumble and power slip from their hands. Rather than turning towards established religions—some of which, like Buddhism and Judaism, have seen a huge increase in interested adherents—these people have embraced a philosophy of meaninglessness. The universe is random, death is inevitable and insignificant, and human intelligence is a quirk of nature.

During my first conversation with Glenn, I asked him if this line of thinking was dangerous. He insisted it was not—that it was practical. However, he did not want to talk about his work and his new endeavor in the interview. (I suspect this is due to the fact that he is busily preparing a magnum opus, a massive volume on nihilism that he hopes to finish next year.) Instead, we spoke at length about the events leading up to the Finality and the turmoil inside the White House.

The marketing pitch on the Ascendant and the Finality was smart.

Most certainly too smart.

President Ballard was impressed.

This wasn't exactly a good time either. The First Gentleman was in a medically induced coma and hanging on to life by a thread, and the country, for all intents and purposes, was in complete chaos.

I'd seen chaos before—weathered all manner of insane political storms—but, of course, there was nothing that compared to the Elevation. It knew no race, no creed, no sex, and no political stripe. If you took one hundred random Americans and lined them up, thirty would be Elevated. Of those thirty, ten would die.

And that wasn't going to change.

Doctors raced to try and find a cure for the Elevation or to reverse or at least halt its progression. But this thing, this biological code, wasn't giving up its secrets easily. I talked to dozens of the world's best biologists and virologists, and they said the same thing: The Elevation cannot be stopped.

So we had to deal with it.

By the end of the first month, the economy was in tatters.

How can a country survive when its future is an open question mark? How do you bet on futures or make meaningful investments? What happened here happened everywhere, frankly. I'm old enough to remember runs on the banks—places like Venezuela, where the government teetered back and forth from socialist to dictatorial and back again. This was before the Elevation, mind you. Every time the currency fluctuated, people pulled their money out of their bank accounts. Stuffed it under their mattresses, maybe. A month after the Elevation, we were in the same exact situation. No one wanted to risk their money. Not with the world going to hell. Not with some strange condition turning people into . . . mystics or nutjobs.

Infrastructure was also crumbling.

Massive potholes were popping up in busy roads seemingly overnight.

Bridges were buckling. I don't think most Americans realize how much re-pair work is done on a daily basis in this country. If you don't have teams of people out there cleaning and clearing, things get bogged up quickly. We're talking sewage, rainwater, roads, trash removal, the whole nine yards. It's a well-oiled machine, and when it seizes up . . . I don't need to tell you: you saw what happened.

So we hunkered down.

While we deployed every asset we had—the National Guard, the Army, the Navy, the Air Force, everyone—those of us working on the messaging locked ourselves into the White House and got serious. Sarah Nagata delivered with her campaign and the President approved it. The trick was the rollout.

People were losing faith out there, to tell the truth.

We needed the President to talk directly to the people, to tell them what we knew and what we were going to do about it. I wrote President Ballard's Disclosure address myself. And I've got to say, I'm pretty proud of it.

Sarah Nagata had her finger on the Pulse, pardon the pun, of what people need. Not necessarily what they want, but what they need at a fundamental level. When faced with the terror of the cold, indifferent unknown, every single one of us reaches for the light. It is intrinsic to who and what we are.

The point of the Disclosure message wasn't information.

It wasn't about advancing science or explaining the code.

It was about bringing people peace of mind.

We had a story to tell and it had to be told right. Dahlia Mitchell, Dr. Xavier Faber—the whole Disclosure Task Force—did their jobs, and we ap-plauded them for that. But at the end of the day, what did they determine? That the Ascendant were changing and killing us for no reason whatsoever. It was just happening like the way the snow falls or the clouds drift. Trust me, I know indifference. I was trained as a nihilist, I still practice what I cur-rently teach, but at that moment the one thing the world needed was hope. We didn't have answers, so we had to make them up. And I will push back to this day: How do you know we were wrong? It's not like the Elevated have ever come back or communicated to tell us.

No, the President and her administration did the right thing.

The only thing.

Think of how bad things could have gotten if we'd told the truth . . .

37

Exactly one month after the Pulse was discovered, President Ballard spoke to the American public in an address broadcast on every national television, cable, satellite, radio, and online channel available.

PRESIDENT BALLARD: Good evening. I know that my message tonight finds our country in disarray. We have encountered something that none of us could have prepared for but that all of us are now having to face directly.

I know many of you have lost family members. Many of you are suffering from symptoms related to what doctors have dubbed the Elevation. This is surely one of the most trying times in our nation's history, and I have been stunned by the amount of compassion and care that I have seen while traveling to meet with affected families and individuals. Our country has truly been blessed with benevolence.

And I have felt that benevolence firsthand. As you may well know, my husband, First Gentleman David Ballard, has been in the hospital. While he was admitted for an acute attack, he appears to be suffering from the Elevation. I'm afraid the outlook is not good. Surely, the days, weeks, months, and years will be challenging for all of us. Not just those who've been affected by the Elevation but those of us caring for the ill and those of us who've lost jobs or otherwise suffered as a result of this strange upheaval of the status quo . . .

But what we are facing today, what is at our doorsteps and in our homes, must be seen in the light of history. As a people we have watched empires rise then crumble. We have endured countless plagues, famines, and floods. We have survived brutal wars and crippling illness. At the same time, we have advanced to unprecedented heights, building technologies that save lives, probe the outer reaches of our universe, and map the bottom of our seas. Writing works of literature that defy the ages and creating art that dazzles our senses. As a people, we have achieved so many incredible things. and I know, that with God's grace, we will accomplish even more.

Over the last month, we have asked why the Elevation has arrived. For some of us, the answer can be found in religion. This is a test? For others, it is merely a biological process we do not yet understand. I am here tonight to tell you that we have answers. Not all of them but many.

For the past four weeks, I have been working closely with my senior advisors and the best and brightest scientific minds in our country to study something we call the "Pulse." A little over a month ago, an astronomer named Dahlia Mitchell intercepted this Pulse and determined it was a radio-transmission from space. This transmission was designed and beamed at our planet by an advanced culture outside of our galaxy. It is a message from an intelligent race and we consider it to be First Contact . . .

As of this moment, we are no longer alone in the universe.

We have named them "the Ascendant" and the Pulse is their way of introducing themselves to us. This is, however, a first step. A handshake, if you will. We do not know what the Ascendant want but we do know that they come to us in peace. I can tell you tonight that the Ascendant have a very simple goal in reaching out to us: they want humanity to achieve greatness and the Pulse is our invitation.

An invitation to what?

The whole of the universe.

We can think of the Elevation as their passport. For our planet, our species, to join the Ascendant, we need to evolve and evolve quickly. Physicians and researchers tell me that the Elevation is a process. It works by remapping our minds, strengthening the neural connections we have and making new associations where there were none before.

We call what happens next "the Finality."

At that moment, the Elevated will leave our planet and move into an overlapping reality where the Ascendant wait to welcome them. I realize that much of what I am saying will sound far-fetched. But, as we have seen with the Elevation thus far, everything we thought we knew about our world has needed to shift to make way for a new understanding.

The Ascendant are a benevolent people.*

Like us, they believe strongly in peace and altruism. Unlike us, they have achieved a state of mutual beneficence. The Ascendant want us to be a part of that shared openheartedness. It sounds rather sentimental, but they love us both for what we are and what we can be.

I know that many have died.

I do not want to downplay the loss that many of you are feeling right now. Those who did not survive the process of the Elevation will always be remembered in our hearts with great fondness. Their deaths were through no fault of their own but merely the vicissitudes of biology and the Ascendant's advanced technology. I have no doubt that those who succumbed have still gone to a better place—whether that place is by our Lord's side or with the Ascendant, I do not know.† This

---

* The use of the word "people" was one of the more controversial parts of President Ballard's address. It makes sense why she'd say it: no one wants to think a race of neon-colored squid or intelligent fragments of stone are genetically altering humanity. The sci-fi stuff—explaining how alien the aliens might be—never sold well, going over the heads of most people. At the same time, we knew nothing about the Ascendant. We might have assumed they were humanlike because of the fact that the Pulse was designed to alter human minds, but there was no proof of it. Calling the Ascendant "people" made them relatable and it made the Elevation a benign if not beneficial thing. Categorizing them as benevolent, well, that was the spin for you . . .

† What can I say about this statement? Clearly, an entire book could be written about the concept of these dead Elevated souls going to a heaven inhabited or designed by the Ascendant. Clearly the inference here is that the Ascendant might be considered angels of a sort, the Elevation being an act of God transmitted through the actions of an alien species. Convoluted thinking, to be sure, but understandable, given how little we know and how badly the government didn't want the populace to panic. As President Ballard later told me, she never imagined herself giving a speech like this but came to believe it was the right thing for the country.

event had no equal—there will be casualties and there will be heart-break—but in the end our world will be transformed for the better . . .

I realize this is a lot to take in. I've just told you that the United States has been contacted by an alien intelligence and that intelligence is behind the Elevation that has been sweeping our country. I want you to know, however, that you are safe and secure. What is happening is happening for a reason—it is being directed by divine providence.

Some of you may be asking about those left behind after the Finality. Do not worry: we will be Elevated soon as well and join our loved ones. Whether this happens next week, next month, or next year, I do not know. All I ask is that you hold tight, stay the course, and remain focused on the future. For the future of mankind is no longer here on Earth but it is in the stars and the new world that the Ascendant are building for us . . .

I will end my speech tonight with some words of wisdom. Johann Kaspar Schmidt, a philosopher,* once said: "If man puts his honor first in relying upon himself, knowing himself and applying himself, this in self-reliance, self-assertion, and freedom, he then strives to rid himself of the ignorance which makes a strange impenetrable object a barrier and a hindrance to his self-knowledge."

I am asking all of you to do the same: Trust in yourselves and do not fear the Elevation or the Ascendant. They may appear strange and impenetrable, but if we are free in our thinking, if our minds are clear, we will know that they mean only the best for us and that our finest days are yet to come.

---

* Schmidt (1806–1856) was better known under the pseudonym Max Stirner. He was a German philosopher seen as a foundational figure in existentialism and psychoanalytic theory. He is perhaps best remembered today for his philosophy of uncompromising individualism.

**38**

PRESIDENT VANESSA BALLARD
DETROIT, MI
SEPTEMBER 18, 2025

President Ballard and I finish our conversation on her front porch.

Large storm clouds have blossomed to the west, sending their anvil heads up into the night sky and blotting out the myriad stars. In the distance I see the flicker of lights in the city, and it takes me a few minutes to realize they're not electric lights but fires. President Ballard tells me there are squatters in a lot of the abandoned skyscrapers. She's seen photos on the local news of office building floors that have been cleared of debris—desks, file cabinets, computers—to make room for gardens. These urban farmers have found success in growing mushrooms and crickets.

The President is in a reflective mood, which is no surprise, given our long conversation, but not necessarily nostalgic.

I said what I said because I believed it was true.

I couldn't go out there and tell the world, let alone the American people, that we had made First Contact with an alien intelligence that didn't give a rat's ass about us. An intelligence that had beamed us a message that meant nothing in the long run. No, I believe that would have doomed our country and we would not be in the position of growth that we find ourselves in now.

The Elevated are gone.

The Ascendant have not returned.

They likely will not.

This doesn't mean that my message to the American people was false. I still believe that the Ascendant wanted us to experience what we're living through now. I trust that the Finality happened for a reason. I do not know if the Elevated are running through beautiful fields in another dimension right now. Perhaps they are. Perhaps they are not. The one truth that we must come to terms with if we are to move forward successfully is this: we will never know and that is okay.

I will tell you that my speech was well received. Ratings were excellent and I think a lot of the tension that had been roiling the country subsided soon afterwards. People look to their leaders for strength and comfort. I think that in a time of great crisis, of unprecedented challenges, I provided both.

After I stepped away from the cameras and lights, Terry pulled me aside and gave me the news. David had passed away while I was speaking. Losing my husband of twenty-seven years was difficult, it was crushing, but knowing that he passed then brought me some measure of comfort. I actually synced up the times once—looking at the video of my speech and strips from David's heart monitors—and the moment that he died was when I said, "Those who have succumbed have gone to a better place." Can you believe that? Gives me chills just remembering it.

So that's your answer: there is order in the universe.

I will say that my message brought a lot of hope to most of our people. It did not, however, bring hope to all of us. There were some who saw the Elevation as the culmination of a doom-filled prophecy. As you well know, there were suicides. Many. There were even attacks on the Elevated. Some, like the hideous events in Indiana, will never be forgotten or forgiven.

**39**

JEAN-PIERRE BRACK, JOURNALIST

SOUTH DUNE, IN

MARCH 19, 2026

I arrive in South Dune, Indiana, to find a thick fog has settled over the area.

This small town on the edge of the Indiana Dunes National Lakeshore bore witness to the worst Elevation-related atrocity in the United States. At one point it was home to roughly 15,000 people but today there are only a few hundred. One of them is Jean-Pierre Brack, a thirty-two-year-old Frenchman who moved here two years ago.

Drawn to the area because of its natural beauty and current "off-the-grid" status, Jean-Pierre enjoys roughing it on the shores of Lake Michigan, spending much of his time exploring the hundreds of abandoned vessels that have washed ashore here.

While Jean-Pierre was born in Paris, he went to graduate school in the States. His English is excellent and before the Elevation he worked as a journalist for the New York Times *and, later, the* Boston Herald. *Today, his writing appears online in various historical journals devoted to documenting some of the lesser-known stories of the Elevation and the Finality.*

Jean-Pierre was one of the first people outside of South Dune to hear of the events that befell a community known as Elevation Camp. He documented Elevation Camp's creation and destruction in a series of social media posts that were then syndicated worldwide. Rather than reprint them here, I asked Jean-Pierre to recount the story as we walked through what remains of Elevation Camp. I should warn some of the more sensitive readers that what fol-

lows is quite disturbing, though I think recording this history is essential to understanding how the Elevation affected various segments of the American population.

We begin on the dunes overlooking Lake Michigan. From this vantage point we can see the Chicago skyline sparkling across the lake, but Jean-Pierre pulls my attention to a series of dilapidated Quonset huts half buried in sand a half mile to the north. This, he tells me, was Elevation Camp.

The founder of Elevation Camp was a woman named Beth Corrado.

Came down with the Elevation and got sick quick.

Seeing things, hearing things, she could taste with her fingertips the way a fly does. Nuts, right?

Beth was a lawyer from Chicago. And within a few days of getting ill, everyone around her freaked out. Sounds really rough, but there had been so much about the Elevation in the media. People were treating it like leprosy. Beth lost her job, her husband left her, and he took the kids. She was left with nothing.

All this over the course of only two weeks.

What I was told was she jumped into her Subaru with her dog, a lab named Max, and drove out here, to the dunes, to just get away from everything. She camped and suffered in silence and posted pictures on her social media feeds. That brought more Elevated people. Within a few days, there were five other Elevated folks down here with her. All of them camping, bonding over their rejection, and going through the stages of the Elevation together.*

It was in that environment, the pressure cooker of people living right up against each other, that the idea of Elevation Camp started. My understanding is that at first it was just a place for the Elevated to be Elevated together.

---

* The history of Beth Corrado that Jean-Pierre presented me with was partially fabricated. I suspect he'd been duped and, despite his research, was unaware of Corrado's real backstory. Rather than fleeing the city because she felt persecuted, Corrado, a patent attorney, was running from a failing marriage and a serious prescription drug addiction. Her husband left her, taking the kids, after police found Corrado in an intersection, passed out behind the wheel of her SUV, with her kids in the back seat. Elevation Camp was less about finding a place for the Elevated to feel free than about Corrado finding a spot to pull her life together. Though it's a more dramatic story, she chose the fabricated history because, just as not all sins are equal, some sinners are more attractive than others.

Safe from prying eyes and people trying to get them help they didn't need. Word spread. More Elevated came. Some guy brought in the Quonset huts and, almost overnight, you had this community out here. Fifty people strong.

That's when it became more than a place to escape to.

It became a state apart.

You'd have to study how religions get their starts. From what I've read, it usually begins with a visionary. I suppose Beth was that for Elevation Camp. She had this vision of the Elevated living apart, away from the hateful glares and the persecution they perceived in the wider society. Not being sent to quarantine camps like they were doing in some states or hospitalized or herded into adult day care facilities. Out here, among the birds and waves, they could be free to transform. To go through the stages to wherever they would lead. You need to remember, no one had reached the final stage yet. People didn't know where the Elevation was going.

We don't know much about what went on inside Elevation Camp.

Beth and the others stopped posting on social media soon after the Quonset huts were built. But a few bits of information trickled out. A lot of it is so colored by what was going on at the time that it's hard to parse it. There were rumors that the people living in Elevation Camp were able to move things with their minds. People said they'd stopped talking and communicated with telepathy. From what we know about the Elevation now, that stuff sounds pretty bogus, but those were the rumors. Well, those were the good rumors.

There were bad rumors too.

The people behind you, back in South Dune, were particularly concerned about the bad rumors going around. The way the townspeople saw it, Elevation Camp was a blight. Not only was it an illegal encampment that the government wasn't clearing up—with good reason: the government was in tatters by this point and almost all the National Guard were up at the border with Canada*—but it was also a population the locals didn't exactly

---

* Though it's little discussed today, the US sent several thousand National Guardsmen to the Michigan-Canada border. There was a standoff that lasted several days between the National Guardsmen and approximately 1,500 Canadian Elevated. While the Canadian government struggled to address the Elevated population, large numbers of people suffering from the Elevation streamed down to the border crossing at Detroit–Windsor Tunnel. The standoff ended peacefully.

want nearby. No one knew what was going to become of the Elevated. There were some online theories that these people might transform into a threat. Tensions built up.

A month after Beth arrived at the dunes, only five days before the Finality, the people in South Dune had had enough. I don't know what exactly set them off, but I've heard it was a post on a town message board. Someone posted a doctored picture of Beth drinking blood from a cut on an Elevated person's arm. I've seen this photo: it's very clearly a fake, and was likely made by someone outside the state as a prank. Regardless, once it hit the town message board, people got really upset.[*]

There was a town meeting. Some residents showed up with guns.

The mayor, Rosemary Cunning, spent the evening riling up the crowd. She was a religious woman and saw the Elevation as a curse from God. This wasn't unusual. There were a lot of rural preachers who condemned the Elevated as being servants of the devil, accusing them of bringing on their illness due to licentious behavior. That sort of stuff spread rapidly over social media. People were scared. And when people are scared, the worst of them bubbles to the surface.

The residents of South Dune were terrified. The world was changing so rapidly around them: the government falling apart, the military weakened, power going out at night, phone service down, Internet spotty, hospitals overcrowded, medicine running low, food overpriced, fuel in short supply, and the idea that there were Elevated weirdos camping in their backyard . . .

That fear needed an outlet.

There is a video recording of what happened that night. Someone shot it on their cell phone. It's pretty grainy and a lot of it is hard to make out, but I've seen that video and I never want to see it again. I think calling it a mob is correct. I've also heard people refer to the tragedy as a lynching; that's correct too.

---

[*] As was the case in Europe, there were many anti-Elevation images floating around the Internet. With the collapse of most of the larger social media sites, these doctored images were spread via text message and email. The one Jean-Pierre describes is certainly unpleasant, but there were many more, even worse images doing the rounds. I saw some linking Elevated people to notorious serial killers, others that suggested the Elevated were pedophiles, and a particularly gruesome series that tried to paint the Elevated as Satanists and Jews out to ritually sacrifice blond-haired, blue-eyed Christian babies on a Luciferian altar.

At ten p.m. two hundred residents of South Dune marched up to the dune with shotguns, axes, and kitchen knives—whatever they could get their hands on. They stormed into Elevation Camp and rounded everyone up. Beth Corrado tried to talk the angry mob down, but she was the first to be killed. A man in a baseball cap shot her in the face with a revolver.

Screams tore through the camp as the Elevated tried to run, but there was nowhere to go, with the lake on one side and the dunes on another. Fifty against two hundred aren't very good odds. What happened thankfully happened quickly. But I have to tell you that it was barbaric. Men, women, and eight children were butchered; in some cases they were set alight while they were still screaming. The worst was the young man . . . His eyes . . . They tore his eyes . . .

Jean-Pierre pauses here, emotional, then recovers and continues.

When it was over, the mob burned the Quonset huts out. I don't know if it was done to cover up their actions, hoping the flames would singe away the evidence. Or if it was by accident, a burning body setting the place on fire. Regardless, if you look just over there you can see what is left: nothing but a few burned-out shells. The people who committed this atrocity were never prosecuted. This was only a few days before the Finality. Today, many of them still live in South Dune.

The media largely ignored the event. Even though it was horrific, it slipped under the radar in the chaos of the Elevation, just another in a long line of similar attacks. The President has talked about some of them before but not all of them. I think her administration likes to downplay that aspect of the Elevation. It doesn't exactly jive with her conception of us being so wonderful that the Ascendant want to bring us to a new world to celebrate our specialness or whatever.

There was one person who came by shortly after the massacre. The people I interviewed told me he was with the government. He seemed pretty shady but was nice enough and didn't go prying where he shouldn't. He only gave his name as Simon. I found one thing I'd heard he said a bit odd. He told one of the perpetrators that he had "done something similar once and that every now and then the world needed to be cleansed by fire."

 **40**

JON HURTADO

SILVER SPRING, MD

APRIL 6, 2026

We're on a patio on the top floor of a building on Georgia Avenue in downtown Silver Spring, Maryland. It is a gloomy day and the cloud ceiling is quite low.

Though it is hard to make out the details of it from our vantage point, Jon assures me there's a tall brick building a mile distant. He chose this location for our meeting because he said we'd get the best view of the particular floor of the brick building, but, alas, the weather is simply not cooperative.

Regardless of the clouds, it is a beautiful day.

The half-light brings out the color in the trees and gives the foliage a vibrancy that a bright, sunny day would flatten. We stay awhile on the patio, drink coffee, and make small talk about traffic—Jon tells me that the other day he drove from Kennedy Airport to Princeton, New Jersey, in twenty-eight minutes, and this was during rush hour*—before Jon gets to why he brought me to this place.

He points across the way to the brick building lurking in the mists, making sure to describe a corner window on the sixth floor. Outside of the fact that it is on a corner, he says, this office is indistinguishable from any of the others.

Well, that is to say the physical properties are indistinguishable. What he found inside was quite the opposite.

---

* Pre-Elevation and -Finality, that same trip would have taken at least an hour and a half. However, I also suspect he was doing at least double the speed limit.

Even when I worked with the CIA, I didn't feel like a spy.

What I did was quiet. I worked at a desk and typed on a computer. Nothing I worked on threatened the life or security of another human being. I wasn't even firearm trained. It wasn't until the Pulse, the Elevation, that I suddenly had to become the agent that I never thought I'd be—the kind who breaks into offices, hacks security systems, rifles through drawers, and then runs off into the night.

It sounds sexier than it was.

An anonymous informant led me to this location. How this person pinpointed me was never clear: the tip came in via an encrypted email and I never knew if they were male or female. I assume it was via the publicity Dahlia had, and my name had been mentioned a few times in connection with the Disclosure Task Force even though, as you know, I wasn't part of the team. Regardless, I wasn't exactly an easy person to get ahold of.

Who sent the email?

I have a few guesses.

Sending someone like me an email is a dangerous thing. It's not just the tools that I have access to but my understanding of how they work. Still, this thing came through some pretty heavy-duty encryption and it was a bear to get any information at all. But I did. I know it was sent from California and I know that the person who sent it was working at an academic institution. The other thing I happen to know—and this wasn't gleaned from the data behind the email but by its contents—is that this person knew Dahlia. How? The anonymous emailer mentioned seeing Dahlia's Pulse Code data before she gave it to me. That narrows it down.

Long story short, I think it was from Frank Kjelgaard.

Maybe he was working with the Twelve and had a change of mind?

Was willing to sell them out now? Or even more: maybe he saw the writing on the wall and knew the Elevation couldn't be stopped. Could have been guilt. Could have been maneuvering. Doesn't matter now.

Anyway, the email contained an address.

The address was the corner office in that building across the way. The message was how to get into that office as well as what to look for when I made it inside. As you can see, this is as nondescript a slice of downtown office building space as you can find. And where's the best place to hide something you don't want anyone to find? In plain sight.

The emailer claimed that this office belonged to the Twelve.

I tell Jon of my research into the Twelve and we compare notes, finding that we've heard much of the same story—though he's eager to tell me the additional information that he's uncovered.

Right, so the Twelve was effectively a CIA special activities division, a covert action group developed to mitigate an "attack" by an outside force unassociated with any known governments or terrorist groups.[*] That's as vague a mission statement as you can find, and folks that I knew within the CIA who'd heard about the Twelve always just referred to them as "the deep-state killers." As far as I knew, the Twelve were working to subvert foreign powers and overthrow governments. Turns out the government they were going after was our own.

So I broke into that office.

It was in the middle of the night and the place was pretty secure. I'd scouted it out beforehand and had what I needed to get in. Took me a few minutes longer than expected, but I'm a bit rusty.

The office was a bit of a mess. Clearly, the folks working there weren't worried about appearances. My guess is they weren't getting many visitors. This was the kind of place people went to get stuff done—a working and storage space. I was able to hack the computers, dig into the paper files. Didn't take me long to realize I'd hit a jackpot. Just like my anonymous informant had suggested, this was one of the Twelve's bases of operation; they were very real.

And they were up to some insane shit.

The files I saw, it was clear they'd been actively suppressing research and investigation into alien contact for decades. A lot of what I saw didn't exactly make sense. Now, looking back and knowing what we know, I get it:

---

[*] Jon's rattling off some jargon here. What he's essentially saying is that the Twelve was outside the reach of normal governmental oversight. What they did they did in the shadows but fully financed by the taxpayers of the United States.

the Pulse traveled back in time and someone associated with the Twelve had picked it up earlier. I saw files about the Pulse—the same code—from the 1970s. They only had tiny snippets of it, not like the more complete version that Dahlia had found, but it was incredible what the Twelve had done with just a few lines of Ascendant code.

I want to say they weaponized it.

They set up a lab in New Mexico and subjected people—most of them were terminal cases from prisons or mentally handicapped folks they'd swept up from God knows where—to their reconfigured Pulse. It was like the Elevation but not quite. The code was altered 'cause they'd filled it in with their own math—and bogus math at that. Think about it for a second: these maniacs were purposefully giving people the Elevation and then sitting back and watching what happened.

They knew about the Pulse, the Elevation, decades ago.

Instead of telling the world about it—instead of trying to advance science and medicine—they were testing it on people. I don't know why. Maybe it was truly to weaponize the Elevation, or maybe it was to study it and understand it better. That's where the videos that I saw came into play. In the computer files was a good fifty-plus hours of video documentation of their experiments. They were disturbing to say the least: a girl with two spines; a man whose muscles had locked up so bad, he couldn't move a fraction of an inch; a child that appeared to have been turned inside out . . . Terrible stuff. War crime kind of stuff.*

And the Twelve certainly weren't happy with what they discovered, because for the next thirty years they pulled out all the stops to keep people

---

* Though Jon is fairly clear in describing what the Twelve were doing, many of the records he claimed to find that day are lost. I have been unable to verify a lot of this information, but, regardless, much of it is corroborated in the interviews and research I have conducted. While Jon says that the Twelve "weaponized" the Pulse Code—and it's an ever-effective bit of imagery—I'm not convinced that this was the goal of the Twelve's work with the code. I suspect they were much more interested in altering the code to figure out how it functioned, sadly resulting in numerous unwitting subjects being altered in horrible ways. Perhaps the Twelve had considered making the Pulse Code a tool of war—a sort of computer age chemical weapon—and it went wrong? But my gut tells me it was much more likely that they had gotten hold of something they didn't understand. Rather than bringing it into the light to find answers, get more eyes on it, they buried it. And then they attempted to make sure it never appeared again. The Pulse had been sent once and forgotten, but—despite the Twelve's best efforts—the second time it appeared it would change the course of human history. As was intended.

from talking about it. Scientists, astronomers, biologists—anyone who stumbled across what they'd found—either had to come into the circle or faced death.

And these guys assassinated a good dozen people.

The most recent was Dr. Cisco and several of her colleagues.

So I made copies of everything I could. Spent a good two hours in the office. When I was finished, I torched the place.

I was careful; I didn't know how far the Twelve's reach really went, so I sent the files to people I could trust.

One of them was Dahlia, of course.

She owed me a sushi dinner.

41

FROM THE PERSONAL JOURNAL OF DAHLIA MITCHELL

ENTRY #331—12.04.2023

Jon and I had the dinner he'd promised a month ago.

But I'll save that for last.

The Disclosure Task Force completed its work, we turned in our report—not that the President actually used it—and the Elevation has progressed to the point that a full 30 percent of the population has been affected.

Even though I can, I try not to watch the news or read too much about what's happening outside of where we're being kept; even though our work is done, the President and her staff want to keep an eye on us. I guess we know too much at this point . . . Not as creepy as it sounds.

Occasionally we get visitors.

Nico and Valerie came the other day. They drove all the way, since flights are hard to come by and incredibly expensive; you wouldn't believe how many pilots have become Elevated.* They're not trusted with planes anymore.

Seeing Nico was truly wonderful. We didn't argue or discuss any-thing upsetting. He hugged me and sat with me, holding hands, and we talked about what was to come.

---

* It is curious to note that one in ten pilots became affected by the Elevation. Researchers who've dug into the reason why have all come up empty-handed. Sure, they've got a few explanations, but all are lacking: it is related to spatial awareness, it has something to do with sleep rhythms, it is the time spent at altitude. None of these suggestions can be effectively proven. Yet another mystery for the heap.

The President called it the Finality—a name made up by a marketing person. The concept might be accurate, but it feels too pat, too carefully constructed to mean something when it likely doesn't. Nico cried. He didn't want to lose me.*

Now it was my turn to comfort my big brother . . .

I told him no one was sure what would happen.

"It might not be like losing someone," I said. "That's the wrong word."

"How sure are you that anything is going to even happen?"

I told Nico what I'd seen. The other place superimposed on this one, our world. I told him that even if I went there, I'd still be here. He didn't understand how that could work, but I assured him that it would. "Think about it in terms of quantum entanglement," I said. "There are photons that are entangled, meaning that changing the state of one will change the state of the other. This happens even if they are separated, with one here and the other at the end of the universe. Einstein called it spooky, but that's only if you look at it as unnatural."

He wasn't sure he got it.

"Will the Elevated die?" he asked me.

"No," I said. "I don't think so."

"That's small comfort."

I wanted to say more about what I'd seen.

And I wanted to tell him how it felt, what I imagined existed beyond those mountains, and the people I imagined were in that other city.

I also wanted to tell Nico about the math that was flooding my brain. It wasn't like anything I'd worked with before. Even the Pulse Code paled in comparison.

If you think of math like music, the Pulse was a simple but beautiful melody—like Mozart's Violin Concerto No. 5 in A Major. The numbers in my head now, they're Bach's Chaconne in D Minor, endlessly intricate and exquisitely complex. It isn't math that can be used here,

---

* Some of the other names that were considered during the Disclosure Task Force's marketing meetings were "the Inevitable," "the Destined," and "the Dominion."

in this world of hotel rooms, siblings, and lovers. It is math for the minds of the Ascendant—math that lives and breathes in that other place. It sounds overly poetic, I know. But it's true.

I don't have the nerve to tell Nico I'm excited to see it.

That this world, this bland hotel room world, isn't for me anymore.

Instead, I hugged him and asked him to see me again in a couple days. He assured me that he would. Before he left, he asked me if I thought I had reached phase 3. I wasn't sure what that meant, but I assumed I'd passed it already.

Earlier tonight was my dinner with Jon.

Yeah, it's time to tell that story.

He brought food into the hotel and we sat in the lobby, in a quiet corner as far from the front desk as we could get. The food was Thai. I was hungry and finished my entire dish of shrimp with pan-fried noodles and caramelized soy sauce. Jon sipped a Thai iced tea and a beer and picked at his food.

He told me he'd been in Silver Spring, Maryland, earlier.

Then he placed a flash drive on the table and pushed it over to me.

"Do you remember what you said the night you gave me one of these?"

I did and I smiled, thinking back on it.

"Feels like a lifetime ago."

More than he could know.

Jon reached out and took my hand and squeezed it.

"This isn't the first time the Pulse has been picked up," he said. "They did awful things before. They hid it because they were scared of its power. I want you to share this, make sure it isn't buried like it has been for the past thirty years. The Twelve need to be put away. I don't know who to talk to, maybe take it to the President, but they need to be held accountable. There are two of them. Simon Household was running the show and he had an assistant named Adalynne Wollheim. We need to find them."

I took the flash drive and pocketed it.

"Jon," I said, "it's time to let this go."

He looked at me like I was crazy.

"I want you to know that everything that happened—the fights, the bad thoughts, the pain, the disappointment, and the anger—I let it all melt away a long time ago. I've missed you. I've missed you since the day I left. And here we are, I'm about to leave, and I don't see a way of ever coming back, but I want you to promise me something: You'll move on. You'll let me go like you'll let your rage go."

"I can't promise—"

"Please. For me."

Jon squeezed my hand again, and for a fraction of a second I saw the other room. I was looking through him, into the distance. I was at another angle, but the field was there and the mountains were hazy along the skyline. The sun was low and the shadows were long. This time, however, I could hear it. There was a hum, like the beat of insect wings. It was rhythmic and lulling.

"Dahlia?"

Jon's voice brought me back and the other place was gone.

"Let's get you back to your place."

We returned to my hotel room. It was locked into place, no shifting light, no doubling of images. Jon tucked me into bed and kissed me gently on the forehead before he took a spare blanket and a pillow and curled up on a love seat in the corner. He looked uncomfortable but he insisted he was not. So sweet.

"Good night," he said. "You'll be here in the morning, right?"

I said nothing. He fell asleep.

I've been writing this, staring at the wall.

Trying to see through it.

From the bed, I can hear Jon's heartbeat.

It sounds as sweet as insect wings . . .

THE FINALITY

42

HARUKI ITO: [*] Thank you, Dr. Mitchell. We have many questions, but first I want to ask how you feel tonight, being the discoverer of the Pulse and our contact with the Ascendant. A lot of people consider you the face of the Elevation.[†]

DAHLIA MITCHELL: I doubt that's true . . . In terms of the Pulse, I just happened to be at the right place at the right time. And I guess I knew what I was looking for.

HARUKI ITO: Tell us about how the Elevation has affected you.

DAHLIA MITCHELL: Like a lot of people, it started with migraines and then visions. I was seeing gravitational waves—things that are normally impossible to see or even sense. That gave way to a new sort of consciousness. I had a . . . well, this is hard to explain on TV . . .

HARUKI ITO: Just give it a try. (laughs) For those non-Elevated folks like me.

---

[*] Haruki Ito (1965–2027) was a Pulitzer Prize–winning journalist known for his series of groundbreaking interviews with Elevated individuals. These interviews were collected in his 2026 book *Talking to the Other Side*. He died in a car accident in Tokyo shortly after the publication of *Talking*.

[†] Dahlia's face was literally on the cover of nearly every magazine in print at the time. She was featured on TV, interviewed online, and appeared on over two dozen radio call-in shows. Though these appearances were brief, they left a lasting impression: Dahlia, discoverer of the Pulse, *was* the Elevation.

DAHLIA MITCHELL: You know the feeling you get when you have what they call a spark of inspiration—when everything just comes together and you suddenly know, or understand, something you've been trying to wrap your head around? Well, I got that sensation, but a flood of information followed it.

HARUKI ITO: What sort?

DAHLIA MITCHELL: Math. The most highly advanced, abstract mathematics I had ever even conceived of. It was like the math at the heart of the Pulse but even more powerful. Really, it was beautiful. And then . . . then I started to see the other side. That's what I call it.

HARUKI ITO: We're talking about the Finality here.

DAHLIA MITCHELL: Yes. That's not . . . That's a term that was thought up by someone, and maybe it's true, but it isn't exactly what I'd call what I've been seeing. The Finality, that's an ending. It's the way that people here—the people who aren't Elevated—will see what's going to happen.

HARUKI ITO: We'll come back to what's going to happen, but tell us a little more about the "other side." What have you been seeing there?

DAHLIA MITCHELL: I'm going to get a little technical again but I can't help it. I have been calling this place the other side, but, really, it's here. It isn't a world apart but one that overlaps our own. And it's beautiful. I want everyone to know that. For those of you who are Elevated, know that where we're shifting to is like here. It is sunny, warm, and it is designed. That's a weird choice of words, but there is an organization there, a purposefulness. For those of you who have family members, loved ones, friends, who are Elevated, I want you to understand that we're not leaving. It's true that you won't see us or hear us or be able to touch us. But that doesn't mean that we won't be alive and near you. We'll still be here, just on the other side of here . . .

HARUKI ITO: That's beautiful.

DAHLIA MITCHELL: I believe it's true.

HARUKI ITO: Dr. Mitchell—

DAHLIA MITCHELL: Dahlia, please . . .

HARUKI ITO: Dahlia, what can you tell us about the Ascendant? Do you see them in the other place, the other side, where you describe the sun and warmth?

DAHLIA MITCHELL: I haven't seen them. I don't know if they're there. I only know the Ascendant from the code they wrote, the Pulse they sent us. They are engineers, builders, and creators. Space travel with machines is archaic to them. They travel without moving, in a sense. The Ascendant are so pure . . . I . . . I don't know how to put it in words, but . . .

When I watch this interview, the last that Dahlia Mitchell ever gave, I freeze the video on this moment right here. Dahlia's expression is one of both awe and sorrow. She knows something that she doesn't want to tell Haruki Ito. She is hiding a truth that would only emerge much later. When you learn it, you understand why she holds back, why she is tongue-tied . . .

HARUKI ITO: Moving on. Tell us about the Finality. What can we expect?

DAHLIA MITCHELL: No one knows when it will happen. That's the first thing to understand. It could be in the next hour or the next month. Though I have a feeling it will happen soon. The Finality will not be frightening. It won't be loud. There won't be fireworks or lightning. What is going to happen will simply . . . happen. I can't explain it any better than that, really. You know how you sense a difference in the light when a cloud passes over the sun? The shift to shade isn't unnerving or shocking. It happens, we understand it, and then it is over. This will be the same way. I will say this: from what I've learned looking over the math that's filled my mind, the Finality will be quite short. Like the Pulse itself, it may also happen in waves.

HARUKI ITO: Waves?

DAHLIA MITCHELL: There might be a few places where it happens first. Or perhaps it will happen to only a handful of Elevated before the rest. Regardless of the rollout, the result will be the same. We're moving on . . .

HARUKI ITO: Some people have suggested this is the end of the world—the apocalypse . . .

DAHLIA MITCHELL: Yes and no. Yes, this is the end of the world as we know it. The word "apocalypse" conjures up all sorts of very negative imagery. It will not be that. We need to come together as one people, as one voice—

This is the moment most everyone watching that day remembers best. It was extraordinary. Depending on which country you were watching the broadcast in, Dahlia began to speak in that language directly to the camera. If you were in France, she shifted from English to French. If you were in India, she switched to Hindi. She spoke in each and every language simultaneously. It cannot be explained, though everyone I've spoken to has said the same thing: she was Elevated; nothing was off the table.

DAHLIA MITCHELL:—and accept what is to come. When the Elevated leave, our world will remain, and those who stay with it will need to rebuild. You have an opportunity that will never come again. Rebuild society to be stronger, better, than it was. Allow the emptiness of the world to fill in naturally. Take your time and do it right, so that it lasts and it is meaningful. The future is unwritten and only you have the tools to write it. Know this: we will be here as well, around you, ineffable but alive, watching but not seeing. It begins . . .

▦ 43

The small town of White Rock, New Mexico, sits approximately thirty-odd miles northeast of the city of Gallup. It was the location of a very unusual case related to the Finality.

While conspiracy theorists have used the incident at White Rock as a rallying cry around a suspected false flag operation to silence people who "knew too much about the truth about the Elevation," the cause of the mass disappearance there is still unknown. Several experts I've spoken with have suggested that this was an incredibly rare instance of mass Elevation, with a whole population being Elevated simultaneously. Whatever the truth behind it, I find it unique and fascinating.

LOS ALAMOS PD: Police Dispatch, what's your emergency?

CALLER 23: This is Kate Molavi. I need . . . Did you hear what's happened? Has anyone called you about what—

LOS ALAMOS PD: Say again? What's happened where?

CALLER 23: I—I'm sorry. Just in a panic here . . . I got . . . I got a call from my daughter Amber in White Rock last night about—they were seeing things, okay? Not just a couple people like you hear on the news, the stuff that I've read about going on across the country, but . . . but all of them . . . all the people . . .

247

LOS ALAMOS PD: Say again? What's happened where?

CALLER 23: I'm in White Rock right now and it's—My daughter called me from here last night . . . Have you been over there? Has anyone called you about it?

LOS ALAMOS PD: No, ma'am. I'm just trying to understand what you're calling in—

CALLER 23: I'm sorry. It's just . . . I'm freaking out . . . I can't find her. The house is empty. The windows and doors are open like . . . people have run out . . .

LOS ALAMOS PD: I understand you're concerned and I'm trying to listen to what you need to tell me. But I need you to take a moment and just . . . just tell me as simply as you can what you know about White Rock. We haven't gotten any calls just yet . . . Don't have anyone down there right now . . .

CALLER 23: Send someone to White Rock, okay? Send as many people as you can because they're gone . . . The people here are gone . . . My daughter . . .

LOS ALAMOS PD: Which people, ma'am? Which people in White Rock?

CALLER 23: All of them. The whole place . . . My daughter called me last night and said she saw something. An opening . . . But it didn't make any sense the way she said it, okay? My daughter has had issues in the past with drugs, all right? I know that. I helped her through those times and I saw her high, listened to her acting crazy. I've been through that, but this was different. I know she's clean—been clean for months— and this . . . She said there was a hole that opened outside her house—

LOS ALAMOS PD: A hole? Like a sinkhole? In a street or—

CALLER 23: Not a sinkhole. Not a normal hole. She said "opening," the way she described it. Like a hole in the air right in front of her. Solid but not. Right in front of everyone.

LOS ALAMOS PD: Where in White Rock are you, ma'am? Can you stay—

CALLER 23: I'm in the lot of the Baptist church. Sun's just coming up and this place—it's just empty. There are cars . . . cars in the street with the doors open and the windows rolled down. All the doors . . . You have to come here now.

LOS ALAMOS PD: Ma'am, I've got several officers on their way over now. I've put in calls with the sheriff there—

CALLER 23: There's no one here. You understand? This place is empty and . . . Hang on, I . . . Oh my God . . . (*rustling sound, then yelling off phone*) What is that? What are you doing . . . Please . . .

LOS ALAMOS PD: Ma'am? Mrs. Molavi, tell me what is happening—

(*Silence on the other end of the line for a few seconds. Rustling sounds and then breathing, rapid, as though running.*)

CALLER 23: I was wrong . . . I was wrong . . . I need to leave . . .

LOS ALAMOS PD: What is going on? Are you okay?

CALLER 23: No. No. No, something's very wrong here.

LOS ALAMOS PD: I have officers on their way right now. They will be there in a matter of minutes. Can you get to a safe place?

CALLER 23: I see them . . . (*Caller is emotional, crying.*) I see them now . . . There is an opening and . . . that is why the doors were open, the windows . . . (*off phone*) Oh, sweetheart. Oh, sweet . . . I knew I'd see you again . . .

LOS ALAMOS PD: Ma'am? My officers are a few blocks from the church. Can you wave to them? Can you signal them and let them know where you are?

(*There is the sound of wind, something brushing against the receiver.*)

LOS ALAMOS PD: Ma'am? Hello?

CALLER 23: (*continuing to speak off phone*) Oh, sweet heaven . . . sweet heaven . . . I knew that you would come back. That I would be with you again . . . Let me . . . Let me . . .

(A second female voice is heard faintly in the background, but what she is saying is indecipherable.)

LOS ALAMOS PD: Please, ma'am. My officers are there right now. Hello? They are by the church and they're telling me they can't see you . . .

(Silence on the other end of the line.)

LOS ALAMOS PD: Ma'am? Hello? Please tell me where you are?

CALLER 23: I am gone . . .

This transcript ends with a note:

Los Alamos, New Mexico, police officers arrived in White Rock to find the entire town of 1,540 people had been abandoned. At local businesses, cash remained untouched in unlocked registers. At homes, cars, valuables, family photos, were all left behind as though the population had suddenly deserted the town en masse. The case report notes that the cause of the incident was never determined and notes that there were no environmental or atmospheric factors involved. The woman who called the police department in Los Alamos was never located.

**44**

PRESIDENT VANESSA BALLARD
DETROIT, MI
SEPTEMBER 18, 2025

President Ballard walks me to my rental car.

I unlock it, the headlights illuminating the darkness around us, and there, just a half block away, I see a woman in fatigues with a machine gun. There are probably a dozen more like her in the shadows. Despite President Ballard's relaxed state, her reflectiveness, she's still a former leader of this country and one who saw our society navigate its most difficult hour. Needless to say, there are a lot of people who'd like to see her dead rather than retired in Detroit.

As I close my car door, President Ballard waves good night. She seems to me to be quite at ease with the way things have ended up. It's hard, at the end of history, to look back and not think: Things could've been much worse . . .

David missed the Finality boat by a handful of days.

Had he survived past the third stage of the Elevation, I have no doubt that he'd be on the other side now. But his body wasn't strong enough. I sometimes lie awake at night staring up at the shadows moving across the ceiling and wonder if he was the lucky one.

We'll never know, of course.

The day the Finality began was much like the others that had preceded it.

Despite Dahlia's message of hope and my own of courage, the nation was racked by turmoil and despair. A funny thing happens when you tell people that their world is ending: They freak out. Some of them go on sprees:

they down every drug they can get their hands on and go out wilding, looking for thrills. That ends badly almost every time. Others do the opposite: they retreat into faith or the forest. At one point there were reports of 3 million people entering Yellowstone National Park and setting up camp.* All those people out on the streets tearing it up or out in the woods looking for salvation—it meant far fewer people manning registers and gas stations and emergency rooms and banks.

At the White House, we were trying to put out fires where we could.

Congress had recessed. DC was shut down, under a curfew. Large sections of the city were burning and there weren't enough fire engines to tackle the flames. The electricity went out around noon and never came back on.†

I was in the Roosevelt Room when a junior staff member on Glenn's team simply vanished. This was a young woman, someone I hadn't even known was suffering from the Elevation. She was there one second, sorting files at the edge of the table, and the next . . . she was gone. The files and her clothes fell to the floor. Paper scattered. Everyone in the room turned to me, totally confused. But our bewilderment didn't last long.

We didn't need to say anything; we all knew what had happened.

At that same millisecond, across the entire globe, several billion people blinked out of existence. A lot of them were in hospitals, being treated— ineffectually—for the Elevation. But the vanishings happened in every situation you can imagine: people walking across the street, people in elevators, people on airplanes, people eating a meal. In a flash, all of them were suddenly gone.

There was no time for farewells. No last glances or cries for help.

I have never heard a silence like the silence that engulfed Washington that day. I emerged from the White House and looked out, past the lawn and fence, to Constitution Avenue, where traffic had stopped. Drivers stepped

---

* From videos I've seen, the bulk of these campers set up their tents by the Old Faithful geyser. They sat around singing songs, playing the guitar. I assume they went there for the beauty but stayed for the consistency. The geyser, a sort of geothermic clock, hinted at stability that they'd likely never really experience again. Those people wanted to hang on to it as long as they possibly could.

† There are plans to rebuild DC and bring the electricity back on, but they remain halted until a stable government comes into power. However, the longer the place remains empty and silent, the more it seems people prefer it that way.

out of their cars and a lot of them were looking up at the sky. It was a crystal clear day.

That moment, I don't know exactly how long it lasted, was so heavy with awe and power. The very air seemed electrified, as though lightning were about to rain down on the city. Then the silence passed, the birds started calling again from the trees, traffic started up, and the rest of us went on with our lives.

I stepped back into the White House, and Glenn Owen and I walked the halls, counting who remained, and assessing the losses. Of the roughly 560 people working in the building that day, 210 had disappeared. Their clothes were gathered up and their valuables—car keys, photos from their desks, wallets and purses—were placed in boxes for their families to retrieve. I don't think the scale of what had happened really struck me then. It's hard to quantify that sort of loss, especially when you consider how quietly they all went: there was no struggle, no one called out for help . . . They simply evaporated.

Jon Hurtado, Dahlia's boyfriend, was in the White House that day.

He came to see me and told me about her last moments. Probably best you talk to him to get the story, but what I recall he told me was this: She was standing at the center of the Ellipse, the circular park just south of the White House fence, and was looking up, eyes closed, at the sun. Feeling the warmth of it on her face. Jon said he was holding her hand when it happened. The way he described it, it sounded as if Dahlia's skin, in that split second of the Finality, turned to light, to warmth.

I didn't go anywhere that night.

I also didn't turn on the television. I couldn't bear to see the breathless coverage of what was happening. Turns out, the coverage didn't last very long. With everyone disappearing, business ground to a halt. Power went out. All cellular phone service stopped; only the landlines worked. The Internet went down and stayed down for a good two weeks. The country, the world, was silent.

My first thought was of David.

I wished he had been there to see it, to experience it.

That sounds strange, considering the Finality was met with so much pain and sorrow, but it was revelatory, a meaningless miracle. Not meaningless in the sense that it was useless or unimportant—quite the opposite. It had no true meaning. It was like a tsunami or an earthquake, an act of nature that devastated us but had no intrinsic, larger meaning.

Wow, I'm starting to sound like Glenn now . . .

The country took a long time to recover.

The world, too, for that matter.

Alabama and Texas were the first two, and so far only, states to leave the union and become their own countries. Oregon and Florida threatened to secede but couldn't find enough votes and enough fortitude to do it. I'm sure many of the Rocky Mountain states—like Colorado—considered leaving as well, but the EMP attack* two years ago ended that pretty quickly.

They won't be out of the darkness for years to come.

In the last year of my presidency, before the institution was reconfigured and the military came in via their soft coup, I did track down the Twelve.

We found Simon Household in Tulsa, Oklahoma.

He put a gun to his head before he could be brought in. The whole scene there was fascinating: the man lived very much as he died. Not only did he not have any fingerprints—the coroner told me he'd had them removed through complicated and painful laser treatments—but there was some suggestion that he was suffering from a form of the Elevation.

Clearly, the mysteries of his past went with him to the grave.

We did find a list of associates and tracked most of them down: assassins, spies, mercenaries, and straight-up criminals. The Twelve were in bed with some pretty bad people. They were all shipped off to various prisons. I have no doubt that a fair number of them were executed.

Simon's right hand, Adalynne, is locked up.

If you want to talk to her, I can get you in.

As you know, most of the people who served in my administration went off to chase their own adventures. I'm sure you've spoken to Glenn. The Disclosure Task Force members have moved on too. Dr. Roberts died of cancer

---

* President Ballard is referring to the electromagnetic pulse (or EMP) attack carried out by a white nationalist group called the Identity Council in an attempt to start a race war. There is still much confusion over how the attack was carried out or the true goal of its formulators. By all accounts it was deemed a failure, and many researchers assume the weapon went off accidentally while en route from Texas to Seattle.

three years back. I know Dr. Mikoyan went east, to Japan, I believe. I've heard Dr. Faber lives in Colorado, at home off the grid, and Dr. Venegas works for the new administration.

I can't really sum it all up for you.

I suppose that's why you're writing the book: to try and find a pattern, a story, inside the chaos. But sometimes the universe doesn't make that easy. It defies our feeble attempts to corral it into trite forms and expected angles. All that being said, I do believe I did my best to lead our country through its most trying time, through humanity's greatest challenge.

Looking out there right now, even with our country divided and our economy crippled, I'm even prouder of us than I was when I was sitting in the Oval Office. You can smell it on the wind. Even though we did not ask to rebuild, it is what we are doing, and we are doing it with such grace.

I believe the world is going to be a wonderful place.

Even better than it was before.

MEXICALI ROSA'S
1001 QUEEN ELIZABETH D
OTTAWA ON

```
TID:                    03117542
SEQ#: 014002   SVR:000019
INV#:                    124982
```

```
CARD      ************8195
CREDIT/VISA                  C
2019/09/14          15:37:27
```

PURCHASE

```
AMOUNT              $119.78
TIP                  $20.00
TOTAL               $139.78
```

```
AUTH#:01830I    B:000463
```

TRANSACTION
APPROVED - 00

```
VISA CREDIT
AID:  A0000000031010
TC:   0BFF7B8B54D65545
TVR:  8000008000
TSI:  7800
```

CUSTOMER COPY

THANK YOU
PLEASE COME AGAIN

MEXICALI ROSA'S
1001 QUEEN ELIZABETH D
OTTAWA ON

TID: 03117542
SEQ#: 010002 SVR:000019
INV#:   124982

CARD   8195************7618
CREDIT/VISA   C
2019/09/14   15:37:27

PURCHASE

AMOUNT $119.78
TIP $20.00
TOTAL $139.78

AUTH#:01301   R:000463

TRANSACTION
APPROVED - 00

VISA CREDIT
AID: A0000000031010
TC: 08F27B8B54D65545
TVR: 8000008000
TSI: 7800

CUSTOMER COPY

THANK YOU.
PLEASE COME AGAIN

45

ADALYNNE WOLLHEIM,
FORMER CIA AGENT AND GUIDING MEMBER OF THE TWELVE
PENNINGTON GAP, VA
APRIL 22, 2026

The thing most people don't think of when they think of prisons is silence.

The buildings are typically very quiet, and when there are noises—the clangs of closing doors, the drumbeat of boots on hallway floors—they can be jarring.

I don't know why my hackles were raised going into United States Penitentiary, Lee, in Lee County, Virginia. Lee used to house only male inmates but with the population changes in the aftermath of the Finality, it became one of the few high-security federal prisons still in operation. The so-called worst of the worst were sent there. I'd been in numerous prisons over my journalistic career, and yet this one gave me the creeps, so to speak. Perhaps it was because I was there to meet with Adalynne Wollheim, considered by many historians to be one of the most dangerous people currently living in the United States.

Dangerous, not because she's particularly strong or fast or violent, but because of what she knows. Adalynne is, for all intents and purposes, the last remaining member of the Twelve, the clandestine "black unit" headed by Simon Household in the years prior to and during the Elevation. While the group had been rumored to exist for many decades—there were fabricated documents purporting to detail minutes from the Twelve's meetings circulated in the 1960s—evidence of their work did not materialize until after the Elevation had reached its peak. And by then it was far too late to hold anyone accountable for the many crimes they were found to have committed—crimes including treason and murder.

Adalynne Wollheim is in her early forties and has her long brown hair pulled back in a tight bun. We meet in the prison atrium, surrounded by five armed security personnel. Adalynne's ankle bracelets never come off.

She has a cool demeanor and speaks quite slowly, carefully choosing her words for maximum impact. While I recorded our conversation, Adalynne insists that I print only the transcript. So that is what I've done.

ME: Thank you for meeting with me. I realize it wasn't an easy decision, considering...

ADALYNNE: Considering what?

ME: You've become one of the most hated people left in the country, possibly even the world. I know professionally that this is probably due to media oversaturation; they put your face and name up all the time. I also know that you didn't work alone.

ADALYNNE: The country needs a scapegoat for what happened.

ME: That's likely true. How do you feel about being that scapegoat?

ADALYNNE: Feel? I don't feel anything about it. I knew what I was getting involved in the minute I was recruited. You don't join a secret mission unless you're willing to accept all potential outcomes. There was never any doubt that when the chips all fell, we were going to be blamed.

ME: And you think that's unfair?

ADALYNNE: Fair, unfair, that's semantics for children. It's a matter of principle. Moral fortitude. I find it funny that soldiers are celebrated with parades and flowers when they arrive home and no one wants to know just what they did overseas. A soldier is a soldier when they are at war. They can't be soldiers at home. It's an insidious Jekyll and Hyde mind-set. Those of us who joined the Twelve, we did so knowing that we'd never be fully accepted again. But we were confident that our work was essential to safeguarding humanity. And we were successful in that mission . . . for a long time . . .

ME: Who was Simon Household?

ADALYNNE: I'll tell you only two things: One, he did not commit suicide in a hotel room in Tulsa. And two, he was always more myth than man.[*]

ME: So he's still out there . . .

ADALYNNE: Maybe. Maybe he was never out there in the first place. Sorry, I'm not going to give you answers.

ME: Tell me about the mission. What were you protecting us from?

ADALYNNE: Seems fairly obvious, doesn't it? *This.* A broken world. I don't know why the earlier instances of the Pulse didn't work. We never figured that out. My guess would be that humanity wasn't ready as a species, as a society. We kept this pandemonium at bay for decades. I think that's worth commendation.

ME: The experiments you ran. What did you learn from them?

ADALYNNE: Only that the human body is capable of incredible transformation. We consider bone and muscle to be locked into place like stone. But it can be manipulated; it can be warped for both good and bad. President Ballard, the Disclosure Task Force scientists—they all looked at the Pulse with optimistic eyes, seeing what they wanted to see: a grand statement about humanity. We are worthy, we are exceptional, we are the Elevation. But that's not true, for the creators of the Pulse—call them the Ascendant if you want to. We were just putty, an experiment, lab rats. You saw Dahlia Mitchell's final interview, the moment that she froze . . . What do you think she was hiding?

---

[*] As far as I've been able to determine, both these things are true. The reports that Simon Household ended his life in a Tulsa hotel room came about the usual way: unsubstantiated rumors after a body was discovered with Household's wallet on it. The corpse had been sitting for a week in a bathtub and was bloated beyond recognition. But it wasn't Household. There were sightings across the country, other bodies that seemed like good fits. Perhaps the myth of Simon Household rose out of those events. Regardless, dead or alive, he'd become notorious: the boogeyman of the Elevation, going down in history as the man who ruined the world.

**46**

JON HURTADO
IRVINE, CA
MAY 10, 2026

My final meeting with Jon Hurtado takes place in an abandoned office park in Irvine, California, just south of Los Angeles.

He flew in the night before and didn't get much sleep. Chugging coffee, he picks me up at my hotel and drives me here, to a place that has not seen more than one or two people a month for well over two years. That is exactly why Jon comes here. He sees it as an escape—not from the reality of the Finality but into an older reality, a time before this landscape was cluttered with human construction.

The buildings around us, all typical office park structures of glass and steel, have been beaten by the weather. Windows are shattered, granite steps are cracked and chipped, and the lobbies—as far as I can see from glancing through the doors—are choked with plants that have run riot as rainwater has leaked in and soil blown through the broken windows. It has a certain beauty.

We stand in a parking lot and watch the sun set.

This is what the Pulse, the Elevation, the Finality, means on a human scale.

Vastness.

We tend to think of the universe as vast, the stars out there far beyond our reach, and the spaces between them impossibly distant. But there is a vastness now here on Earth. Overnight, the spaces between people have lengthened from feet to miles. Wars do that; natural disasters do that too.

But they leave their marks, right? Scars in the earth and shattered glass everywhere.

But here, there are no marks, no signs.

Just emptiness.

It's only been three years or so since this place was abandoned. The first time I came, there were squatters in a few of the buildings over there.

He points off to my left and I turn to see a low structure. There are a few dozen bicycles chained to a fence in front of it, all of them missing tires.

The squatters left the place busted up—windows shattered and doors knocked down, more than enough space for the elements to scream through it and the wildlife to get a foothold. Now the place is home to several families of raccoons and a pack of coyotes. And those are the carnivores. I bet if you went floor by floor, you'd find a full ecosystem in each. From fungi chewing through the discarded manuals and office reports to the feral cats hunting sparrows and field crickets.

But come here, this is what I wanted you to see.

Flashlight in hand, we enter one of the buildings—this one rather intact—and make our way up the pitch-black staircase to the fifth floor, where we emerge onto a landing. Before the Finality, this likely served as a lunch spot for office workers looking to smoke cigarettes or get fresh air. Today, its moss-coated railing looks out over a circular park that was once crisscrossed with concrete paths.

This reminds me of the Ellipse in DC.[*]

The day of the Finality, Dahlia and I were there. She must have felt it coming; she said there was an electricity in the air that made me need to move, to get out. So we left the hotel where we'd been holed up and walked to the park.

I think Dahlia had it all timed just right.

---

[*] The Ellipse is one of Washington, DC's, most recognizable features. A circular open space just south of the White House, it was originally used as a corral for horses in the early 1800s. Fittingly, that is what it is used for now.

She knew exactly what she was doing. At the park, we walked across the lawn holding hands. Dahlia didn't want to talk about the Finality. She didn't want to talk about the Pulse or the Elevation. She wanted to keep things simple, like they'd never be again.

"The first time we met," she said, "we looked up at the stars together."

"I was looking," I said. "You came in and told me what I was seeing."

"The Seven Sisters. The Pleiades."

"I didn't forget."

"They're one of the brightest constellations," Dahlia said, "and one of the earliest written about. The Maori, the Persians, the Sioux and Cherokee—all of them have legends about the Seven Sisters. They're even in the Bible. The Blackfoot people have a legend about them being orphans: they weren't cared for by the people, so the Sun Man turned them into stars . . ."

"Like the Elevated."

Dahlia didn't answer that.

I asked her to give me some wisdom, something I would never know—something only the Elevated, only the Ascendant, knew. To leave me with a message, a bit of knowledge. She pulled a letter from the back pocket of her jeans and handed it to me. Then she kissed me and said, "We end but we continue."

I didn't get it. I still don't.

We stopped walking and she asked me to tell her a joke.

I could only think of some corny jokes my grandfather had told me. Dahlia still laughed at them. Then she told me she loved me and would always be nearby. We were still holding hands when she looked up at the sky and raised her arms as though she were going to just drift upwards. She didn't.

She vanished.

I didn't see it happen.

I was holding air and her clothes fluttered to the ground.

Look . . . there . . .

The sun's last rays hit the circle of overgrown grass beneath us. I see movement near the closest building and several deer emerge from the long shadows to graze. As we watch them, Jon turns to me, smiles. There are tears in his eyes. We watch for a moment and then make our way back to his car. He hands me the letter that Dahlia gave him the day of the Finality.

I will close this book with it.

∷47

I used to have nightmares about alien invasions as a kid.

In my dreams, the aliens appeared in complicated spacecraft that resembled massive, nearly invisible snowflakes that blinked into existence above our cities. Colored lights flashing in roiling fogbanks that washed over the buildings. Then there were waves of fire as the ships let loose their destruction, skyscrapers flooded with flames, black smoke choking out all visibility. I would see this from my parents' apartment building, and in the dream I'd try to run down the stairs and beat the tsunami of fire. Sometimes I made it; sometimes I was engulfed.

I'd wake up terrified and awed either way.

These dreams are vivid even now.

Maybe it was Nico and me sneaking into too many bad movies. But I always assumed this was how it was going to happen. If they came, when they came, it would be riding a never-ending wave of annihilation. We would be conquered by force and broken by our own weakness.

But that never happened, of course.

Some people saw the Elevation as an invasion.

It wasn't quite like that.

Sure, we were colonized by the Pulse Code, but there was no force.

And there was no other to arrive.

When the Finality comes and the Elevated shift from our reality to the next one, there will be no one to greet us, no outside intelligence to lay down the welcome mat and show us the way. Over the past twenty-four hours, my vision of the other side has gotten stronger. I've seen it for what it is: a ready-made community, a prefabricated world, that was never inhabited. It has sat empty, abandoned, since before we'd even left the treetops.

The last Ascendant died 5 million years ago.

They made the Pulse and sent it out when their society was flagging, their civilization in tatters. They designed and sent the Pulse hoping upon hope that it would find another, similar race, a species they could "download" themselves into. See, that's what the Elevation did: it changed our brains, rewired them, to inherit theirs.

We were to be vehicles, bodies, for the Ascendant to inhabit. The Pulse was not so much a message in a bottle as it was a life vessel—an escape pod.

And it failed.

When I think of the Pulse now, the Elevation, I can't help but think of Spanish conquistadors—how their sixteenth-century culture emerged from out of nowhere to subsume the Aztecs and Incas, to take their land, their resources, and their workforce. But the Ascendant, they didn't want to colonize our world; they wanted to colonize us. Why bother with the difficulty of building ships to navigate light-years' worth of empty space when you could just send your mind? The closest parallel, really, is a parasite.

Of course, when the Pulse finally reached the Earth, we weren't ready to receive it, and the Ascendant were already long dead. They gambled a little too late and they lost.

The Pulse, the Elevation, the Finality—the reason why I paused during my last interview was simple. I didn't want to tell the world the truth: that the Ascendant, our saviors, were dust.

But I should have.

You see, Jon, this was always about acceptance.

We cannot find true meaning in the world, in life, if we're always hedging our bets that some miracle will arrive to bail us out. We are special ourselves. That should be enough. That should have always been enough.

There was always only us.

ACKNOWLEDGMENTS

I want to thank everyone I interviewed for taking the time (and answering my repeated phone calls) to sit and talk with me about sometimes very difficult and painful events.

This is your story and I hope I told it properly.

I want to thank my assistants along the way: Yves Appel, Nat Whetstone, Rose Blassingame, and J. Quinliven. I could not have done any of this without your very generous and strong support.

To the following individuals, organizations, and institutions for their help in illuminating the past: Susan O'Connell, Rinka, Engage Astrophysics, Patti Heckert, Glyph, Jock Foster, Leslie Korenbrot, the Overlook Crew, Radio 5, Juno Vale, the staff of the New York Public Library, Black Moon, Sam Sachs, Doris Matsumoto, Dr. Lester Shizue, Dr. Jadine Chang, Fizzy, Tomoko, the Space Mapping Project, Tanis Chaisson, the Air Loom Gang, Alex Ward, R. R. Ryan, Dr. Emet Pilsk, Survival Research Laboratories II, Abednego, Charles Halein, and the Skells, Starkies, Diggers, Trolls, and Roaches (you know who you are).

I also want to extend my gratitude to the University of California, Santa Cruz; the University of Wyoming; the University of Nevada; Cornell University; the University of Washington; and the University of Pennsylvania. I really appreciate how graciously you opened the doors to your offices and libraries for me.

To my wife and my family: Thank you for every day.

SELECTED BIBLIOGRAPHY

Carter, August. *Faith Enough to Shout: Life After the Finality*. Spectrum, 2026.

Childs-Briddle, Nieves. *The Elevation: A Case Study*. Oxford University Press, 2025.

Curwen, Alfred. *The Ascendant: Voices from the Fold?* Zothique, 2026.

Eymery, Jean-Pierre. *The Science of the Elevation*. Duke University Press, 2024.

Hu, Dylan. *The Fundamentals of Plasticity*. Keystone, 2024.

Ito, Haruki. *Talking to the Other Side*. Dell, 2026.

Kudryashev, Viacheslav. *Romans: How Hating Thy Neighbor Became Loving Yourself*. University of Notre Dame Press, 2025.

Liebovicci, Chaim. *Breaking New Physics*. Institute of Physics, 2025.

Matsumoto, Doris. *Forgetting to Breathe: How the Finality Reinvented American Culture*. University Press of Florida, 2025.

Owen, Glenn. *Beneath the Darkness: Nihilism and Youth*. Yale University Press, 2019.

Ruckkehr, Esther. *The Elevation Casebook*. Human Rights Watch, 2026.

Schwader, Ruthanna. *Paradigm Shifts: Culture in Collapse*. Overlook, 2023.

Stableford, Lois. *Encountering the Imaginable*. Gauntlet, 2024.

Tanzer, Melissa. *Who Is Elevated?* University Press of Colorado, 2024.

Van den Broek, Fritz. *The Finality: A Study of Transformation*. Bruna, 2025.

Vanhee, Livia. *The Last 24 Hours: The Finality and Fragility*. Éditions Denoë, 2025.

ACKNOWLEDGMENTS

Thank you to everyone who helped make this book possible.
Primarily: Leo, Jonah, Lisa, Loan, Rakesh, Jess, Molish, Landheart, and Ita.

ABOUT THE AUTHOR

Keith Thomas is an author and filmmaker. Prior to writing for film and television, he worked as a clinical researcher at the University of Colorado School of Medicine and National Jewish Health.